Great French Short Stories

EDITED BY
PAUL NEGRI

DOVER PUBLICATIONS, INC.
Mineola, New York

DOVER THRIFT EDITIONS

SERIES EDITOR: PAUL NEGRI

Bibliographical Note

This Dover edition, first published in 2004, is an unabridged republication of twelve stories.
The present translations of "The Legend of St. Julian the Hospitaler," "The Return of the Prodigal Son," and "Micromegas" are taken from *French Stories/Contes Français: A Bantam Dual-Language Book*, edited and translated by Wallace Fowlie, published by Bantam Books, Inc., New York, in 1960, and reprinted by Dover as *French Stories/Contes Français: A Dual-Language Book* in 1990.
The present translations of "The Dark Lantern" and "Salome," by William E. Smith, and "Emilie," by William M. Davis, are taken from *Nineteenth Century French Tales*, edited by Angel Flores, published by Doubleday & Company, Inc., Garden City, in 1960, and reprinted by Dover as *Great Nineteenth-Century French Short Stories* in 1990.
The present translation of "The Necklace" is taken from *The Works of Guy de Maupassant: Short Stories*, published by Black's Readers Service, Roslyn, n.d.
The present translation of "The Unknown Masterpiece" is taken from *Honoré de Balzac: Selected Short Stories/Contes Choisis: A Dual-Language Book*, edited and translated by Stanley Appelbaum, published by Dover in 2000.
The present translations of "The Attack on the Mill," "Mateo Falcone," and "The Pope's Mule" are taken from *Nineteenth-Century French Short Stories/Contes et Nouvelles Français du XIXe Siècle: A Dual-Language Book*, edited and translated by Stanley Appelbaum, published by Dover in 2000.
"The Horla" is reprinted from a standard translated edition.

Library of Congress Cataloging-in-Publication Data

Great French short stories / edited by Paul Negri.
    p. cm. — (Dover thrift editions)
    ISBN 0-486-43470-2 (pbk.)
    1. Short stories, French—Translations into English. 2. French fiction—19th century—Translations into English. I. Negri, Paul. II. Series.

PQ1278.G74 2004
843'.0108—dc22

2004043940

Manufactured in the United States by Courier Corporation
43470203
www.doverpublications.com

Note

The nineteenth-century rise of newspapers and periodicals created a new demand and appreciation for short fiction. In the hands of the great French writers of the day, the genre of the short story flourished. Under the influence of foreign authors (notably Edgar Allan Poe and E. T. A. Hoffmann), many of the classic French short stories explored themes of the fantastic and supernatural. The Realist movement, by contrast, spawned stories that portrayed everyday subjects in as respectful and unpretentious a manner as possible. The competing Symbolist movement sought to bring profound truths into focus through the use of mysterious and often dark imagery. The result of these many disparate influences was a short story literature of tremendous range and variety.

This volume contains twelve of the finest and best-known short stories by French writers, most of them written during the nineteenth-century "golden age" of French short fiction. In addition, this collection includes a selection by the great eighteenth-century satirist Voltaire as well as a story by the twentieth-century master André Gide. These stories still maintain their power to surprise and enthrall readers.

Contents

Gustave Flaubert

THE LEGEND OF ST. JULIAN THE HOSPITALER

La Légende de Saint Julien l'Hospitalier

I

Julian's father and mother lived in a castle, in the middle of a forest, on the slope of a hill.

The four towers at the corners had pointed roofs covered with scales of lead, and the base of the walls rested on shafts of rock which fell steeply to the bottom of the moat.

The pavement of the courtyard was as clean as the flagstones of a church. Long gutter-spouts, representing dragons, with their mouths hanging down, spat rainwater into the cistern; and on the window ledges, at every floor, in a pot of painted earthenware, a basil or heliotrope blossomed.

A second enclosure, made with stakes, contained first an orchard of fruit trees, then a flower-bed where flowers were patterned into the form of figures, and then a trellis with arbors where you could take a walk, and a mall where the pages could play. On the other side were the kennels, the stables, the bakery, the wine-presses and the barns. A pasture of green grass spread round about, itself enclosed by a stout thorn-hedge.

They had lived at peace for so long that the portcullis was never lowered. The moats were full of water, birds made their nests in the cracks of the battlements, and when the blaze of the sun was too strong, the archer, who all day long walked back and forth on the curtain wall, went into the watch-tower and slept like a monk.

Inside, the ironwork glistened everywhere. Tapestries in the bedrooms were protection against the cold. Cupboards overflowed with linen, casks of wine were piled up in the cellars, and oak coffers creaked with the weight of bags of money.

In the armory, between standards and heads of wild beasts, you could see weapons of every age and nation, from the slings of the Amalekites and the javelins of the Garamantes, to the short swords of the Saracens and the Norman coats-of-mail.

The large spit in the kitchen could roast an ox. The chapel was as

1

sumptuous as the oratory of a king. There was even, in a remote corner, a Roman steam-bath; but the good lord did not use it, considering it a pagan practice.

Always wrapped in a coat lined with fox fur, he walked about his house, meting out justice to his vassals and settling the quarrels of his neighbors. During the winter, he would watch the snowflakes fall or have stories read to him. With the first fine days he went off on his mule along the small lanes, beside the wheat turning green, and chatted with the peasants, to whom he gave advice. After many adventures, he had taken as his wife a young lady of high lineage.

Her skin was very white, and she was a bit proud and serious. The horns of her coif grazed the lintel of the doors, and the train of her dress trailed three paces behind her. Her household was run like the inside of a monastery. Each morning she distributed the work to her servants, supervised the preserves and unguents, span at her distaff or embroidered altar-cloths. After much praying to God, a son was born to her.

There was great rejoicing then, and a banquet which lasted three days and four nights, on leaves strewn about, under the illumination from torches and the playing of harps. They ate the rarest spices, with chickens as fat as sheep. For amusement, a dwarf came out of a pastry-pie, and as the bowls gave out because the crowd was constantly increasing, they were obliged to drink from horns and helmets.

The new mother was not present at this festivity. She quietly stayed in her bed. One evening she awoke and saw, under a moonbeam which came through the window, something like a moving shadow. It was an old man in a frieze robe, with a rosary at his side, a wallet on his shoulder, and resembling a hermit. He came near to her bedside and said to her, without opening his lips.

"Rejoice, O mother, your son will be a saint!"

She was going to cry out, but, gliding along the moonbeam, he gently rose up into the air and disappeared. The banquet songs broke out louder. She heard the voices of angels and her head fell back on her pillow over which hung a martyr's bone in a frame of carbuncles.

The next day all the servants were questioned and declared they had seen no hermit. Dream or reality, it must have been a message from heaven, but she was careful to say nothing about it, for fear she would be accused of pride.

The guests departed at day-break, Julian's father was outside of the postern gate where he had just accompanied the last one to go, when suddenly a beggar rose up before him in the mist. He was a Gypsy with plaited beard and silver rings on his two arms, and flaming eyes. Like one inspired, he stammered these disconnected words:

"Ah, ah! your son! . . . much blood! . . . much glory! . . . always happy! . . . an emperor's family."

And bending down to pick up his alms, he was lost in the grass and disappeared.

The good castellan looked right and left, and called as loud as he could. No one! The wind whistled and the morning mist flew away.

He attributed this vision to the weariness of his head for having slept too little. "If I speak of this, they will make fun of me," he said to himself. Yet the glory destined to his son dazzled him, although the promise was not clear and he even doubted he had heard it.

The husband and wife kept their secret. But both cherished the child with an equal love, and respecting him as one marked by God, they had infinite care for his person. His crib was padded with the finest down, a lamp in the form of a dove burned over it, three nurses rocked him, and, tightly wrapped in his swaddling-clothes, with rosy face and blue eyes, dressed in a brocade mantle and a bonnet set with pearls, he looked like a little Lord Jesus. He teethed without crying once.

When he was seven, his mother taught him to sing. To make him brave, his father lifted him up on to a large horse. The child smiled with pleasure and was not long in knowing everything about chargers.

A very learned old monk taught him Holy Scripture, Arabic numerals, Latin letters, and how to make charming pictures on vellum. They worked together, high up in a turret, away from noise.

When the lesson was over, they went down into the garden where they studied flowers as they walked slowly about.

Sometimes they saw, passing below in the valley, a file of beasts of burden, led by a man walking, dressed in an Oriental fashion. The castellan, recognizing him for a merchant, would send a page to him. The stranger, when he felt confidence, turned off from his road. When led into the parlor, he would take out of his coffers strips of velvet and silk, jewelry, spices and strange things of unknown use. After this, the fellow, having suffered no violence, would go off, with a large profit. At other times, a group of pilgrims would knock at the door. Their wet clothes steamed before the hearth. When they had eaten heartily, they told the story of their travels: the courses of the ships on the foamy sea, the journeyings on foot in the burning sand, the cruelty of the pagans, the caves of Syria, the Manger and the Sepulcher. Then they would give the young lord shells from their cloaks.

Often the castellan would give a feast for his old companions-at-arms. As they drank, they recalled their wars, the storming of fortresses with the crash of war machines and huge wounds. As he listened to them, Julian uttered cries; his father then did not doubt that one day he would be a conqueror. But at evening, coming from the Angelus, when he passed among the poor, with their heads bowed, he took money from his purse with such modesty and so noble an air, that his mother was sure she would see him one day an archbishop.

His place in chapel was beside his parents, and no matter how long the services, he remained kneeling on his prayer-stool, his cap on the floor and his hands clasped.

One day, during mass, he saw, on raising his head, a small white mouse coming out of a hole in the wall. It trotted over the first step of the altar and after two or three turns to right and left, scampered back from where it had come. The next Sunday, he was disturbed by the thought that he might see it again. It came back, and each Sunday, he waited for it, was upset by it, grew to hate it and made up his mind to get rid of it.

So, having shut the door and spread on the steps some cake-crumbs, he took his place in front of the hole, with a stick in his hand.

After a long time, a pink nose appeared, and then the entire mouse. He struck a light blow, and stood lost in stupefaction before the small body that did not move again. A drop of blood spotted the pavement. He quickly wiped it with his sleeve, threw the mouse outdoors, and did not mention the matter to anyone.

All kinds of small birds were pecking at the seeds in the garden. He had the idea of putting peas in a hollow reed. When he heard the birds chirping in a tree, he came up to it quietly, then raised his pipe and blew out his cheeks. The little creatures rained down on his shoulders in such numbers that he could not keep from laughing with delight over his malice.

One morning, as he was coming back along the curtain wall, he saw on the top of the rampart a fat pigeon strutting in the sun. Julian stopped to look at it. The wall at that spot had a breach and a fragment of stone lay close to his fingers. He swung his arm and the stone struck down the bird which fell like a lump into the moat.

He rushed down after it, tearing himself on the undergrowth, ferreting about everywhere, more nimble than a young dog.

The pigeon, its wings broken, hung quivering in the branches of a privet.

Its persistence to live irritated the boy. He began to strangle it. The bird's convulsions made his heart beat and filled him with a wild tumultuous pleasure. When it stiffened for the last time, he felt himself fainting.

During the evening meal, his father declared it was time for him to learn venery, and went to look for an old copybook containing, in the form of questions and answers, the entire pastime of hunting. In it a teacher demonstrated to his pupil the art of training dogs and taming falcons, of setting traps, of how to recognize the stag by his droppings, the fox by its track, the wolf by its scratchings; the right way to make out their tracks, the way in which to start them, where their lairs are usually found, which winds are the most favorable, with a list of the calls and the rules for the quarry.

When Julian could recite all these things by heart, his father made up a pack of hounds for him.

First you could see twenty-four greyhounds from Barbary, swifter than gazelles, but subject to over-excitement; then seventeen pairs of Breton hounds, with red coats and white spots, unshakably dependable, broad-chested and great howlers. For an attack on the wild boar and for dangerous redoublings, there were forty griffons, as shaggy as bears. Mastiffs from Tartary, almost as tall as asses, flame-colored, with broad backs and straight legs, were intended to hunt aurochs. The black coats of the spaniels shone like satin. The yapping of the talbots was equal to the chanting of the beagles. In a yard by themselves, as they shook their chains and rolled their eyes, growled eight Alain bulldogs, formidable beasts which fly at the belly of a horseman and have no fear of lions.

All ate wheat bread, drank from stone troughs, and bore sonorous names.

The falconry, possibly, was better chosen than the pack. The good lord, thanks to money, had secured tercelets from the Caucasus, sakers from Babylonia, gerfalcons from Germany, and peregrines, caught on the cliffs, at the edge of cold seas, in distant countries. They were housed in a shed with a thatched roof, and attached according to size on the perching-bar. Before them was a strip of grass where from time to time they were placed to unstiffen their legs.

Rabbit-nets, hooks, wolf-traps and all kinds of snares were constructed.

They often took into the country setters which quickly came to a point. Then grooms, advancing step by step, cautiously spread over their motionless bodies an immense net. A word of command made them bark; the quail took wing; and ladies from nearby, invited with their husbands, children, handmaids, — the entire group fell on the birds and easily caught them.

On other occasions, to start the hares, they would beat drums. Foxes fell into pits, or a trap would spring and catch a wolf by its paw.

But Julian scorned these easy devices. He preferred to hunt far from the others, with his horse and falcon. It was almost always a large Scythian tartaret, white as snow. Its leather hood was topped with a plume, gold bells shook on its blue feet. It stood firm on its master's arm while the horse galloped and the plains unrolled. Julian, untying the jesses, would suddenly release it. The bold bird rose straight as an arrow into the air, and you saw two uneven specks turn, meet and disappear in the high blue of the sky. The falcon was not long in coming down, tearing apart some bird, and returned to perch on the gauntlet, its two wings quivering.

In this way, Julian flew his falcon at the heron, the kite, the crow and the vulture.

As he blew his horn, he loved to follow his dogs when they ran over the side of the hills, jumped the streams, and climbed back to the woods. When the stag began to groan under the bites of the dogs, he killed it quickly and then revelled in the fury of the mastiffs as they devoured it, cut into pieces on its steaming skin.

On foggy days he would go down into a marsh to ambush geese and otters and wild-duck.

At dawn three squires were waiting for him at the foot of the steps, and the old monk, leaning out of his dormer-window, vainly made signs to call him back. Julian would not turn. He went out in the heat of the sun, in the rain, in storms, drank the water of the springs out of his hand, ate crab-apples as he trotted, rested under an oak if he were tired; and came back in the middle of the night, covered with blood and mire, with thorns in his hair and the smell of wild beasts on him. He became one of them. When his mother kissed him, he accepted her embrace coldly and seemed to be dreaming of deep things.

He killed bears with blows of his knife, bulls with the axe, wild boars with the boar-spear, and once, even, with only a stick he defended himself against wolves which were gnawing corpses at the foot of a gibbet.

One winter morning, he left before daybreak, well equipped, with a crossbow on his shoulder and a bunch of arrows at his saddle-bow.

His Danish jennet, followed by two bassets, made the earth resound under its even tread. Drops of ice stuck to his cloak. A strong wind was blowing. One side of the horizon lighted up, and in the whiteness of the early light, he saw rabbits hopping at the edge of their burrows. Immediately the two bassets rushed on them, and quickly throwing them back and forth broke their backs.

Soon he went into a forest. At the end of a branch, a wood grouse, numbed by the cold, slept with its head under its wing. With a back-stroke of his sword, Julian cut off its two feet, and without picking it up, went on his way.

Three hours later, he was on the top of a mountain, so high that the sky seemed almost black. In front of him, a rock like a long wall sloped down, hanging over a precipice. At its farther end, two wild rams were looking into the chasm. Since he did not have his arrows (his horse had stayed behind), he decided to go down to them. Barefoot and half bent-over, he finally reached the first of the rams, and plunged a dagger under its ribs. The second, terrified, jumped into the chasm. Julian jumped in order to strike it, and slipping on his right foot, fell over the body of the other one, his face over the abyss and his two arms spread out.

Coming down again onto the plain, he followed a line of willows which bordered a river. Cranes, flying very low, passed overhead from time to time. Julian killed them with his whip and did not miss one.

In the meantime the warmer air had melted the hoarfrost, broad streaks of mist floated in the air and the sun came out. At a distance he saw a still lake glistening as if it were of lead. In the middle of the lake there was an animal which Julian did not know, a beaver with a black snout. In spite of the distance, an arrow killed it, and he was disconsolate at not being able to carry off the skin.

Then he advanced along an avenue of tall trees, forming with their tops a kind of triumphal arch, at the entrance of a forest. A roebuck bounded out of a thick wood, a deer appeared at a crossing, a badger came out of a hole, a peacock spread its tail on the grass; and when he had slain them all, more roebucks appeared, more deer, more badgers, more peacocks, and blackbirds, jays, polecats, foxes, hedgehogs, lynxes, an endless number of animals, more numerous at every step. They circled around him, trembling and looking at him gently and entreatingly. But Julian did not tire of killing, by turns bending his crossbow, unsheathing his sword, thrusting with his cutlass, and having no thought, no memory of anything at all. He had been hunting in some vague country, for an indefinite time, by the sole fact of his own existence, and everything had been accomplished with the ease you experience in dreams. An extraordinary spectacle brought him to a halt. A valley in the form of an amphitheater was filled with stags crowded close together and warming one another with their breath which could be seen steaming in the fog.

The perspective of such a slaughter choked him with pleasure for a few minutes. Then he dismounted, rolled up his sleeves and began to shoot.

At the whistle of the first arrow, all the stags turned their heads at once. Some openings were made in their mass. Plaintive cries rose up and a great stir shook the herd.

The brim of the valley was too high to climb. They leapt about in the enclosure, trying to escape. Julian kept aiming and shooting, and his arrows fell like shafts of rain in a storm. The maddened stags fought, reared, and climbed over each other. Their bodies with their entangled antlers made a broad hillock which collapsed as it moved about.

At last they died, stretched out on the sand, frothing at the nostrils, their entrails coming out, and the heaving of their bellies slowly diminishing. Then all was motionless.

Night was approaching. Behind the woods, in the interspaces of the branches, the sky was red like a cloth of blood.

Julian leaned against a tree. With staring eyes he looked at the vastness of the massacre, and did not understand how he could have done it.

On the other side of the valley, on the edge of the forest, he saw a stag, a hind and its fawn.

The stag, which was black and huge in size, carried antlers of sixteen tines and a white beard. The hind, of a dull yellow like dead leaves, was grazing, and the spotted fawn, without hindering her walk, was suckling her udder.

Once more the crossbow hummed. The fawn was killed at once. Then its mother, raising her head toward the sky, belled with a deep, heart-rending, human cry. Exasperated, Julian, with one shot full in the breast, stretched her out on the ground.

The large stag had seen this and made one bound. Julian shot his last arrow at him. It pierced him in the forehead and stuck fast there.

The large stag did not seem to feel it. Stepping over the dead bodies, it kept coming, and was going to charge and disembowel him. Julian drew back in unspeakable fear. The monstrous animal stopped. With his eyes flaming, as solemn as a patriarch and a judge, he repeated three times, while a bell tolled far off:

"A curse on you! A curse on you! A curse on you! One day, ferocious heart, you will murder your father and your mother!"

His knees bent, he gently closed his eyes, and died.

Julian was stupefied and then crushed by a sudden fatigue. Disgust and an immense sadness overcame him. His head in his two hands, he wept for a long time.

His horse was lost, his dogs had abandoned him, and the solitude which surrounded him seemed to threaten him with vague perils. Impelled by fright, he made his way across the countryside, chose a path at random, and found himself almost immediately at the gate of the castle.

That night he did not sleep. In the flickering of the hanging lamp he kept seeing the large black stag. Its prophecy obsessed him. He fought against it. "No, no, no, it is impossible for me to kill them!" Then he thought, "And yet, what if I wished to . . . ?" And he feared that the devil might inspire him with this desire.

For three months his anguished mother prayed by his bedside, and his father with groans walked back and forth in the corridors. He sent for the most famous master physicians who prescribed quantities of drugs. They said that the malady of Julian had been caused by some deadly wind or by a love-desire. But the young man, at every question, shook his head.

His strength came back, and he was taken for walks in the courtyard, the old monk and the good lord supporting him on either side.

When he had completely recovered, he stubbornly refused to hunt.

His father, wanting to cheer him, made him a present of a large Saracen sword.

It was at the top of a pillar, in a trophy-stand. To reach it, a ladder was necessary. Julian climbed up. The sword was so heavy that it slipped from his fingers and as it fell, it grazed the good lord so close that it cut his great-coat. Julian thought he had killed his father and fainted.

From then on, he dreaded weapons. The sight of a bare blade made him turn pale. This weakness was a sorrow for his family.

Finally the old monk, in the name of God, of his honor and his ancestors, ordered him to resume his exercises of a noble.

Every day the squires amused themselves by practising with the javelin. Very soon Julian excelled in this. He could hurl his into the neck of bottles, or break off the teeth of weather-vanes, or hit the nails on doors at a hundred paces.

One summer evening, at the hour when the fog makes things indistinct, he was under the vine-arbor of the garden and saw at the end of it two white wings fluttering at the same height as the espalier. He thought beyond doubt it was a stork, and threw his javelin.

A piercing cry rang out.

It was his mother whose bonnet with long flaps was nailed to the wall.

Julian fled from the castle and was not seen there again.

II

He joined up with a troop of adventurers who happened to pass by. He knew hunger, thirst, fever and vermin. He grew accustomed to the din of fights, and to the sight of dying men.

The wind tanned his skin. His limbs hardened through contact with armor; and as he was very strong, courageous, temperate and prudent, he received without difficulty the command of a company.

At the beginning of the battles, he would urge on his soldiers with a flourish of his sword. With a knotted rope he scaled the walls of citadels at night, swinging with the wind, while sparks of Greek fire stuck to his cuirass, and boiling resin and molten lead poured from the battlements. Often a stone would strike and shatter his shield. Bridges overladen with men collapsed under him. By swinging his mace, he got rid of fourteen horsemen. In the lists, he overcame all his challengers. More than twenty times he was believed dead.

Thanks to divine favor, he always recovered, because he protected churchmen, orphans, widows, and most of all, old men. When he saw one walking in front of him, he called out to see his face, as if he were afraid of killing him by mistake.

Runaway slaves, peasants in revolt, bastards without fortune, all kinds of daring men crowded under this banner, and he formed an army of his own.

It grew large. He became famous. He was sought after.

In turn, he helped the French Dauphin and the King of England, the Templars of Jerusalem, the Surena of the Parthians, the Negus of Abyssinia, and the Emperor of Calicut. He fought Scandinavians covered with fish-scales, Negroes equipped with round shields of hippopotamus hide and mounted on red asses, gold-colored Indians brandishing over their diadems broadswords brighter than mirrors. He conquered the Troglodytes and the Anthropophagi. He crossed lands so torrid that under the burning sun the hair on the head caught fire of itself, like a torch. And other regions were so glacial that the arms snapped from the body and fell to the ground. And still other countries where there was so much fog that you walked surrounded by ghosts.

Republics in distress consulted him. When he interviewed ambassadors, he obtained unhoped-for terms. If a monarch behaved too badly, Julian appeared suddenly and admonished him. He liberated peoples. He freed queens locked in towers. It was he, and no other, who slew the viper of Milan and the dragon of Oberbirbach.

Now, the Emperor of Occitania, having triumphed over the Spanish Moslems, had taken as concubine the sister of the Caliph of Cordova. By her he had a daughter whom he had brought up as a Christian. But the Caliph, pretending he wanted to be converted, came to visit him, accompanied by a numerous escort, and massacred his entire garrison. He threw the Emperor into a dungeon underground where he treated him harshly in order to extort treasures from him.

Julian hastened to his aid, destroyed the army of the Infidels, besieged the city, killed the Caliph, cut off his head, and threw it like a ball over the ramparts. Then he released the Emperor from prison and set him back on his throne, in the presence of his entire court.

For such a service, the Emperor presented him with a great deal of money in baskets. Julian wanted none of it. Believing that he desired more, he offered him three quarters of his wealth. He was refused again. Then he offered to share his kingdom and Julian declined. The Emperor wept through vexation, not knowing how to express his gratitude, when suddenly he tapped his forehead, and said some words in a courtier's ear. The curtains of a tapestry lifted and a young girl appeared.

Her large black eyes shone like two very gentle lamps. Her lips parted in a charming smile. The ringlets of her hair caught in the jewels of her half dress, and under the transparency of her tunic the youthfulness of her body could be guessed. She had a slim figure and was entrancing and soft.

Julian was dazzled with love, all the more so because he had lived until then very chastely.

So, he took the Emperor's daughter in marriage, and a castle which she received from her mother. When the wedding was over, the two families separated after endless courtesies on both sides.

It was a palace of white marble, built in the Moorish style, on a promontory, in a grove of orange trees. Terraces of flowers sloped down to the edge of a bay, where pink shells crunched underfoot. Behind the castle, a forest spread in the shape of a fan. The sky was continually blue, and the trees bent by turns under the sea breeze and the wind from the mountains which enclosed the horizon far off.

The bedrooms, full of twilight, were lighted from inlays in the walls. High columns, as slender as reeds, supported the vault of the cupolas, decorated with bas-reliefs imitating stalactites in caves.

There were fountains in the large rooms, mosaics in the courtyards, festooned partitions, numberless delicacies of architecture, and everywhere such silence that you heard the rustle of a scarf or the echo of a sigh.

Julian no longer waged war. He rested, in the midst of a quiet people. Each day a crowd passed in front of him with genuflections and hand-kissing in the Oriental style.

Dressed in purple, he remained leaning on his elbows in the embrasure of a window, recalling the hunts he used to go on. He would have liked to race over the desert after gazelles and ostriches, hide in the bamboo to wait for leopards, go through forests full of rhinoceroses, climb to the summit of the most inaccessible mountains in order to take better aim at eagles, and fight white bears on ice floes.

Sometimes, in a dream, he saw himself as our father Adam in the middle of Paradise, among all the animals. By stretching out his arm, he had them die. Or they would file by, two by two, according to size, from elephants and lions to ermines and ducks, as on the day when they entered Noah's Ark. In the dark of a cavern, he hurled on them infallible javelins. Others appeared, and there was no end to them. He woke up rolling his wild eyes.

Some princes among his friends invited him to hunt. He always refused, believing that by this kind of penance, he would turn aside his misfortune, for it seemed to him that the fate of his parents depended upon the slaughter of animals. But he was grieved at not seeing them, and his other desire became unbearable.

His wife had jugglers and dancing-girls come to amuse him.

She traveled with him, in an open litter, throughout the countryside. On other occasions, lying over the edge of a shallop they would watch fish swimming aimlessly in water as clear as the sky. Often she threw flowers in his face, or crouching at his feet she drew melodies from a three-stringed mandolin. Then, placing her two clasped hands on his shoulders, said timidly:

"What troubles you, dear lord?"

He did not answer, or burst into sobs. At last, one day he confessed his horrible thought.

She fought it with good arguments. His father and mother were probably dead. If ever he did see them again, by what chance or for what reason, would he perform that abomination? So, his fears had no cause and he should take up hunting again.

Julian smiled as he listened to her, but did not decide to fulfill his desire.

One evening in the month of August when they were in their rooms, she had just gone to bed and he was kneeling for his prayers when he heard the yapping of a fox and then light steps under the window. In the shadows he caught a glimpse of something like the forms of animals. The temptation was too strong. He took down his quiver.

She showed surprise.

"It is to obey you!" he said. "I shall be back at sunrise."

Yet she feared a fatal adventure.

He reassured her and then left, surprised at the inconsistency of her mood.

Shortly afterwards, a page came to announce that two strangers were insisting upon seeing the wife of the lord immediately, since the lord was absent.

Soon there came into the room an old man and an old woman, bent over, covered with dust, dressed in rough cloth and each leaning on a staff.

They took courage and declared they were bringing Julian news of his parents.

She leaned over in order to hear them.

But first, exchanging glances of agreement, they asked her if he still loved them and if he ever spoke of them.

"Oh, yes!" she said.

Then they cried:

"We are his parents!"

And they sat down, being very weary and exhausted with fatigue.

There was nothing to assure the young wife that her husband was their son.

They gave proof of this by describing some particular marks he had on his body.

She leapt from her bed, called her page and had food served to them.

Although they were very hungry, they could hardly eat; and, off to one side, she watched the trembling of their bony hands as they took the goblets.

They asked countless questions about Julian. She answered each one, but was careful to conceal the deadly idea in which they were concerned.

When he did not return home, they had left their castle and had been walking for several years, on vague clues, without losing hope. So much money had been needed for river-tolls and for hostelries, for the taxes of princes and the demands of thieves, that the bottom of their purse was empty and now they begged. But this was of no consequence, since they would soon embrace their son. They extolled his happiness at having such a pretty wife, and did not grow weary of looking at her and kissing her.

The richness of the apartment astonished them, and the old man, examining the walls, asked why the coat-of-arms of the Emperor of Occitania was on them.

She replied:

"He is my father!"

At that he trembled, remembering the prophecy of the Gypsy, and the old woman thought of the hermit's words. Her son's glory doubtless was only the dawn of eternal splendor. Both of them sat open-mouthed, under the light of the candelabrum on the table.

They must have been very handsome in their youth. The mother still had all her hair and its fine plaits, like drifts of snow, hung to the bottom of her cheeks. The father, with his tall figure and long beard, resembled a church statue.

Julian's wife urged them not to wait for him. She herself put them into her own bed, and then closed the casement window. They fell asleep. The day was about to dawn and on the other side of the stained-glass window, small birds were beginning to sing.

Julian had crossed the park and he walked with a nervous stride in the forest enjoying the softness of the grass and the mildness of the air.

Shadows from the trees spread over the moss. At times the moon made white spots in the glades, and he hesitated to continue, thinking he saw a pool of water, or the surface of the still ponds merged with the color of the grass. A deep silence was everywhere. He found not one of the beasts which a few minutes earlier were wandering around his castle.

The wood thickened and the darkness grew more dark. Puffs of warm wind passed by, full of enervating smells. He sank into piles of dead leaves, and he leaned against an oak in order to catch his breath.

Suddenly, behind his back, a blacker mass leapt out. It was a wild boar. Julian had only time enough to seize his bow, and he was grieved at this as if by a misfortune.

Then, after leaving the woods, he saw a wolf trotting along a hedge.

Julian shot an arrow at it. The wolf stopped, turned its head to look at him, and went on again. As it trotted on, it always kept the same distance, stopped from time to time, and as soon as it was aimed at, began again to run.

In this manner, Julian covered an endless plain, then some small sand-hills, and finally came out on a plateau which looked over a large expanse of country. Flat stones were scattered about between ruined burial vaults. You stumbled over bones of dead men. In some places worm-eaten crosses leaned over in a mournful way. But forms stirred in the indistinct shadows of the tombs. Hyenas, terrified and panting, rose out of them. With their nails clattering on the paving-stones, they came up to him and sniffed at him, showing their gums as they yawned. He unsheathed his sword. They went off at once in every direction, and continuing their limping precipitous gallop, they disappeared in a distant cloud of dust.

One hour later, in a ravine he came upon a mad bull, its horns lowered and pawing the sand with its foot. Julian thrust his lance under its dew-lap. The weapon was shattered as if the animal had been of bronze. He closed his eyes, expecting his death. When he opened them again, the bull had disappeared.

Then his soul sank with shame. A superior power was destroying his strength. In order to return home, he went back into the forest.

It was tangled with creepers. He was cutting them with his sword when a marten slipped abruptly between his legs. A panther made a bound over his shoulder and a serpent coiled its way up an ash tree.

A monstrous jackdaw in the foliage was looking at Julian. Here and there, between the branches appeared quantities of large sparks, as if the firmament had showered all of its stars into the forest. They were eyes of animals, wildcats, squirrels, owls, parrots and monkeys.

Julian shot his arrows at them, and the arrows with their feathers alighted on the leaves like white butterflies. He threw stones at them, and the stones, without touching anything, fell to the ground. He cursed himself, wanted to fight, shouted imprecations, and choked with rage.

And all the animals he had hunted appeared again forming around him a narrow circle. Some sat on their haunches and others were fully erect. He stayed in the middle, frozen with horror, incapable of the slightest movement. Through a supreme effort of his will, he took one step. The ones perched on trees opened their wings, those treading on the ground stretched their limbs, and all went with him.

The hyenas walked in front of him, the wolf and the boar behind. The bull, on his right, swayed its head, and on his left, the serpent wound through the grass, while the panther, arching its back, advanced with long velvet-footed strides. He went as slowly as possible in order not to irritate them. He saw coming out from the dark of the bushes porcupines, foxes, vipers, jackals and bears.

Julian began to run, and they ran. The serpent hissed, the stinking beasts slavered. The boar rubbed Julian's heels with his tusks, the wolf the inside of his hands with the hairs of its snout. The monkeys pinched him and made faces. The marten rolled over his feet. A bear, with a backhanded swipe of its paw, knocked off his hat, and the panther scornfully dropped an arrow which it had been holding in its mouth.

An irony was apparent in their sly movements. While watching him from the corner of their eyes, they seemed to be meditating a plan of revenge. Deafened by the buzzing of insects, lashed by the tails of birds, suffocated by all the breathing around him, he walked with his arms stretched out and his eyes closed like a blind man, without even having the strength to cry for mercy.

The crow of a cock rang through the air. Others answered it. It was day and he recognized, beyond the orange trees, the ridge of his palace roof.

Then, at the edge of a field he saw, three paces off, some red-legged partridge fluttering in the stubble. He unfastened his cloak and cast it over them like a net. When he uncovered them, he found only one, dead for a long time and rotten.

This disappointment exasperated him more than all the others. His thirst for slaughter seized him again. Since there were no animals, he would willingly massacre humans.

He climbed the three terraces, broke open the door with a blow of his fist, but at the bottom of the staircase, the thought of his dear wife softened his heart. She was doubtless sleeping and he would surprise her.

Taking off his sandals, he gently turned the lock and went in.

The pallor of the dawn was darkened as it came through the leaded stained-glass windows. Julian's feet caught in some clothes on the floor, and a bit farther on, he knocked against a buffet still laden with dishes. "She must have been eating," he said to himself, and he moved toward the bed which was lost in the darkness at the end of the room. When he reached the edge of the bed, in order to kiss his wife, he leaned over the pillow where the two heads were lying one close to the other. Then against his mouth he felt the touch of a beard.

He drew back, believing that he was losing his mind. But he came back close to the bed, and as his fingers felt about, they touched very long hair. To convince himself of his error, he again slowly passed his hand over the pillow. It was really a beard this time and a man! A man in bed with his wife!

Overcome with unbounded rage, he leaped on them and struck with his dagger. He stamped and foamed, with roars of a wild beast. Then he stopped. The dead, pierced to the heart, had not even moved. He listened closely to their death-rattles which were almost the same, and as they grew feebler, another groan from far off took them up. At first indistinct, this plaintive long-drawn voice came closer, swelled and became cruel. Terrified, he recognized the belling of the large black stag.

As he turned around, he thought he saw, in the frame of the door, his wife's ghost, with a light in her hand.

She had been drawn there by the din of the murder. In one wide glance she understood everything, and fleeing in horror, dropped her torch.

He picked it up.

Before him his mother and father were lying on their backs, with a hole in their breasts. Their faces, of a majestic gentleness, seemed to be keeping an eternal secret. Splashes and pools of blood spread over their white skin, over the sheets of the bed, on the floor, and over an ivory crucifix hanging in the alcove. The scarlet reflection from the stained-glass window, which the sun was striking, lit up the red patches and cast many others throughout the apartment. Julian walked toward the two dead figures, saying to himself, and wanting to believe, that this was not possible, that he was mistaken, that at times there are inexplicable resemblances. Finally he bent down slightly to look at the old man close to, and he saw, between the partly closed eyelids, a glazed eyeball which burned him like fire. Then he went to the other side of the bed, where the other body lay, whose white hair covered a part of her face. Julian passed his fingers under the plaits and raised the head. He looked at it as he held it at arm's length in one hand, while in his other hand he held up a torch for light. Drops, oozing from the mattress, fell one by one on the floor.

At the end of the day, he presented himself before his wife. In a voice not his own, he first ordered her not to answer him, not to approach him, not even to look at him, and to follow, under pain of damnation, all his instructions, which were irrevocable.

The funeral was carried out according to the directions he had left in writing, on a prie-Dieu, in the chamber of the dead. He left to her his palace, his vassals, all his possessions, without even retaining the clothes of his body and his sandals which would be found at the head of the stairs.

She had obeyed the will of God in causing his crime, and she was to pray for his soul because henceforth he did not exist.

The dead were buried with great pomp, in the church of a monastery three days' journey from the castle. A monk, with his hood pulled down, followed the procession, far from all the others, and no one dared to speak to him.

During the mass, he remained flat on his stomach, in the middle of the portal, his arms like a cross and his forehead in the dust.

After the burial, they saw him take the road which led to the mountains. He turned to look back several times, and finally disappeared.

III

He went off, begging his way through the world.

He held out his hand to horsemen on the roads, and approached harvesters with genuflections, or remained motionless before the gate of courtyards. His face was so sad that he was never refused alms.

In a spirit of humility, he would tell his story. Then all would flee from him, as they made the sign of the cross. In villages which he had already passed through, as soon as he was recognized, people would shut their doors, threaten him with words, and throw stones at him. The most charitable placed a bowl on their window-sill, then closed the shutters so as not to see him.

Being repulsed everywhere, he avoided men. He lived on roots, plants, spoiled fruit and shellfish which he found along the beaches.

Sometimes, at the turn of a hillside, he saw down below a jumble of crowded roofs, with stone spires, bridges, towers, dark streets crisscrossing, from which a continuous hum rose up to him.

The need to mingle with other beings made him go down into the town. But the brutish expressions on the faces, the uproar of the crafts, the emptiness of the words froze his heart. On feast days, when the ringing of the cathedral bells made everyone joyful from daybreak, he watched the inhabitants leave their houses, and the dancing on the squares, the barley-beer jugs at the crossroads, the damask hangings in front of the houses of princes; and when evening came, he watched through the windows of the ground floor the long family table where grandparents held small children on their knees. Sobs would choke him and he would go back toward the country.

With feelings of love he watched colts in the pasture, birds in their nests, insects on the flowers. But all, as he drew near, would run off, or hide in terror or quickly fly away.

He sought solitary places. But the wind brought to his ears sounds like the death-rattle. The drops of dew falling to the ground reminded him of other drops of heavier weight. Every evening the sun spread blood over the clouds, and every night, in his dreams, his parricide began over again.

He made himself a hair shirt with iron spikes. On his knees he climbed every hill which had a chapel at the top. But his pitiless thought darkened the splendor of the tabernacles, and tortured him throughout the maceration of his penance.

He did not revolt against God who had inflicted this action on him, and yet he was in despair through having been able to commit it.

His own person filled him with such horror that, hoping for release from it, he risked his life in dangers. He saved paralytics from fires and children from the bottom of chasms. The abyss threw him back and the flames spared him.

Time did not relieve his suffering. It grew intolerable. He resolved to die.

One day when he was on the brink of a fountain and leaning over in order to judge the depths of the water, he saw appear opposite him an emaciated old man, with a white beard and so sorrowful a look that he could not hold back his weeping. The other also was weeping. Without recognizing his image, Julian vaguely remembered a face which resembled that one. He uttered a cry. It was his father. He thought no more of killing himself.

Thus, bearing the weight of his memory, he traveled through many countries. He came to a river which was dangerous to cross because of its violence and because there was on its banks a large stretch of mud. For a long time no one had dared cross it.

An old boat, whose stern was embedded, raised its prow among the reeds. On examining it, Julian discovered a pair of oars, and the thought came to him to spend his life in the service of others.

He began by constructing on the banks a kind of roadway which would permit people to reach the channel. He broke his nails in moving gigantic stones, and pressed them against his stomach in order to carry them, slipped in the mud, sank into it, and almost perished several times.

Then he repaired the boat with pieces of ship wreckage and made a hut for himself with clay and tree-trunks.

Since the crossing was known, travelers appeared. They called to him from the other bank, by waving flags. Quickly Julian jumped into his barge. It was very heavy, and they would overweigh it with all kinds of baggage and bundles, not to mention the beasts of burden which increased the crowding as they kicked in fear. He asked nothing for his work. Some would give him the remains of food which they pulled out of their wallets or worn-out clothes they no longer wanted. The roughest of them shouted blasphemies. Julian reproved them gently and they answered with words of abuse. He was content to bless them.

His only furniture was a small table, a stool, a bed of dry leaves and three clay cups. Two holes in the wall served as windows. On one side barren plains stretched out as far as the eye could see, dotted here and there with pale ponds. In front of him, the great river rolled forth its greenish waves. In the spring, the damp earth had a smell of decay. Then, a riotous wind raised up the dust in whirling clouds. It came in everywhere, muddied the water, and made a crunching sound under the gums. A little later, there were swarms of mosquitoes, which did not stop buzzing and stinging day or night. Then, terrible frosts would come which gave to everything the rigidity of stone, and aroused a mad need to eat meat.

Months passed when Julian saw no one. He often closed his eyes and tried in his memory to return to his youth. The courtyard of the castle would appear with greyhounds on the steps, page boys in the armory, and, under a vine arbor, a blond-haired adolescent between an old man dressed in furs and a lady wearing a large coif. Suddenly, the two corpses were there. He threw himself flat on his stomach, on his bed, and repeated through his tears:

"Ah! poor father! poor mother! poor mother!"
And fell into a drowsiness where funereal visions continued.
One night when he was sleeping, he thought he heard someone calling him. He listened and could only make out the roar of the waves.
But the same voice called out again:
"Julian!"
It came from the other bank, which seemed extraordinary to him, considering the breadth of the river.
A third time someone called:
"Julian!"
And that loud voice had the resonance of a church bell.

He lit his lantern and went out of the hut. A furious hurricane filled the night. There was total darkness, pierced here and there by the whiteness of the leaping waves.

After a moment's hesitation, Julian untied the painter. Instantly the water became calm. The barge glided over it and reached the other bank where a man was waiting.

He was wrapped in a tattered cloth. His face was like a plaster mask and his two eyes were redder than coals. As he brought the lantern close to him, Julian saw that he was covered with a hideous leprosy; yet his bearing had the majesty of a king.

As soon as he entered the barge, it sank prodigiously, overwhelmed by his weight. It rose again with a shake, and Julian began to row.

At each stroke of the oar, the backwash of the waves raised its bow. Blacker than ink, the water raced furiously on both sides of the planking. It hollowed out chasms and made mountains. The shallop leaped over them, then went down again into the depths where it whirled, tossed about by the wind.

Julian bent his body, stretched out his arms, and propping himself with his feet, swung back with a twist of his waist, in order to get more power. The hail lashed his hands, the rain rolled down his back, the fierceness of the wind stifled him and he stopped. Then the boat was set adrift. But, feeling that something momentous was at stake, an order which he should not disobey, he took up his oars again. The banging of the tholes cut through the uproar of the storm.

The small lantern burned in front of him. Birds as they fluttered about hid it from time to time. But he could always see the eyeballs of the Leper who stood at the stern, motionless as a pillar.

That lasted a long time, a very long time.

When they came to the hut, Julian shut the door. He saw the Leper sitting on the stool. The kind of shroud which covered him had fallen to his hips. His shoulders, his chest and his thin arms were hidden under a coating of scaly pustules. Immense wrinkles furrowed his brow. Like a skeleton, he had a hole in place of a nose, and his bluish lips exhaled a breath as thick as fog and nauseous.

"I am hungry!" he said.

Julian gave him what he had, an old gammon of bacon and the crusts of a loaf of black bread.

When he had devoured them, the table, the bowl and knife handle bore the same spots that were seen on his body.

Next, he said:

"I am thirsty."

Julian went to get his pitcher, and as he took it, it gave forth an aroma which dilated heart and nostrils! It was wine—what luck! But the Leper put out his arm and emptied the whole pitcher at one draught.

Then he said:

"I am cold!"

With his candle Julian lighted a pile of fern in the middle of the hut. The Leper drew near to warm himself. Crouching on his heels, he trembled in every limb and grew weaker. His eyes no longer shone, his ulcers ran, and in an almost lifeless voice, he murmured:

"Your bed!"

Julian helped him gently to drag himself to it and even spread over him, to cover him, the sail from his boat.

The Leper groaned. His teeth showed at the corners of his mouth, a faster rattle shook his chest, and his stomach at each breath was hollowed to his backbone.

Then he closed his eyelids.

"It is like ice in my bones! Come close to me!"

And Julian, lifting the sail, lay down on the dry leaves, near him, side by side.

The Leper turned his head.

"Undress, so that I can have the warmth of your body!"

Julian took off his clothes; then, naked as on the day of his birth, got back into the bed. And he felt against his thigh the Leper's skin, colder than a serpent and rough as a file.

He tried to give him courage, and the other answered panting:

"Ah! I am dying! . . . Come closer, warm me! Not with your hands! no! with your whole body."

Julian stretched out completely over him, mouth to mouth, chest to chest.

Then the Leper clasped him and his eyes suddenly took on the light of the stars. His hair became as long as the rays of the sun. The breath of his nostrils was as sweet as roses. A cloud of incense rose up from the hearth and the waves sang. Meanwhile an abundance of happiness, a super-human joy came down like a flood into Julian's soul as it swooned. The one whose arms still clasped him, grew and grew until he touched with his head and his feet the two walls of the hut. The roof flew off, the firmament unrolled, and Julian ascended toward the blue spaces, face to face with Our Lord Jesus, who carried him to heaven.

And that is the story of St. Julian the Hospitaler, more or less as you find it, on a stained-glass window of a church in my town.

Guy de Maupassant

THE NECKLACE

La Parure

She was one of those pretty, charming young ladies, born, as if through an error of destiny, into a family of clerks. She had no dowry, no hopes, no means of becoming known, appreciated, loved, and married by a man either rich or distinguished; and she allowed herself to marry a petty clerk in the office of the Board of Education.

She was simple, not being able to adorn herself; but she was unhappy, as one out of her class; for women belong to no caste, no race; their grace, their beauty, and their charm serving them in the place of birth and family. Their inborn finesse, their instinctive elegance, their suppleness of wit are their only aristocracy, making some daughters of the people the equal of great ladies.

She suffered incessantly, feeling herself born for all delicacies and luxuries. She suffered from the poverty of her apartment, the shabby walls, the worn chairs, and the faded stuffs. All these things, which another woman of her station would not have noticed, tortured and angered her. The sight of the little Breton, who made this humble home, awoke in her sad regrets and desperate dreams. She thought of quiet antechambers, with their Oriental hangings, lighted by high, bronze torches, and of the two great footmen in short trousers who sleep in the large armchairs, made sleepy by the heavy air from the heating apparatus. She thought of large drawing-rooms, hung in old silks, of graceful pieces of furniture carrying bric-à-brac of inestimable value, and of the little perfumed coquettish apartments, made for five o'clock chats with most intimate friends, men known and sought after, whose attention all women envied and desired.

When she seated herself for dinner, before the round table where the tablecloth had been used three days, opposite her husband who uncovered the tureen with a delighted air, saying: "Oh! the good potpie! I know nothing better than that—" she would think of the elegant dinners, of the shining silver, of the tapestries peopling the walls with ancient personages and rare birds in the midst of fairy forests; she thought of the exquisite food served on marvelous dishes, of the whispered gallantries, listened to with the smile of the sphinx, while eating the rose-colored flesh of the trout or a chicken's wing.

She had neither frocks nor jewels, nothing. And she loved only those things. She felt that she was made for them. She had such a desire to please, to be sought after, to be clever, and courted.

She had a rich friend, a schoolmate at the convent, whom she did not like to visit, she suffered so much when she returned. And she wept for whole days from chagrin, from regret, from despair, and disappointment.

*   *   *

One evening her husband returned elated bearing in his hand a large envelope.

"Here," he said, "here is something for you."

She quickly tore open the wrapper and drew out a printed card on which were inscribed these words:

> "The Minister of Public Instruction and Madame George Ramponneau ask the honor of Mr. and Mrs. Loisel's company Monday evening, January 18, at the Minister's residence."

Instead of being delighted, as her husband had hoped, she threw the invitation spitefully upon the table murmuring:

"What do you suppose I want with that?"

"But, my dearie, I thought it would make you happy. You never go out, and this is an occasion, and a fine one! I had a great deal of trouble to get it. Everybody wishes one, and it is very select; not many are given to employees. You will see the whole official world there."

She looked at him with an irritated eye and declared impatiently:

"What do you suppose I have to wear to such a thing as that?"

He had not thought of that; he stammered:

"Why, the dress you wear when we go to the theater. It seems very pretty to me—"

He was silent, stupefied, in dismay, at the sight of his wife weeping. Two great tears fell slowly from the corners of her eyes toward the corners of her mouth; he stammered:

"What is the matter? What is the matter?"

By a violent effort, she had controlled her vexation and responded in a calm voice, wiping her moist cheeks:

"Nothing. Only I have no dress and consequently I cannot go to this affair. Give your card to some colleague whose wife is better fitted out than I."

He was grieved, but answered:

"Let us see, Matilda. How much would a suitable costume cost, something that would serve for other occasions, something very simple?"

She reflected for some seconds, making estimates and thinking of a sum that she could ask for without bringing with it an immediate refusal and a frightened exclamation from the economical clerk.

Finally she said, in a hesitating voice:

"I cannot tell exactly, but it seems to me that four hundred francs ought to cover it."

He turned a little pale, for he had saved just this sum to buy a gun that he might be able to join some hunting parties the next summer, on the plains at Nanterre, with some friends who went to shoot larks up there on Sunday. Nevertheless, he answered:

"Very well. I will give you four hundred francs. But try to have a pretty dress."

*   *   *

The day of the ball approached and Mme. Loisel seemed sad, disturbed, anxious. Nevertheless, her dress was nearly ready. Her husband said to her one evening:

"What is the matter with you? You have acted strangely for two or three days."

And she responded: "I am vexed not to have a jewel, not one stone, nothing to adorn myself with. I shall have such a poverty-laden look. I would prefer not to go to this party."

He replied: "You can wear some natural flowers. At this season they look very *chic*. For ten francs you can have two or three magnificent roses."

She was not convinced. "No," she replied, "there is nothing more humiliating than to have a shabby air in the midst of rich women."

Then her husband cried out: "How stupid we are! Go and find your friend Mrs. Forestier and ask her to lend you her jewels. You are well enough acquainted with her to do this."

She uttered a cry of joy: "It is true!" she said. "I had not thought of that."

The next day she took herself to her friend's house and related her story of distress. Mrs. Forestier went to her closet with the glass doors, took out a large jewel-case, brought it, opened it, and said: "Choose, my dear."

She saw at first some bracelets, then a collar of pearls, then a Venetian cross of gold and jewels and of admirable workmanship. She tried the jewels before the glass, hesitated, but could neither decide to take them nor leave them. Then she asked:

"Have you nothing more?"

"Why, yes. Look for yourself. I do not know what will please you."

Suddenly she discovered, in a black satin box, a superb necklace of diamonds, and her heart beat fast with an immoderate desire. Her hands trembled as she took them up. She placed them about her throat against her dress, and remained in ecstasy before them. Then she asked, in a hesitating voice, full of anxiety:

"Could you lend me this? Only this?"

"Why, yes, certainly."

She fell upon the neck of her friend, embraced her with passion, then went away with her treasure.

*   *   *

The day of the ball arrived. Mme. Loisel was a great success. She was the prettiest of all, elegant, gracious, smiling, and full of joy. All the men noticed her, asked her name, and wanted to be presented. All the members of the Cabinet wished to waltz with her. The Minister of Education paid her some attention.

She danced with enthusiasm, with passion, intoxicated with pleasure, thinking of nothing, in the triumph of her beauty, in the glory of her success, in a kind of cloud of happiness that came of all this homage, and all this admiration, of all these awakened desires, and this victory so complete and sweet to the heart of woman.

She went home toward four o'clock in the morning. Her husband had been half asleep in one of the little salons since midnight, with three other gentlemen whose wives were enjoying themselves very much.

He threw around her shoulders the wraps they had carried for the coming home, modest garments of everyday wear, whose poverty clashed with the elegance of the ball costume. She felt this and wished to hurry away in order not to be noticed by the other women who were wrapping themselves in rich furs.

Loisel retained her: "Wait," said he. "You will catch cold out there. I am going to call a cab."

But she would not listen and descended the steps rapidly. When they were in the street, they found no carriage; and they began to seek for one, hailing the coachmen whom they saw at a distance.

They walked along toward the Seine, hopeless and shivering. Finally they found on the quay one of those old, nocturnal *coupés* that one sees in Paris after nightfall, as if they were ashamed of their misery by day.

It took them as far as their door in Martyr street, and they went wearily up to their apartment. It was all over for her. And on his part, he remembered that he would have to be at the office by ten o'clock.

She removed the wraps from her shoulders before the glass, for a final view of herself in her glory. Suddenly she uttered a cry. Her necklace was not around her neck.

Her husband, already half undressed, asked: "What is the matter?"

She turned toward him excitedly:

"I have—I have—I no longer have Mrs. Forestier's necklace."

He arose in dismay: "What! How is that? It is not possible."

And they looked in the folds in the dress, in the folds of the mantle, in the pockets, everywhere. They could not find it.

He asked: "You are sure you still had it when we left the house?"

"Yes, I felt it in the vestibule as we came out."

"But if you had lost it in the street, we should have heard it fall. It must be in the cab."

"Yes. It is probable. Did you take the number?"

"No. And you, did you notice what it was?"

"No."

They looked at each other utterly cast down. Finally, Loisel dressed himself again.

"I am going," said he, "over the track where we went on foot, to see if I can find it."

And he went. She remained in her evening gown, not having the force to go to bed, stretched upon a chair, without ambition or thoughts.

Toward seven o'clock her husband returned. He had found nothing.

He went to the police and to the cab offices, and put an advertisement in the newspapers, offering a reward; he did everything that afforded them a suspicion of hope.

She waited all day in a state of bewilderment before this frightful disaster. Loisel returned at evening with his face harrowed and pale; and had discovered nothing.

"It will be necessary," said he, "to write to your friend that you have broken the clasp of the necklace and that you will have it repaired. That will give us time to turn around."

She wrote as he dictated.

* * *

At the end of a week, they had lost all hope. And Loisel, older by five years, declared:

"We must take measures to replace this jewel."

The next day they took the box which had inclosed it, to the jeweler whose name was on the inside. He consulted his books:

"It is not I, Madame," said he, "who sold this necklace; I only furnished the casket."

Then they went from jeweler to jeweler seeking a necklace like the other one, consulting their memories, and ill, both of them, with chagrin and anxiety.

In a shop of the Palais-Royal, they found a chaplet of diamonds which seemed to them exactly like the one they had lost. It was valued at forty thousand francs. They could get it for thirty-six thousand.

They begged the jeweler not to sell it for three days. And they made an arrangement by which they might return it for thirty-four thousand francs if they found the other one before the end of February.

Loisel possessed eighteen thousand francs which his father had left him. He borrowed the rest.

He borrowed it, asking for a thousand francs of one, five hundred of another, five louis of this one, and three louis of that one. He gave notes, made ruinous promises, took money of usurers and the whole race of lenders. He compromised his whole existence, in fact, risked his signature, without even knowing whether he could make it good or not, and, harassed by anxiety for the future, by the black misery which surrounded him, and by the prospect of all physical privations and moral torture, he went to get the new necklace, depositing on the merchant's counter thirty-six thousand francs.

When Mrs. Loisel took back the jewels to Mrs. Forestier, the latter said to her in a frigid tone:

"You should have returned them to me sooner, for I might have needed them."

She did open the jewel-box as her friend feared she would. If she should perceive the substitution, what would she think? What should she say? Would she take her for a robber?

*   *   *

Mrs. Loisel now knew the horrible life of necessity. She did her part, however, completely, heroically. It was necessary to pay this frightful debt. She would pay it. They sent away the maid; they changed their lodgings; they rented some rooms under a mansard roof.

She learned the heavy cares of a household, the odious work of a kitchen. She washed the dishes, using her rosy nails upon the greasy pots and the bottoms of the stewpans. She washed the soiled linen, the chemises and dishcloths, which she hung on the line to dry; she took down the refuse to the street each morning and brought up the water, stopping at each landing to breathe. And, clothed like a woman of the people, she went to the grocer's, the butcher's, and the fruiterer's, with her basket on her arm, shopping, haggling to the last sou her miserable money.

Every month it was necessary to renew some notes, thus obtaining time, and to pay others.

The husband worked evenings, putting the books of some merchants in order, and nights he often did copying at five sous a page.

And this life lasted for ten years.

At the end of ten years, they had restored all, all, with interest of the usurer, and accumulated interest besides.

Mrs. Loisel seemed old now. She had become a strong, hard woman, the crude woman of the poor household. Her hair badly dressed, her skirts awry, her hands red, she spoke in a loud tone, and washed the floors in large pails of water. But sometimes, when her husband was at the office, she would seat herself before the window and think of that evening party of former times, of that ball where she was so beautiful and so flattered.

How could it have been if she had not lost that necklace? Who knows? Who knows? How singular is life, and how full of changes! How small a thing will ruin or save one!

* * *

One Sunday, as she was taking a walk in the Champs-Elysées to rid herself of the cares of the week, she suddenly perceived a woman walking with a child. It was Mrs. Forestier, still young, still pretty, still attractive. Mrs. Loisel was affected. Should she speak to her? Yes, certainly. And now that she had paid, she would tell her all. Why not?

She approached her. "Good morning, Jeanne."

Her friend did not recognize her and was astonished to be so familiarly addressed by this common personage. She stammered:

"But, Madame—I do not know—You must be mistaken—"

"No, I am Matilda Loisel."

Her friend uttered a cry of astonishment: "Oh! my poor Matilda! How you have changed—"

"Yes, I have had some hard days since I saw you; and some miserable ones—and all because of you—"

"Because of me? How is that?"

"You recall the diamond necklace that you loaned me to wear to the Commissioner's ball?"

"Yes, very well."

"Well, I lost it."

"How is that, since you returned it to me?"

"I returned another to you exactly like it. And it has taken us ten years to pay for it. You can understand that it was not easy for us who have nothing. But it is finished and I am decently content."

Madame Forestier stopped short. She said:

"You say that you bought a diamond necklace to replace mine?"

"Yes. You did not perceive it then? They were just alike."

And she smiled with a proud and simple joy. Madame Forestier was touched and took both her hands as she replied:

"Oh! my poor Matilda! Mine were false. They were not worth over five hundred francs!"

Guy de Maupassant

Guy de Maupassant

THE HORLA

Le Horla

May 8. What a lovely day! I have spent all the morning lying in the grass in front of my house, under the enormous plane tree that shades the whole of it. I like this part of the country and I like to live here because I am attached to it by old associations, by those deep and delicate roots which attach a man to the soil on which his ancestors were born and died, which attach him to the ideas and usages of the place as well as to the food, to local expressions, to the peculiar twang of the peasants, to the smell of the soil, of the villages and of the atmosphere itself.

I love my house in which I grew up. From my windows I can see the Seine which flows alongside my garden, on the other side of the high road, almost through my grounds, the great and wide Seine, which goes to Rouen and Havre, and is covered with boats passing to and fro.

On the left, down yonder, lies Rouen, that large town, with its blue roofs, under its pointed Gothic towers. There are innumerable, slender or broad, dominated by the spire of the cathedral, and full of bells which sound through the blue air on fine mornings, sending their sweet and distant iron clang even as far as my home; that song of the metal, which the breeze wafts in my direction, now stronger and now weaker, according as the wind is stronger or lighter.

What a delicious morning it was!

About eleven o'clock, a long line of boats drawn by a steam tug as big as a fly, and which scarcely puffed while emitting its thick smoke, passed my gate.

After two English schooners, whose red flag fluttered in space, there came a magnificent Brazilian three-master; it was perfectly white, and wonderfully clean and shining. I saluted it, I hardly knew why, except that the sight of the vessel gave me great pleasure.

May 12. I have had a slight feverish attack for the last few days, and I feel ill, or rather I feel low-spirited.

Whence come those mysterious influences which change our happiness into discouragement, and our self-confidence into diffidence? One might almost say that the air, the invisible air, is full of unknowable Powers whose mysterious presence we have to endure. I wake up in the best spirits, with an inclination to sing. Why? I go down to the edge of the water, and suddenly, after walking a short distance, I return home wretched, as if some misfortune were awaiting me there. Why? Is it a cold shiver which, passing over my skin, has upset my nerves and given me low spirits? Is it the form of the clouds, the color of the sky, or the color of the surrounding objects which is so changeable, that has troubled my thoughts as they passed before my eyes? Who can tell? Everything that surrounds us, everything that we see, without looking at it, everything that we touch, without knowing it, everything that we handle, without feeling it, all that we meet, without clearly distinguishing it, has a rapid, surprising and inexplicable effect upon us and upon our senses, and, through them, on our ideas and on our heart itself.

How profound that mystery of the Invisible is! We cannot fathom it with our miserable senses, with our eyes which are unable to perceive what is either too small or too great, too near us, or too far from us— neither the inhabitants of a star nor of a drop of water; nor with our ears that deceive us, for they transmit to us the vibrations of the air in sonorous notes. They are fairies who work the miracle of changing these vibrations into sound, and by that metamorphosis give birth to music, which makes the silent motion of nature musical . . . with our sense of smell which is less keen than that of a dog . . . with our sense of taste which can scarcely distinguish the age of a wine!

Oh! If we only had other organs which would work other miracles in our favor, what a number of fresh things we might discover around us!

May 16. I am ill, decidedly! I was so well last month! I am feverish, horribly feverish, or rather I am in a state of feverish enervation, which makes my mind suffer as much as my body. I have, continually, that horrible sensation of some impending danger, that apprehension of some coming misfortune, or of approaching death; that presentiment which is, no doubt, an attack of some illness which is still unknown, which germinates in the flesh and in the blood.

May 17. I have just come from consulting my physician, for I could no longer get any sleep. He said my pulse was rapid, my eyes dilated, my nerves highly strung, but there were no alarming symptoms. I must take a course of shower baths and of bromide of potassium.

May 25. No change! My condition is really very peculiar. As the evening comes on, an incomprehensible feeling of disquietude seizes me, just as if night concealed some threatening disaster. I dine hurriedly, and then try to read, but I do not understand the words, and can scarcely distinguish the letters. Then I walk up and down my drawing-room, oppressed by a feeling of confused and irresistible fear, the fear of sleep and fear of my bed.

About ten o'clock I go up to my room. As soon as I enter it I double-lock and bolt the door; I am afraid . . . of what? Up to the present time I have been afraid of nothing . . . I open my cupboards, and look under my bed; I listen . . . to what? How strange it is that a simple feeling of discomfort, impeded or heightened circulation, perhaps the irritation of a nerve filament, a slight congestion, a small disturbance in the imperfect delicate functioning of our living machinery, may turn the most light-hearted of men into a melancholy one, and make a coward of the bravest? Then, I go to bed, and wait for sleep as a man might wait for the executioner. I wait for its coming with dread, and my heart beats and my legs tremble, while my whole body shivers beneath the warmth of the bedclothes, until all at once I fall asleep, as though one should plunge into a pool of stagnant water in order to drown. I do not feel it coming on as I did formerly, this perfidious sleep which is close to me and watching me, which is going to seize me by the head, to close my eyes and annihilate me.

I sleep—a long time—two or three hours perhaps—then a dream—no—a nightmare lays hold on me. I feel that I am in bed and asleep . . . I feel it and I know it . . . and I feel also that somebody is coming close to me, is looking at me, touching me, is getting on to my bed, is kneeling on my chest, is taking my neck between his hands and squeezing it . . . squeezing it with all his might in order to strangle me.

I struggle, bound by that terrible sense of powerlessness which para-lyzes us in our dreams; I try to cry out—but I cannot; I want to move—I cannot do so; I try, with the most violent efforts and breathing hard, to turn over and throw off this being who is crushing and suffocating me—I cannot!

And then, suddenly, I wake up, trembling and bathed in perspiration; I light a candle and find that I am alone, and after that crisis, which occurs every night, I at length fall asleep and slumber tranquilly till morning.

June 2. My condition has grown worse. What is the matter with me? The bromide does me no good, and the shower baths have no effect. Sometimes, in order to tire myself thoroughly, though I am fatigued enough already, I go for a walk in the forest of Roumare. I used to think at first that the fresh light and soft air, impregnated with the odor of herbs and leaves, would instill new blood into my veins and impart fresh energy to my heart. I turned into a broad hunting road, and then turned toward La Bouille, through a narrow path, between two rows of exceedingly tall trees, which placed a thick green, almost black, roof between the sky and me.

A sudden shiver ran through me, not a cold shiver, but a strange shiver of agony, and I hastened my steps, uneasy at being alone in the forest, afraid, stupidly and without reason, of the profound solitude. Suddenly it seemed to me as if I were being followed, that somebody was walking at my heels, close, quite close to me, near enough to touch me.

I turned round suddenly, but I was alone. I saw nothing behind me except the straight, broad path, empty and bordered by high trees, horribly empty; before me it also extended until it was lost in the distance, and looked just the same, terrible.

I closed my eyes. Why? And then I began to turn round on one heel very quickly, just like a top. I nearly fell down, and opened my eyes; the trees were dancing round me and the earth heaved; I was obliged to sit down. Then, ah! I no longer remembered how I had come! What a strange idea! What a strange, strange idea! I did not the least know. I started off to the right, and got back into the avenue which had led me into the middle of the forest.

June 3. I have had a terrible night. I shall go away for a few weeks, for no doubt a journey will set me up again.

July 2. I have come back, quite cured, and have had a most delightful trip into the bargain. I have been to Mont Saint-Michel, which I had not seen before.

What a sight, when one arrives as I did, at Avranches toward the end of the day! The town stands on a hill, and I was taken into the public garden at the extremity of the town. I uttered a cry of astonishment. An extraordinarily large bay lay extended before me, as far as my eyes could reach, between two hills which were lost to sight in the mist; and in the middle of this immense yellow bay, under a clear, golden sky, a peculiar hill rose up, sombre and pointed in the midst of the sand. The sun had just disappeared, and under the still flaming sky appeared the outline of that fantastic rock which bears on its summit a fantastic monument.

At daybreak I went out to it. The tide was low, as it had been the night before, and I saw that wonderful abbey rise up before me as I approached it. After several hours' walking, I reached the enormous mass of rocks which supports the little town, dominated by the great church. Having climbed the steep and narrow street, I entered the most wonderful Gothic building that has ever been built to God on earth, as large as a town, full of low rooms which seem buried beneath vaulted roofs, and lofty galleries supported by delicate columns.

I entered this gigantic granite gem, which is as light as a bit of lace, covered with towers, with slender belfries with spiral staircases, which raise their strange heads that bristle with chimeras, with devils, with fantastic animals, with monstrous flowers, to the blue sky by day, and to the black sky by night, and are connected by finely carved arches.

When I had reached the summit I said to the monk who accompanied me: "Father, how happy you must be here!" And he replied: "It is very windy here, monsieur"; and so we began to talk while watching the rising tide, which ran over the sand and covered it as with a steel cuirass.

And then the monk told me stories, all the old stories belonging to the place, legends, nothing but legends.

One of them struck me forcibly. The country people, those belonging to the Mount, declare that at night one can hear voices talking on the sands, and then that one hears two goats bleating, one with a strong, the other with a weak voice. Incredulous people declare that it is nothing but the cry of the sea birds, which occasionally resembles bleatings, and occasionally, human lamentations; but belated fishermen swear that they have met an old shepherd wandering between tides on the sands around the little town. His head is completely concealed by his cloak and he is followed by a billy goat with a man's face, and a nanny goat with a woman's face, both having long, white hair and talking incessantly and quarreling in an unknown tongue. Then suddenly they cease and begin to bleat with all their might.

"Do you believe it?" I asked the monk. "I scarcely know," he replied, and I continued: "If there are other beings besides ourselves on this earth, how comes it that we have not known it long since, or why have *you* not seen them? How is it that *I* have not seen them?" He replied: "Do we see the hundred-thousandth part of what exists? Look here; there is the wind, which is the strongest force in nature, which knocks down men, and blows down buildings, uproots trees, raises the sea into mountains of water, destroys cliffs and casts great ships on the rocks; the wind which kills, which whistles, which sighs, which roars—have you ever seen it, and can you see it? It exists for all that, however."

I was silent before this simple reasoning. That man was a philosopher, or perhaps a fool; I could not say which exactly, so I held my tongue. What he had said had often been in my own thoughts.

July 3. I have slept badly; certainly there is some feverish influence here, for my coachman is suffering in the same way as I am. When I went back home yesterday, I noticed his singular paleness, and I asked him: "What is the matter with you, Jean?" "The matter is that I never get any rest, and my nights devour my days. Since your departure, monsieur, there has been a spell over me."

However, the other servants are all well, but I am very much afraid of having another attack myself.

July 4. I am decidedly ill again; for my old nightmares have returned. Last night I felt somebody leaning on me and sucking my life from between my lips. Yes, he was sucking it out of my throat, like a leech.

Then he got up, satiated, and I woke up, so exhausted, crushed and weak that I could not move. If this continues for a few days, I shall certainly go away again.

July 5. Have I lost my reason? What happened last night is so strange that my head wanders when I think of it!

I had locked my door, as I do now every evening, and then, being thirsty, I drank half a glass of water, and accidentally noticed that the water bottle was full up to the cut-glass stopper.

Then I went to bed and fell into one of my terrible sleeps, from which I was aroused in about two hours by a still more frightful shock.

Picture to yourself a sleeping man who is being murdered and who wakes up with a knife in his lung, and whose breath rattles, who is covered with blood, and who can no longer breathe and is about to die, and does not understand—there you have it.

Having recovered my senses, I was thirsty again, so I lit a candle and went to the table on which stood my water bottle. I lifted it up and tilted it over my glass, but nothing came out. It was empty! It was completely empty! At first I could not understand it at all, and then suddenly I was seized by such a terrible feeling that I had to sit down, or rather I fell into a chair! Then I sprang up suddenly to look about me; then I sat down again, overcome by astonishment and fear, in front of the transparent glass bottle! I looked at it with fixed eyes, trying to conjecture, and my hands trembled! Somebody had drunk the water, but who? I? I without any doubt. It could surely only be I. In that case I was a somnambulist; I lived, without knowing it, that mysterious double life which makes us doubt whether there are not two beings in us, or whether a strange, unknowable and invisible being does not at such moments, when our soul is in a state of torpor, animate our captive body, which obeys this other being, as it obeys us, and more than it obeys ourselves.

Oh! Who will understand my horrible agony? Who will understand the emotion of a man who is sound in mind, wide awake, full of common sense, who looks in horror through the glass of a water bottle for a little water that disappeared while he was asleep? I remained thus until it was daylight, without venturing to go to bed again.

July 6. I am going mad. Again all the contents of my water bottle have been drunk during the night—or rather, I have drunk it!

But is it I? Is it I? Who could it be? Who? Oh! God! Am I going mad? Who will save me?

July 10. I have just been through some surprising ordeals. Decidedly I am mad! And yet! . . .

On July 6, before going to bed, I put some wine, milk, water, bread and strawberries on my table. Somebody drank—I drank—all the water and a little of the milk, but neither the wine, bread, nor the strawberries were touched.

On the seventh of July I renewed the same experiment, with the same results, and on July 8, I left out the water and the milk, and nothing was touched.

Lastly, on July 9, I put only water and milk on my table, taking care to wrap up the bottles in white muslin and to tie down the stoppers. Then I rubbed my lips, my beard and my hands with pencil lead, and went to bed.

Irresistible sleep seized me, which was soon followed by a terrible awakening. I had not moved, and there was no mark of lead on the sheets. I rushed to the table. The muslin round the bottles remained intact; I undid the string, trembling with fear. All the water had been drunk, and so had the milk! Ah! Great God! . . .

I must start for Paris immediately.

July 12. Paris. I must have lost my head during the last few days! I must be the plaything of my enervated imagination, unless I am really a somnambulist, or that I have been under the power of one of those hitherto unexplained influences which are called suggestions. In any case, my mental state bordered on madness, and twenty-four hours of Paris sufficed to restore my equilibrium.

Yesterday, after doing some business and paying some visits which instilled fresh and invigorating air into my soul, I wound up the evening at the *Théâtre-Français*. A play by Alexandre Dumas the younger was being acted, and his active and powerful imagination completed my cure. Certainly solitude is dangerous for active minds. We require around us men who can think and talk. When we are alone for a long time, we people space with phantoms.

I returned along the boulevards to my hotel in excellent spirits. Amid the jostling of the crowd I thought, not without irony, of my terrors and surmises of the previous week, because I had believed—yes, I had believed—that an invisible being lived beneath my roof. How weak our brains are, and how quickly they are terrified and led into error by a small incomprehensible fact.

Instead of saying simply: "I do not understand because I do not know the cause," we immediately imagine terrible mysteries and supernatural powers.

July 14. Fête of the Republic. I walked through the streets, amused as a child at the firecrackers and flags. Still it is very foolish to be merry on a fixed date, by Government decree. The populace is an imbecile flock of sheep, now stupidly patient, and now in ferocious revolt. Say to it: "Amuse yourself," and it amuses itself. Say to it: "Go and fight with your neighbor," and it goes and fights. Say to it: "Vote for the Emperor," and it votes for the Emperor, and then say to it: "Vote for the Republic," and it votes for the Republic.

Those who direct it are also stupid; only, instead of obeying men, they obey principles which can only be stupid, sterile, and false, for the very reason that they are principles, that is to say, ideas which are considered as certain and unchangeable, in this world where one is certain of nothing, since light is an illusion and noise is an illusion.

July 16. I saw some things yesterday that troubled me very much.

I was dining at the house of my cousin, Madame Sablé, whose husband is colonel of the 76th Chasseurs at Limoges. There were two young women there, one of whom had married a medical man, Dr. Parent, who devotes much attention to nervous diseases and to the remarkable manifestations taking place at this moment under the influence of hypnotism and suggestion.

He related to us at some length the wonderful results obtained by English scientists and by the doctors of the Nancy school; and the facts which he adduced appeared to me so strange that I declared that I was altogether incredulous.

"We are," he declared, "on the point of discovering one of the most important secrets of nature; I mean to say, one of its most important secrets on this earth, for there are certainly others of a different kind of importance up in the stars, yonder. Ever since man has thought, ever since he has been able to express and write down his thoughts, he has felt himself close to a mystery which is impenetrable to his gross and imperfect senses, and he endeavors to supplement through his intellect the inefficiency of his senses. As long as that intellect remained in its elementary stage, these apparitions of invisible spirits assumed forms that were commonplace, though terrifying. Thence sprang the popular belief in the supernatural, the legends of wandering spirits, of fairies, of gnomes, ghosts, I might even say the legend of God; for our conceptions of the workman-creator, from whatever religion they may have come down to us, are certainly the most mediocre, the most stupid and the most incredible inventions that ever sprang from the terrified brain of any human beings. Nothing is truer than what Voltaire says: 'God made man in His own image, but man has certainly paid Him back in his own coin.'

"However, for rather more than a century men seem to have had a presentiment of something new. Mesmer and some others have put us on an unexpected track, and, especially within the last two or three years, we have arrived at really surprising results."

My cousin, who is also very incredulous, smiled, and Dr. Parent said to her: "Would you like me to try and send you to sleep, madame?"
"Yes, certainly."

She sat down in an easy chair, and he began to look at her fixedly, so as to fascinate her. I suddenly felt myself growing uncomfortable, my heart beating rapidly and a choking sensation in my throat. I saw Madame Sablé's eyes becoming heavy, her mouth twitching and her bosom heaving, and at the end of ten minutes she was asleep.

"Go behind her," the doctor said to me, and I took a seat behind her. He put a visiting card into her hands, and said to her: "This is a looking-glass; what do you see in it?" And she replied, "I see my cousin." "What is he doing?" "He is twisting his mustache." "And now?" "He is taking a photograph out of his pocket." "Whose photograph is it?" "His own."

That was true, and the photograph had been given me that same evening at the hotel.

"What is his attitude in this portrait?" "He is standing up with his hat in his hand."

She saw, therefore, on that card, on that piece of white pasteboard, as if she had seen it in a mirror.

The young women were frightened, and exclaimed: "That is enough! Quite, quite enough!"

But the doctor said to Madame Sablé authoritatively; "You will rise at eight o'clock to-morrow morning; then you will go and call on your cousin at his hotel and ask him to lend you five thousand francs which your husband demands of you, and which he will ask for when he sets out on his coming journey."

Then he woke her up.

On returning to my hotel, I thought over this curious séance, and I was assailed by doubts, not as to my cousin's absolute and undoubted good faith, for I had known her as well as if she were my own sister ever since she was a child, but as to a possible trick on the doctor's part. Had he not, perhaps, kept a glass hidden in his hand, which he showed to the young woman in her sleep, at the same time as he did the card? Professional conjurors do things that are just as singular.

So I went home and to bed, and this morning, at about half-past eight, I was awakened by my valet, who said to me: "Madame Sablé has asked to see you immediately, monsieur." I dressed hastily and went to her.

She sat down in some agitation, with her eyes on the floor, and without raising her veil she said to me: "My dear cousin, I am going to ask a great favor of you." "What is it, cousin?" "I do not like to tell you, and yet I must. I am in absolute need of five thousand francs." "What, you?" "Yes, I, or rather my husband, who has asked me to procure them for him."

I was so thunderstruck that I stammered out my answers. I asked myself whether she had not really been making fun of me with

Dr. Parent, if it was not merely a very well-acted farce which had been rehearsed beforehand. On looking at her attentively, however, all my doubts disappeared. She was trembling with grief, so painful was this step to her, and I was convinced that her throat was full of sobs.

I knew that she was very rich and I continued: "What! Has not your husband five thousand francs at his disposal? Come, think. Are you sure that he commissioned you to ask me for them?"

She hesitated for a few seconds, as if she were making a great effort to search her memory, and then she replied: "Yes . . . yes, I am quite sure of it." "He has written to you?"

She hesitated again and reflected, and I guessed the torture of her thoughts. She did not know. She only knew that she was to borrow five thousand francs of me for her husband. So she told a lie. "Yes, he has written to me." "When, pray? You did not mention it to me yesterday." "I received his letter this morning." "Can you show it me?" "No; no . . . no . . . it contained private matters . . . things too personal to ourselves . . . I burned it." "So your husband runs into debt?"

She hesitated again, and then murmured: "I do not know." Thereupon I said bluntly: "I have not five thousand francs at my disposal at this moment, my dear cousin."

She uttered a kind of cry as if she were in pain and said: "Oh! oh! I beseech you, I beseech you to get them for me. . . ."

She got excited and clasped her hands as if she were praying to me! I heard her voice change its tone; she wept and stammered, harassed and dominated by the irresistible order that she had received.

"Oh! oh! I beg you to . . . if you knew what I am suffering . . . I want them to-day."

I had pity on her: "You shall have them by and by, I swear to you." "Oh! thank you! thank you! How kind you are."

I continued: "Do you remember what took place at your house last night?" "Yes." "Do you remember that Dr. Parent sent you to sleep?" "Yes." "Oh! Very well, then; he ordered you to come to me this morning to borrow five thousand francs, and at this moment you are obeying that suggestion."

She considered for a few moments, and then replied: "But as it is my husband who wants them—"

For a whole hour I tried to convince her, but could not succeed, and when she had gone I went to the doctor. He was just going out, and he listened to me with a smile, and said: "Do you believe now?" "Yes, I cannot help it." "Let us go to your cousin's."

She was already half asleep on a reclining chair, overcome with fatigue. The doctor felt her pulse, looked at her for some time with one hand raised toward her eyes, which she closed by degrees under the irresistible power of this magnetic influence, and when she was asleep, he said:

"Your husband does not require the five thousand francs any longer! You must, therefore, forget that you asked your cousin to lend them to you, and, if he speaks to you about it, you will not understand him."

Then he woke her up, and I took out a pocketbook and said: "Here is what you asked me for this morning, my dear cousin." But she was so surprised that I did not venture to persist; nevertheless, I tried to recall the circumstance to her, but she denied it vigorously, thought I was making fun of her, and, in the end, very nearly lost her temper.

* * *

There! I have just come back, and I have not been able to eat any lunch, for this experiment has altogether upset me.

July 19. Many people to whom I told the adventure laughed at me. I no longer know what to think. The wise man says: "It may be!"

July 21. I dined at Bougival, and then I spent the evening at a boatmen's ball. Decidedly everything depends on place and surroundings. It would be the height of folly to believe in the supernatural on the Île de la Grenouillière . . . but on the top of Mont Saint-Michel? . . . and in India? We are terribly influenced by our surroundings. I shall return home next week.

July 30. I came back to my own house yesterday. Everything is going on well.

August 2. Nothing new; it is splendid weather, and I spend my days in watching the Seine flowing past.

August 4. Quarrels among my servants. They declare that the glasses are broken in the cupboards at night. The footman accuses the cook, who accuses the seamstress, who accuses the other two. Who is the culprit? It is a clever person who can tell.

August 6. This time I am not mad. I have seen . . . I have seen . . . I have seen! . . . I can doubt no longer . . . I have seen it! . . .

I was walking at two o'clock among my rose trees, in the full sunlight . . . in the walk bordered by autumn roses which are beginning to fall. As I stopped to look at a Géant de Bataille, which had three splendid blossoms, I distinctly saw the stalk of one of the roses near me bend, as if an invisible hand had bent it, and then break, as if that hand had picked it! Then the flower raised itself following the curve which a hand would have described in carrying it toward a mouth, and it remained suspended in the transparent air, all alone and motionless, a terrible red spot, three yards from my eyes. In desperation I rushed at it to take it! I found nothing; it had disappeared. Then I was seized with furious rage against myself, for a reasonable and serious man should not have such hallucinations.

But was it an hallucination? I turned round to look for the stalk, and I found it at once, on the bush, freshly broken, between two other roses which remained on the branch. I returned home then, my mind greatly disturbed; for I am certain now, as certain as I am of the alternations of day and night, that there exists close to me an invisible being that lives on milk and water, that can touch objects, take them and change their places; that is, consequently, endowed with a material nature, although it is imperceptible to our senses, and that lives as I do, under my roof—

August 7. I slept tranquilly. He drank the water out of my decanter, but did not disturb my sleep.

I wonder if I am mad. As I was walking just now in the sun by the river side, doubts as to my sanity arose in me; not vague doubts such as I have had hitherto, but definite, absolute doubts. I have seen mad people, and I have known some who have been quite intelligent, lucid, even clear-sighted in every concern of life, except on one point. They spoke clearly, readily, profoundly on everything, when suddenly their mind struck upon the shoals of their madness and broke to pieces there, and scattered and floundered in that furious and terrible sea, full of rolling waves, fogs and squalls, which is called *madness*.

I certainly should think that I was mad, absolutely mad, if I were not conscious, did not perfectly know my condition, did not fathom it by analyzing it with the most complete lucidity. I should, in fact, be only a rational man who was laboring under an hallucination. Some unknown disturbance must have arisen in my brain, one of those disturbances which physiologists of the present day try to note and to verify; and that disturbance must have caused a deep gap in my mind and in the sequence and logic of my ideas. Similar phenomena occur in dreams which lead us among the most unlikely phantasmagoria, without causing us any surprise, because our verifying apparatus and our organ of control are asleep, while our imaginative faculty is awake and active. Is it not possible that one of the imperceptible notes of the cerebral keyboard has been paralyzed in me? Some men lose the recollection of proper names, of verbs, or of numbers, or merely of dates, in consequence of an accident. The localization of all the variations of thought has been established nowadays; why, then, should it be surprising if my faculty of controlling the unreality of certain hallucinations were dormant in me for the time being?

I thought of all this as I walked by the side of the water. The sun shone brightly on the river and made earth delightful, while it filled me with a love for live, for the swallows, whose agility always delights my eye, for the plants by the river side, the rustle of whose leaves is a pleasure to my ears.

By degrees, however, an inexplicable feeling of discomfort seized me. It seemed as if some unknown force were numbing and stopping me, were preventing me from going further, and were calling me back. I felt that painful wish to return which oppresses you when you have left a beloved invalid at home, and when you are seized with a presentiment that he is worse.

I, therefore, returned in spite of myself, feeling certain that I should find some bad news awaiting me, a letter or a telegram. There was nothing, however, and I was more surprised and uneasy than if I had had another fantastic vision.

August 8. I spent a terrible evening yesterday. He does not show himself any more, but I feel that he is near me, watching me, looking at me, penetrating me, dominating me, and more redoubtable when he hides himself thus than if he were to manifest his constant and invisible presence by supernatural phenomena. However, I slept.

August 9. Nothing, but I am afraid.

August 10. Nothing; what will happen to-morrow?

August 11. Still nothing; I cannot stop at home with this fear hanging over me and these thoughts in my mind; I shall go away.

August 12. Ten o'clock at night. All day long I have been trying to get away, and have not been able. I wished to accomplish this simple and easy act of freedom—to go out—to get into my carriage in order to go to Rouen—and I have not been able to do it. What is the reason?

August 13. When one is attacked by certain maladies, all the springs of our physical being appear to be broken, all our energies destroyed, all our muscles relaxed; our bones, too, have become as soft as flesh, and our blood as liquid as water. I am experiencing these sensations in my moral being in a strange and distressing manner. I have no longer any strength, any courage, any self-control, not even any power to set my own will in motion. I have no power left to will anything; but some one does it for me and I obey.

August 14. I am lost! Somebody possesses my soul and dominates it. Somebody orders all my acts, all my movements, all my thoughts. I am no longer anything in myself, nothing except an enslaved and terrified spectator of all the things I do. I wish to go out; I cannot. He does not wish to, and so I remain, trembling and distracted, in the armchair in which he keeps me sitting. I merely wish to get up and to rouse myself; I cannot! I am riveted to my chair, and my chair adheres to the ground in such a manner that no power could move us.

Then, suddenly, I must, I must go to the bottom of my garden to pick some strawberries and eat them, and I go there. I pick the strawberries and eat them! Oh, my God! My God! Is there a God? If there be one, deliver me! Save me! Succor me! Pardon! Pity! Mercy! Save me! Oh, what sufferings! What torture! What horror!

August 15. This is certainly the way in which my poor cousin was possessed and controlled when she came to borrow five thousand francs of me. She was under the power of a strange will which had entered into her, like another soul, like another parasitic and dominating soul. Is the world coming to an end?

But who is he, this invisible being that rules me? This unknowable being, this rover of a supernatural race?

Invisible beings exist, then! How is it, then, that since the beginning of the world they have never manifested themselves precisely as they do to me? I have never read of anything that resembles what goes on in my house. Oh, if I could only leave it, if I could only go away, escape, and never return! I should be saved, but I cannot.

August 16. I managed to escape to-day for two hours, like a prisoner who finds the door of his dungeon accidentally open. I suddenly felt that I was free and that he was far away, and so I gave orders to harness the horses as quickly as possible, and I drove to Rouen. Oh, how delightful to be able to say to a man who obeys you: "Go to Rouen!"

I made him pull up before the library, and I begged them to lend me Dr. Herrmann Herestauss' treatise on the unknown inhabitants of the ancient and modern world.

Then, as I was getting into my carriage, I intended to say: "To the railway station!" but instead of this I shouted—I did not say, but I shouted—in such a loud voice that all the passers-by turned round: "Home!" and I fell back on the cushion of my carriage, overcome by mental agony. He had found me again and regained possession of me.

August 17. Oh, what a night! What a night! And yet it seems to me that I ought to rejoice. I read until one o'clock in the morning! Herestauss, doctor of philosophy and theogony, wrote the history of the manifestation of all those invisible beings which hover around man, or of whom he dreams. He describes their origin, their domain, their power; but none of them resembles the one which haunts me. One might say that man, ever since he began to think, has had a foreboding fear of a new being, stronger than himself, his successor in this world, and that, feeling his presence, and not being able to foresee the nature of that master, he has, in his terror, created the whole race of occult beings, of vague phantoms born of fear.

Having, therefore, read until one o'clock in the morning, I went and sat down at the open window, in order to cool my forehead and thoughts, in the calm night air. It was very pleasant and warm! How I should have enjoyed such a night formerly!

There was no moon, but the stars darted out their rays in the dark heavens. Who inhabits those worlds? What forms, what living beings, what animals are there yonder? What do the thinkers in those distant worlds know more than we do? What can they do more than we can? What do they see which we do not know? Will not one of them, some day or other, traversing space, appear on our earth to conquer it, just as the Norsemen formerly crossed the sea in order to subjugate nations more feeble than themselves?

We are so weak, so defenseless, so ignorant, so small, we who live on this particle of mud which revolves in a drop of water.

I fell asleep, dreaming thus in the cool night air, and when I had slept for about three-quarters of an hour, I opened my eyes without moving, awakened by I know not what confused and strange sensation. At first I saw nothing, and then suddenly it appeared to me as if a page of a book which had remained open on my table turned over of its own accord. Not a breath of air had come in at my window, and I was surprised, and waited. In about four minutes, I saw, I saw, yes, I saw with my own eyes, another page lift itself up and fall down on the others, as if a finger had turned it over. My armchair was empty, appeared empty, but I knew that he was there, he, and sitting in my place, and that he was reading. With a furious bound, the bound of an enraged wild beast that springs at its tamer, I crossed my room to seize him, to strangle him, to kill him! But before I could reach it, the chair fell over as if somebody had run away from me—my table rocked, my lamp fell and went out, and my window closed as if some thief had been surprised and had fled out into the night, shutting it behind him.

So he had run away; he had been afraid; he, afraid of me!

But—but—to-morrow—or later—some day or other—I should be able to hold him in my clutches and crush him against the ground! Do not dogs occasionally bite and strangle their masters?

August 18. I have been thinking the whole day long. Oh, yes, I will obey him, follow his impulses, fulfill all his wishes, show myself humble, submissive, a coward. He is the stronger; but the hour will come—

August 19. I know—I know—I know all! I have just read the following in the *Revue du Monde Scientifique:* "A curious piece of news comes to us from Rio de Janeiro. Madness, an epidemic of madness, which may be compared to that contagious madness which attacked the people of Europe in the Middle Ages, is at this moment raging in the Province of San-Paolo. The terrified inhabitants are leaving their houses, saying that they are pursued, possessed, dominated like human cattle by invisible, though tangible beings, a species of vampire, which feed on their life while they are asleep, and who, besides, drink water and milk without appearing to touch any other nourishment.

"Professor Don Pedro Henriques, accompanied by several medical savants, has gone to the Province of San-Paolo, in order to study the origin and the manifestations of this surprising madness on the spot, and to propose such measures to the Emperor as may appear to him to be most fitted to restore the mad population to reason."

Ah! Ah! I remember now that fine Brazilian three-master which passed in front of my windows as it was going up the Seine, on the 8th day of last May! I thought it looked so pretty, so white and bright! That Being was on board of her, coming from there, where its race originated. And it saw me! It saw my house which was also white, and it sprang from the ship on to the land. Oh, merciful heaven!

Now I know, I can divine. The reign of man is over, and he has come. He who was feared by primitive man; whom disquieted priests exorcised; whom sorcerers evoked on dark nights, without having seen him appear, to whom the imagination of the transient masters of the world lent all the monstrous or graceful forms of gnomes, spirits, genii, fairies and familiar spirits. After the coarse conceptions of primitive fear, more clear-sighted men foresaw it more clearly. Mesmer divined it, and ten years ago physicians accurately discovered the nature of his power, even before he exercised it himself. They played with this new weapon of the Lord, the sway of a mysterious will over the human soul, which had become a slave. They called it magnetism, hypnotism, suggestion—what do I know? I have seen them amusing themselves like rash children with this horrible power! Woe to us! Woe to man! He has come, the—the—what does he call himself—the—I fancy that he is shouting out his name to me and I do not hear him—the—yes—he is shouting it out—I am listening—I cannot—he repeats it—the—Horla—I hear—the Horla—it is he—the Horla—he has come!

Ah! the vulture has eaten the pigeon; the wolf has eaten the lamb; the lion has devoured the sharp-horned buffalo; man has killed the lion with an arrow, with a sword, with gunpowder; but the Horla will make of man what we have made of the horse and of the ox; his chattel, his slave and his food, by the mere power of his will. Woe to us!

But, nevertheless, the animal sometimes revolts and kills the man who has subjugated it. I should also like—I shall be able to—but I must know him, touch him, see him! Scientists say that animals' eyes, being different from ours, do not distinguish objects as ours do. And my eye cannot distinguish this newcomer who is oppressing me.

Why? Oh, now I remember the words of the monk at Mont Saint-Michel: "Can we see the hundred-thousandth part of what exists? See here; there is the wind, which is the strongest force in nature, which knocks down men, and blows down buildings, uproots trees, raises the sea into mountains of water, destroys cliffs and casts great ships on the breakers; the wind which kills, which whistles, which sighs, which roars—have you ever seen it, and can you see it? It exists for all that however!"

And I went on thinking; my eyes are so weak, so imperfect, that they do not even distinguish hard bodies, if they are as transparent as glass! If a glass without tinfoil behind it were to bar my way, I should run into it, just as a bird which has flown into a room breaks its head against the window-panes. A thousand things, moreover, deceive man and lead him astray. Why should it then be surprising that he cannot perceive an unknown body through which the light passes?

A new being! Why not? It was assuredly bound to come! Why should we be the last? We do not distinguish it any more than all the others created before us! The reason is, that its nature is more perfect, its body finer and more finished than ours, that ours is so weak, so awkwardly constructed, encumbered with organs that are always tired, always on the strain like machinery that is too complicated, which lives like a plant and like a beast, nourishing itself with difficulty on air, herbs and flesh, an animal machine which is a prey to maladies, to malformations, to decay; broken-winded, badly regulated, simple and eccentric, ingeniously badly made, at once a coarse and a delicate piece of workmanship, the rough sketch of a being that might become intelligent and grand.

We are only a few, so few in this world, from the oyster up to man. Why should there not be one more, once that period is passed which separates the successive apparitions from all the different species?

Why not one more? Why not, also, other trees with immense, splendid flowers, perfuming whole regions? Why not other elements besides fire, air, earth and water? There are four, only four, those nursing fathers of various beings! What a pity! Why are there not forty, four hundred, four thousand? How poor everything is, how mean and wretched! grudgingly produced, roughly constructed, clumsily made! Ah, the elephant and the hippopotamus, what grace! And the camel, what elegance!

But the butterfly, you will say, a flying flower! I dream of one that should be as large as a hundred worlds, with wings whose shape, beauty, colors and motion I cannot even express. But I see it—it flutters from star to star, refreshing them and perfuming them with the light and harmonious breath of its flight! And the people up there look at it as it passes in an ecstasy of delight!

*   *   *

What is the matter with me? It is he, the Horla, who haunts me, and who makes me think of these foolish things! He is within me, he is becoming my soul; I shall kill him!

August 19. I shall kill him. I have seen him! Yesterday I sat down at my table and pretended to write very assiduously. I knew quite well that he would come prowling round me, quite close to me, so close that I might perhaps be able to touch him, to seize him. And then—then I should have the strength of desperation; I should have my hands, my knees, my chest, my forehead, my teeth to strangle him, to crush him, to bite him, to tear him to pieces. And I watched for him with all my over-excited senses.

I had lighted my two lamps and the eight wax candles on my mantelpiece, as if with this light I could discover him.

My bedstead, my old oak post bedstead, stood opposite to me; on my right was the fireplace; on my left, the door which was carefully closed, after I had left it open for some time in order to attract him; behind me was a very high wardrobe with a looking-glass in it, before which I stood to shave and dress every day, and in which I was in the habit of glancing at myself from head to foot every time I passed it.

I pretended to be writing in order to deceive him, for he also was watching me, and suddenly I felt—I was certain that he was reading over my shoulder, that he was there, touching my ear.

I got up, my hands extended, and turned round so quickly that I almost fell. Eh! well? It was as bright as at midday, but I did not see my reflection in the mirror! It was empty, clear, profound, full of light! But my figure was not reflected in it—and I, I was opposite to it! I saw the large, clear glass from top to bottom, and I looked at it with unsteady eyes; and I did not dare to advance; I did not venture to make a movement, feeling that he was there, but that he would escape me again, he whose imperceptible body had absorbed my reflection.

How frightened I was! And then, suddenly, I began to see myself in a mist in the depths of the looking-glass, in a mist as it were a sheet of water; and it seemed to me as if this water were flowing clearer every moment. It was like the end of an eclipse. Whatever it was that hid me did not appear to possess any clearly defined outlines, but a sort of opaque transparency which gradually grew clearer.

At last I was able to distinguish myself completely, as I do every day when I look at myself.

I had seen it! And the horror of it remained with me, and makes me shudder even now.

August 20. How could I kill it, as I could not get hold of it? Poison? But it would see me mix it with the water; and then, would our poisons have any effect on its impalpable body? No—no—no doubt about the matter——Then—then?—

August 21. I sent for a blacksmith from Rouen, and ordered iron shutters for my room, such as some private hotels in Paris have on the ground floor, for fear of burglars, and he is going to make me an iron door as well. I have made myself out a coward, but I do not care about that!

*   *   *

September 10.—Rouen, Hotel Continental. It is done—it is done—but is he dead? My mind is thoroughly upset by what I have seen.

Well then, yesterday, the locksmith having put on the iron shutters and door, I left everything open until midnight, although it was getting cold.

Suddenly I felt that he was there, and joy, mad joy, took possession of me. I got up softly, and walked up and down for some time, so that he might not suspect anything; then I took off my boots and put on my slippers carelessly; then I fastened the iron shutters, and, going back to the door, quickly double-locked it with a padlock, putting the key into my pocket.

Suddenly I noticed that he was moving restlessly round me, that in his turn he was frightened and was ordering me to let him out. I nearly yielded; I did not, however, but, putting my back to the door, I half opened it, just enough to allow me to go out backward, and as I am very tall my head touched the casing. I was sure that he had not been able to escape, and I shut him up quite alone, quite alone. What happiness! I had him fast. Then I ran downstairs; in the drawing-room, which was under my bedroom, I took the two lamps and I poured all the oil on the carpet, the furniture, everywhere; then I set fire to it and made my escape, after having carefully double-locked the door.

I went and hid myself at the bottom of the garden, in a clamp of laurel bushes. How long it seemed! How long it seemed! Everything was dark, silent, motionless, not a breath of air and not a star, but heavy banks of clouds which one could not see, but which weighed, oh, so heavily on my soul.

I looked at my house and waited. How long it was! I already began to think that the fire had gone out of its own accord, or that he had extinguished it, when one of the lower windows gave way under the violence of the flames, and a long, soft, caressing sheet of red flame mounted up the white wall, and enveloped it as far as the roof. The light fell on the trees, the branches, and the leaves, and a shiver of fear pervaded them also! The birds awoke, a dog began to howl, and it seemed to me as if the day were breaking! Almost immediately two other windows flew into fragments, and I saw that the whole of the lower part of my house was nothing but a terrible furnace. But a cry, a horrible, shrill, heartrending cry, a woman's cry, sounded through the night, and two garret windows were opened! I had forgotten the servants! I saw their terror-stricken faces, and their arms waving frantically.

Then, overwhelmed with horror, I set off to run to the village, shouting: "Help! help! fire! fire!" I met some people who were already coming to the scene, and I returned with them.

By this time the house was nothing but a horrible and magnificent funeral pile, a monstrous funeral pile which lit up the whole country, a funeral pile where men were burning, and where he was burning also, He, He, my prisoner, that new Being, the new master, the Horla!

Suddenly the whole roof fell in between the walls, and a volcano of flames darted up to the sky. Through all the windows which opened on that furnace, I saw the flames darting, and I thought that he was there, in that kiln, dead.

Dead? Perhaps?——His body? Was not his body, which was transparent, indestructible by such means as would kill ours?

If he were not dead?——Perhaps time alone has power over that Invisible and Redoubtable Being. Why this transparent, unrecognizable body, this body belonging to a spirit, if it also has to fear ills, infirmities and premature destruction?

Premature destruction? All human terror springs from that! After man, the Horla. After him who can die every day, at any hour, at any moment, by any accident, came the one who would die only at his own proper hour, day, and minute, because he had touched the limits of his existence!

No—no—without any doubt—he is not dead——Then—then—I suppose I must kill myself! . . .

Honoré de Balzac

THE UNKNOWN MASTERPIECE

Le Chef-d'Oeuvre Inconnu

To a Lord. 1845.

1. Gillette

Toward the end of the year 1612, on a cold December morning, a young man whose clothing looked very thin was walking to and fro in front of the door to a house located on the Rue des Grands-Augustins in Paris. After walking on that street for quite some time with the indecision of a lover who lacks the courage to visit his first mistress, no matter how easy her virtue, he finally crossed the threshold of that door and asked whether master François Pourbus was at home. On the affirmative reply made by an old woman busy sweeping a downstairs room, the young man slowly climbed the steps, stopping from stair to stair like some recently appointed courtier worried about how the king will receive him. When he reached the top of the spiral staircase, he remained on the landing for a while, unsure about seizing the grotesque knocker that decorated the door to the studio in which Henri IV's painter, abandoned by Marie de Médicis in favor of Rubens, was no doubt working. The young man was experiencing that profound emotion that must have stirred the heart of all the great artists when, at the height of their youth and love of art, they approached a man of genius or some masterpiece. There exists in all human feelings a pristine purity, engendered by a noble enthusiasm, that gradually grows weaker until happiness is only a memory, and glory a lie. Among these delicate emotions, the one most resembling love is the youthful ardor of an artist beginning the delicious torture of his destiny of glory and misfortune, an ardor full of audacity and shyness, of vague beliefs and inevitable discouragements. The man who, short of money but of budding genius, has never felt a sharp thrill when introducing himself to a master, will always be lacking a string in his heart, some stroke of the brush, a certain feeling in his work, some poetic expressiveness. If a few braggarts, puffed up with themselves, believe in their future too soon,

49

only fools consider them wise. Judging by this, the young stranger seemed to possess real merit, if talent can be measured by that initial shyness, by that indefinable modesty that men slated for glory are prone to lose during the practice of their art, just as pretty women lose theirs in the habits of coquetry. Being accustomed to triumph lessens one's self-doubt, and modesty may be a form of doubt.

Overwhelmed with poverty and, at that moment, surprised at his own presumptuousness, the poor novice wouldn't have entered the studio of the painter to whom we owe the admirable portrait of Henri IV if it hadn't been for an unusual helping hand sent his way by chance. An old man came up the stairs. From the oddness of his clothes, from the magnificence of his lace collar, from the exceptional self-assurance of his gait, the young man guessed that this person must be the painter's protector or friend; he moved back on the landing to give him room and studied him with curiosity, hoping to find in him the good nature of an artist or the helpful disposition of an art lover; but he discerned something diabolical in that face, and especially that indefinable something which attracts artists. Imagine a bald, convex, jutting forehead, sloping down to a small, flat nose turned up at the end like Rabelais's or Socrates'; a smiling, wrinkled mouth; a short chin, lifted proudly and adorned with a gray beard cut in a point; sea-green eyes apparently dimmed by age but which, through the contrast of the pearly white in which the irises swam, must sometimes cast hypnotic looks at the height of anger or enthusiasm. In addition, his face was singularly withered by the labors of old age, and still more by the kind of thoughts that hollow out both the soul and the body. His eyes had no more lashes, and only a few traces of eyebrows could be made out above their protruding ridges. Place this head on a thin, weak body, encircle it with sparkling-white lace of openwork like that of a fish slice, throw onto the old man's black doublet a heavy gold chain, and you will have an imperfect picture of that character, whom the feeble daylight of the staircase lent an additional tinge of the fantastic. You would have thought him a Rembrandt painting, walking silently without a frame in the dark atmosphere which that great painter made all his own. The old man cast a glance imbued with wisdom at the young man, knocked three times at the door, and said to the sickly man of about forty, who opened it: "Good day, master."

Pourbus bowed respectfully; he let the young man in, thinking the old man had brought him along, and didn't trouble himself over him, especially since the novice was under the spell that born painters must undergo at the view of the first studio they've seen, where they can discover some of the practical methods of their art. A skylight in the vaulted ceiling illuminated Master Pourbus's studio. Falling directly

onto a canvas attached to the easel, on which only three or four white
lines had been placed, the daylight didn't reach the black depths of the
corners of that vast room; but a few stray reflections in that russet
shadow ignited a silvery flash on the belly of a knight's breastplate hung
on the wall; streaked with a sudden furrow of light the carved, waxed
cornice of an antique sideboard laden with curious platters; or jabbed
with brilliant dots the grainy weave of some old curtains of gold brocade with large, sharp folds, thrown there as models. Plaster anatomi-
cal figures, fragments and torsos of ancient goddesses, lovingly polished
by the kisses of the centuries, were strewn over the shelves and con-
soles. Innumerable sketches, studies in three colors of crayon, in san-
guine, or in pen and ink, covered the walls up to the ceiling.
Paintboxes, bottles of oil and turpentine, and overturned stools left only
a narrow path to reach the aureole projected by the tall window, whose
beams fell directly onto Pourbus's pale face and the peculiar man's
ivory-colored cranium. The young man's attention was soon claimed
exclusively by a painting which, in that time of chaos and revolutions,
had already become famous and was visited by some of those obstinate
men to whom we owe the preservation of the sacred fire in dark days.
That beautiful canvas depicted Saint Mary of Egypt preparing to pay
her boat fare. That masterpiece, painted for Marie de Médicis, was sold
by her when she had become destitute.

"I like your saint," the old man said to Pourbus, "and I'd pay ten gold
écus for it over and above what the queen is paying; but, compete with
her? Never!"

"You find it good?"

"Hm, hm!" said the old man. "Good? Yes and no. Your lady isn't
badly set up, but she's not alive. You people think you've done it all
when you've drawn a figure correctly and you've put everything in the
right place according to the laws of anatomy! You color in that outline
with a flesh tone prepared in advance on your palette, making sure to
keep one side darker than the other, and because from time to time you
look at a naked woman standing on a table, you think you've copied
nature, you imagine you're painters and that you've stolen God's
secrets! Brrr! To be a great poet, it's not enough to have a full command
of syntax and avoid solecisms of language! Look at your saint, will you,
Pourbus? At first glance she seems admirable; but at the second look,
you notice that she's glued to the background and that you could never
walk all around her. She's a silhouette with only one side, she's a cut-
out likeness, an image that couldn't turn around or shift position. I feel
no air between this arm and the field of the picture; space and depth
are lacking; and yet the perspective is quite correct, and the atmos-
pheric gradation of tones is precisely observed; but, despite such laudable

efforts, I can't believe that that beautiful body is animated by the warm breath of life. It seems to me that, if I placed my hand on that bosom so firm and round, I'd find it as cold as marble! No, my friend, the blood isn't flowing beneath that ivory skin, life is not swelling with its crimson dew the veins and capillaries that intertwine in networks beneath the transparent amber of the temples and chest. This spot is throbbing, but this other spot is rigid; life and death are locked in combat in every detail: here she's a woman, there she's a statue, over there she's a corpse. Your creation is incomplete. You've been able to breathe only a portion of your soul into your beloved work. Prometheus's torch has gone out more than once in your hands, and many places in your painting haven't been touched by the heavenly flame."

"But why is that, dear master?" Pourbus respectfully asked the old man, while the youngster had difficulty repressing a strong urge to strike him.

"Ah! This is it," said the little old man. "You've wavered indecisively between the two systems, between drawing and color, between the painstaking stolidity and precise stiffness of the old German masters and the dazzling fervor and felicitous richness of the Italian painters. You wanted to imitate Hans Holbein and Titian, Albrecht Dürer and Paolo Veronese, at the same time. Certainly that was a magnificent ambition! But what happened? You haven't achieved either the austere charm of dryness or the deceptive magic of chiaroscuro. In this spot here, like molten bronze cracking a mold that's too weak for it, Titian's rich, blonde color has smashed through the thin outline à la Dürer into which you had poured it. In other places, the outline resisted, and restrained the magnificent outpouring of the Venetian palette. Your figure is neither perfectly drawn nor perfectly painted, and everywhere it bears the traces of that unfortunate indecisiveness. If you didn't feel strong enough to weld together in the flame of your genius the two competing manners, you should have opted openly for one or the other, so you could achieve that unity which simulates one of the conditions of life. You are true only in the interior sections; your outlines are false, they fail to join up properly, and they don't indicate that there's anything behind them. There's truth here," said the old man, pointing to the saint's chest. "And then here," he continued, indicating the place on the painting where the shoulder ended. "But here," he said, returning to the center of the bosom, "everything is false. Let's not analyze it, it would drive you to despair."

The old man sat down on a stool, held his head in his hands, and fell silent.

"Master," Pourbus said to him, "all the same, I studied that bosom from a nude live model; but, to our misfortune, there are true effects in nature that are no longer lifelike on the canvas . . ."

"The mission of art is not to copy nature but to express it! You're not a cheap copyist but a poet!" the old man exclaimed hotly, interrupting Pourbus with a lordly gesture. "Otherwise a sculptor would be through with all his labors if he just took a cast of a woman! Well now, just try taking a cast of your sweetheart's hand and setting it down in front of you; you'll find a hideous corpse that's not at all like the real thing, and you'll be compelled to seek out the chisel of a man who wouldn't copy it exactly for you, but would depict its movement and its life for you. Our job is to grasp the spirit, the soul, the face of objects and living beings. Effects! Effects! They're merely the incidental phenomena of life, not life itself. A hand, since I've chosen that example, a hand isn't merely part of a body, it expresses and prolongs an idea that must be grasped and rendered. Neither the painter, nor the poet, nor the sculptor should separate the effect from the cause, since they're inevitably interconnected! The real struggle is there! Many painters achieve an instinctive sort of success without knowing that theme of art. You draw a woman, but you don't see her! That's not the way to make nature yield up her secrets. Your hand, without any thought on your part, reproduces the model you had copied in your teacher's studio. You don't delve sufficiently into the intimate depths of the form, you don't pursue it with sufficient love and perseverance through its twists and turns and its elusive maneuvers. Beauty is something austere and difficult that cannot be attained that way; you have to wait for the right moment, spy it out, seize it, and hug it tight to force it to surrender. Form is a Proteus much more unseizable and rich in hidden secrets than the Proteus of legend; it's only after lengthy struggles that you can compel it to show itself in its true guise; all of you are satisfied with the first semblance it yields to you, or at most the second, or the third; that's not how victorious fighters go about it! Those unvanquished painters don't allow themselves to be deceived by all those subterfuges; they persevere until nature is forced to show itself bare, in its true spirit. That's how Raphael went about it," said the old man, taking off his black velvet cap to show the respect he felt for the king of art; "his great superiority is due to the intimate sense which, in his works, seems set on breaking through form. In his figures, form is what it is in us, an interpreter of ideas and feelings, a great poetry. Every figure is a world, a portrait whose model appeared in a sublime vision, colored by light, pointed out by an inner voice, stripped bare by a heavenly finger that showed the sources of expression within the past of an entire lifetime. You make beautiful robes of flesh for your women, beautiful draperies of hair, but where is the blood that produces either calm or passion and causes particular effects? Your saint is a brunette, but this here, my poor Pourbus, is suitable for a blonde! And so your figures are pale, colored-in phantoms that you trot out before us, and you call that painting and art. Because you've produced something that looks more like a woman than like a house, you think you've hit the mark; and, really proud because you no longer need to label your figures *currus venustus* or *pulcher homo*, the way the earliest painters did, you imagine you're wonderful artists! Ha, ha! You're not there yet, my worthy friends, you'll have to use up many a crayon and cover many a canvas before you get there. Of course, a woman carries her head this way, she holds her skirt like that, her eyes grow languid and melt with that air of resigned gentleness, that's the way that the fluttering shadow of her lashes hovers over her cheeks! It's right, and it isn't. What's missing? A trifle, but that trifle is everything. You have the semblance of life, but you aren't expressing its overflowing superabundance, that indefinable something, which may be the soul, hovering like a cloud above the outer husk; in short, that bloom of life which Titian and Raphael captured. Starting out from where you've left off, some excellent painting might be achieved; but you get tired too soon. The layman admires you, but the true connoisseur merely smiles. O Mabuse, my teacher," that odd character added, "you're a thief, you stole life when you died!—Aside from that," he resumed, "this canvas is better than the paintings of that brute Rubens, with his mountains of Flemish meat, sprinkled with vermilion, his tidal waves of red hair, and his glaring colors. At least you've got color, feeling, and drawing there, the three essential components of art."

"But that saint is sublime, my good man!" the young man called out loudly, emerging from his deep daydreams. "These two figures, the saint and the boatman, have a subtlety of purpose that the Italian painters have no notion of; I don't know one of them who could have created the indecisiveness of the boatman."

"Does this little rascal belong to you?" Pourbus asked the old man.

"Alas, master, forgive my boldness," replied the novice, blushing. "I'm a nobody, a dauber of pictures by instinct who has recently arrived in this city, which is the fount of all knowledge."

"Get to work!" Pourbus said to him, offering him a red crayon and a sheet of paper.

The stranger nimbly made a line copy of the Saint Mary.

"Oh, ho!" cried the old man. "Your name?"

The young man signed "Nicolas Poussin" at the bottom.

"That's not bad for a beginner," said the odd character who had been speaking so extravagantly. "I see that it's possible to talk about painting in your presence. I don't blame you for having admired Pourbus's saint. It's a masterpiece for the world at large, and only those initiated into the deepest secrets of art can discover what's wrong with it. But, since you're worthy of the lesson, and able to understand, I'm going to show you just how little it would take to complete this picture. Be all eyes and give me complete attention; another opportunity to teach you like this may never occur again! Your palette, Pourbus?"

Pourbus went to get a palette and brushes. The little old man rolled up his sleeves in a convulsively brusque fashion, stuck his thumb into the palette, mottled and laden with paints, that Pourbus held out to him; he not so much took as ripped from his hands a fistful of brushes of all sizes, and his pointy beard suddenly started bobbing in menacing motions that expressed the urgings of an ardent imagination. While loading his brush with paint, he muttered between his teeth: "Here are tints that are only good enough to be thrown out the window along with the man who mixed them; they're revoltingly crude and false, how can I paint with this?" Then, with feverish energy, he dipped the tip of his brush into the various gobs of paint, at times running through their entire gamut more rapidly than a cathedral organist races from one end of his keyboard to another during the Easter O Filii.

Pourbus and Poussin remained motionless on either side of the canvas, sunk in the most vehement contemplation.

"Do you see, young man," said the old man without turning away, "do you see how, with three or four strokes and a little bluish glaze, it was possible to make the air circulate around the head of this poor saint, who must have been stifled, trapped in that thick atmosphere? See how this drapery now flutters and how one now realizes that the breeze is lifting it! Before, it looked like a starched cloth held up by pins. Do you notice how the gleaming gloss I've just put on her chest reproduces the plump suppleness of a girl's skin, and how the tint blended of red-brown and burnt ocher warms up the gray chill of this large shadow, in which the blood was coagulating instead of flowing? Young man, young man, what I'm showing you here, no master could teach you. Mabuse alone possessed the secret of giving figures life. Mabuse had only one pupil: me. I never had any, and I'm old! You have enough intelligence to guess the rest from what I allow you to glimpse."

While speaking, the old man was placing strokes on every part of the painting: here two brushstrokes, there just one, but always so felicitously that you would have said it was a different picture, one bathed in light. He worked with such passionate fervor that beads of sweat stood out on his hairless brow; he moved so rapidly, with short movements that were so impatient and jerky, that it seemed to young Poussin as if the body of that peculiar character contained a demon acting through his hands, seizing them eerily as if against the man's will. The preternatural brightness of his eyes, the convulsions that looked like the effects of resistance, lent that notion a semblance of truth that had to affect a young imagination. The old man kept saying: "Bang, bang,

bang! That's how it takes on consistency, young man! Come, little brushstrokes, make that icy tint grow red for me! Let's go!—Boom, boom, boom!" he would say, while adding warmth to the areas he had accused of lacking life, while eliminating the differences in feeling with a few patches of color, and restoring the unity of tone that an ardent Egyptian woman demanded.

"You see, youngster, it's only the final brushstroke that counts. Pourbus laid on a hundred and I've laid on just one. No one is going to thank us for what's underneath. Remember that!"

Finally that demon halted and, turning around to address Pourbus and Poussin, who were speechless with admiration, he said: "This is still not as good as my *Quarrelsome Beauty*, and yet it would be possible to put one's name at the bottom of a picture like this. Yes, I'd sign it," he added, standing up to fetch a mirror, in which he looked at it. "Now let's go dine," he said. "Both of you come to my house. I have smoked ham, I have good wine! Ho, ho! Despite the unfortunate era we live in, we'll chat about painting! We're equally matched. Here's a little fellow," he added, tapping Nicolas Poussin on the shoulder, "who has some aptitude."

Then, catching sight of the Norman's wretched coat, he drew a leather purse from his belt, rummaged in it, drew out two gold coins, and, showing them to him, said: "I'll buy your drawing."

"Take it," said Pourbus to Poussin, seeing him give a start and blush with shame, for that young adept had a poor man's pride. "Go on and take it; he's got enough in his moneybag to ransom two kings!"

The three of them left the studio and walked, conversing about the arts, until they reached a beautiful wooden house located near the Saint-Michel Bridge; its decorations, its door knocker, the frames of its casement windows, its arabesques, all amazed Poussin. The aspiring painter suddenly found himself in a downstairs room, in front of a good fire, near a table laden with appetizing food, and, by unusual good fortune, in the company of two great artists who were exceptionally good-natured.

"Young man," Pourbus said to him, seeing him dumbfounded in front of a painting, "don't look at that picture too long, or it will drive you to despair."

It was the *Adam* that Mabuse painted to get out of the prison where his creditors kept him so long. Indeed, that figure gave such a strong impression of being real that, from that moment on, Nicolas Poussin began to understand the true meaning of the confused words the old man had uttered. The old man looked at the picture with seeming satisfaction, but without enthusiasm, and appeared to be saying: "I've done better!"

"There's life in it," he said. "My poor master outdid himself in it; but there was still a little truth missing in the background of the picture. The man is really alive; he's getting up and is going to approach us. But the air, sky, and wind that we breathe, see, and feel aren't there. Besides, he's still just a man! Now, the only man who ever came directly from the hands of God ought to have something divine about him, which is missing. Mabuse used to say so himself, with vexation, when he wasn't drunk."

Poussin was looking back and forth between the old man and Pourbus with restless curiosity. He came up to Pourbus as if to ask him their host's name; but the painter put a finger to his lips with an air of mystery, and the young man, though keenly interested, kept silent, hoping that sooner or later some remark would allow him to learn the name of his host, whose wealth and talents were sufficiently attested to by the respect Pourbus showed him and by the wonders assembled in that room.

Seeing a magnificent portrait of a woman on the somber oak paneling, Poussin exclaimed: "What a beautiful Giorgione!"

"No," replied the old man, "you're looking at one of my first smears."

"Damn! Then I'm in the home of the god of painting," Poussin said naïvely.

The old man smiled like a man long accustomed to such praise.

"Master Frenhofer," said Pourbus, "could you possibly send for a little of your good Rhenish wine for me?"

"Two casks," replied the old man. "One to repay you for the pleasure I had this morning looking at your pretty sinner, and the other as a present to a friend."

"Oh, if I weren't always under the weather," continued Pourbus, "and if you were willing to let me see your *Quarrelsome Beauty*, I could paint some tall, wide, deep picture in which the figures were life-size."

"Show my painting!" cried the old man, quite upset. "No, no, I still have to perfect it. Yesterday, toward evening," he said, "I thought I had finished it. Her eyes seemed moist to me, her flesh was stirring. The locks of her hair were waving. She was breathing! Even though I've found the way to achieve nature's relief and three-dimensionality on a flat canvas, this morning, when it got light, I realized my mistake. Oh, to achieve this glorious result, I've studied thoroughly the great masters of color, I've analyzed and penetrated layer by layer the paintings of Titian, that king of light; like that sovereign painter, I sketched in my figure in a light tint with a supple, heavily loaded brush—for shadow is merely an incidental phenomenon, remember that, youngster. Then I went back over my work and, by means of gradations and glazes that I made successively less transparent, I rendered the heaviest shadows and even the deepest blacks; for the shadows of ordinary painters are of a different nature from their bright tints; they're wood, bronze, or whatever you want, except flesh in shadow. You feel that, if their figure shifted position, the areas in shadow would never be cleared up and wouldn't become bright. I avoided that error, into which many of the most illustrious have fallen, and in my picture the whiteness can be discerned beneath the opacity of even the most dense shadow! Unlike that pack of ignoramuses who imagine they're drawing correctly because they produce a line carefully shorn of all rough edges, I haven't indicated the outer borders of my figure in a dry manner, bringing out even the slightest detail of the anatomy, because the human body isn't bounded by lines. In that area, sculptors can come nearer the truth than we can. Nature is comprised of a series of solid shapes that dovetail into one another. Strictly speaking, there's no such thing as drawing! Don't laugh, young man! As peculiar as that remark may sound to you, you'll understand the reasons behind it some day. Line is the means by which man renders the effect of light on objects; but there are no lines in nature, where everything is continuous: it's by modeling that we draw; that is, we separate things from the medium in which they exist; only the distribution of the light gives the body its appearance! Thus, I haven't fixed any outlines, I've spread over the contours a cloud of blonde, warm intermediate tints in such a way that no one can put his finger on the exact place where the contours meet the background. From close up, this work looks fleecy and seems lacking in precision, but, at two paces, everything firms up, becomes fixed, and stands out; the body turns, the forms project, and you feel the air circulating all around them. And yet I'm still not satisfied, I have some doubts. Perhaps it's wrong to draw a single line, perhaps it would be better to attack a figure from the center, first concentrating on the projecting areas that catch most of the light, and only then moving on to the darker sections. Isn't that how the sun operates, that divine painter of the universe? O nature, nature, who has ever captured you in your inmost recesses? You see, just like ignorance, an excess of knowledge leads to a negation. I have doubts about my painting!"

The old man paused, then resumed: "It's ten years now, young man, that I've been working on it; but what are ten short years when it's a question of struggling with nature? We don't know how long it took Sir Pygmalion to make the only statue that ever walked!"

The old man dropped into deep musing, and sat there with fixed eyes, mechanically playing with his knife.

"Now he's in converse with his 'spirit,'" said Pourbus quietly.

At that word, Nicholas Poussin felt himself under the power of an unexplainable artistic curiosity. That old man with white eyes, attentive and in a stupor, had become more than a man to him; he seemed like a whimsical genius living in an unknown sphere. He awakened a thousand confused ideas in his soul. The moral phenomenon of that type of fascination can no more be defined than one can render in words the emotion caused by a song that reminds an exiled man's heart of his homeland. The scorn this old man affected to express for beautiful artistic endeavors, his wealth, his ways, Pourbus's deference toward him, that painting kept a secret for so long—a labor of patience, a labor of genius, no doubt, if one were to judge by the head of the Virgin that young Poussin had so candidly admired, and which, still beautiful even alongside Mabuse's *Adam*, bespoke the imperial talents of one of the princes of art—everything about that old man exceeded the boundaries of human nature. The clear, perceivable image that Nicholas Poussin's rich imagination derived from his observation of that preternatural being was a total image of the artistic nature, that irrational nature to which such great powers have been entrusted, and which all too often abuses those powers, leading cool reason, the bourgeois, and even some connoisseurs over a thousand rocky roads where there is nothing for them, while that white-winged lass, a madcap of fantasies, discovers there epics, castles, works of art. Nature—mocking and kind, fertile and poor! And so, for the enthusiastic Poussin, that old man, through a sudden transformation, had become art itself, art with its secrets, its passions, and its daydreams.

"Yes, my dear Pourbus," Frenhofer resumed, "up to now I've been unable to find a flawless woman, a body whose contours are perfectly beautiful, and whose complexion . . . But," he said, interrupting himself, "where is she in the living flesh, that undiscoverable Venus of the ancients, so often sought for, and of whose beauty we scarcely come across even a few scattered elements here and there? Oh, if I could see for a moment, just once, that divine, complete nature—in short, that ideal—I'd give my entire fortune; but I'd go after you in the underworld, heavenly beauty! Like Orpheus, I'd descend to the Hades of art to bring back life from there."

"We can leave," said Pourbus to Poussin; "he can't hear us anymore or see us anymore!"

"Let's go to his studio," replied the amazed young man.

"Oh, the sly old customer has taken care to block all entry to it. His treasures are too well guarded for us to reach them. I didn't wait for your suggestion or your fancies to attempt an attack on the mystery."

"So there is a mystery?"

"Yes," Pourbus replied. "Old Frenhofer is the only pupil Mabuse was ever willing to train. Having become his friend, his rescuer, his father,

Frenhofer sacrificed the largest part of his treasures in satisfying Mabuse's passions; in exchange, Mabuse transmitted to him the secret of three-dimensionality, the power to give figures that extraordinary life, that natural bloom, which is our eternal despair, but the technique of which he possessed so firmly that, one day, having sold for drink the flowered damask with which he was supposed to make garments to wear at Emperor Charles V's visit to the city, he accompanied his patron wearing paper clothing painted like damask. The particular brilliance of the material worn by Mabuse surprised the emperor, who, wanting to compliment the old drunkard's protector on it, discovered the deception. Frenhofer is a man who's impassioned over our art, who sees higher and further than other painters. He has meditated profoundly on color, on the absolute truth of line; but, by dint of so much investigation, he has come to have his doubts about the very thing he was investigating. In his moments of despair, he claims that there is no such thing as drawing and that only geometric figures can be rendered in line; that is going beyond the truth, because with line and with black, which isn't a color, we can create a figure; which proves that our art, like nature, is made up of infinite elements: drawing supplies a skeleton, color supplies life; but life without the skeleton is even more incomplete than the skeleton without life. Lastly, there's something truer than all this: practice and observation are everything to a painter, and if reasoning and poetry pick a fight with our brushes, we wind up doubting like this fellow here, who is as much a lunatic as he is a painter. Although a sublime painter, he had the misfortune of being born into wealth, and that allowed his mind to wander. Don't imitate him! Work! Painters shouldn't meditate unless they have their brushes in their hand."

"We'll make our way in!" cried Poussin, no longer listening to Pourbus and no longer troubled by doubts.

Pourbus smiled at the young stranger's enthusiasm, and left him, inviting him to come and see him.

Nicolas Poussin went back slowly toward the Rue de la Harpe, walking past the modest hostelery in which he lodged, without noticing it. Climbing his wretched staircase with restless speed, he reached an upstairs room located beneath a half-timbered roof, that naïve, lightweight covering of old Parisian houses. Near the dark window, the only one in his room, he saw a girl, who, at the sound of the door, suddenly stood up straight, prompted by her love; she had recognized the painter by the way he had jiggled the latch.

"What's the matter?" she asked.

"The matter, the matter," he cried, choking with pleasure, "is that I really felt I was a painter! I had doubted myself up to now, but this morning I began to believe in myself! I can be a great man! Come, Gillette, we'll be rich and happy! There's gold in these brushes."

But he suddenly fell silent. His serious, energetic face lost its expression of joy when he compared the immensity of his hopes to the insignificance of his resources. The walls were covered with plain pieces of paper full of crayon sketches. He didn't own four clean canvases. Paints were expensive at the time, and the poor gentleman's palette was nearly bare. Living in such destitution, he possessed and was aware of incredible riches of the heart and the superabundance of a devouring genius. Brought to Paris by a nobleman who had befriended him, or perhaps by his own talent, he had suddenly found a sweetheart there, one of those noble, generous souls who accept suffering at the side of a great man, adopting his poverty and trying to understand his whims; brave in poverty and love just as other women are fearless in supporting luxury and making a public show of their lack of feelings. The smile that played on Gillette's lips gilded that garret, competing with the brightness of the sky. The sun didn't always shine, whereas she was always there, communing with his passion, devoted to his happiness and his suffering, consoling the genius that overflowed with love before seizing art.

"Listen, Gillette, come."

The joyful, obedient girl leaped onto the painter's knees. She was all grace, all beauty, lovely as springtime, adorned with all feminine riches and illumining them with the flame of a beautiful soul.

"Oh, God!" he cried, "I'll never have the courage to tell her."

"A secret?" she asked. "I want to hear it."

Poussin remained quiet, lost in thought.

"Well, talk."

"Gillette, my poor sweetheart!"

"Oh, you want something from me?"

"Yes."

"If you want me to pose for you again the way I did the other day," she continued in a rather sulky way, "I'll never agree to it again, because, at times like that, your eyes no longer tell me anything. You no longer think about me, even though you're looking at me."

"Would you prefer to see me drawing another woman?"

"Maybe," she said, "if she were good and ugly."

"So, then," Poussin went on in a serious tone, "what if, for my future glory, in order to make me a great painter, it were necessary to pose for someone else?"

"You want to test me," she said. "You know very well I wouldn't go."

Poussin's head dropped onto his chest, like that of a man succumbing to a joy or sorrow too strong for his soul.

"Listen," she said, tugging the sleeve of Poussin's threadbare doublet, "I've told you, Nick, that I'd give my life for you; but I've never promised you to give up my love for you while I was alive."

"Give it up?" cried Poussin.

"If I showed myself that way to somebody else, you wouldn't love me anymore. And I myself would feel unworthy of you. Isn't catering to your whims a natural, simple thing? In spite of myself, I'm happy, and even proud to do everything you ask me to. But for somebody else—oh, no."

"Forgive me, Gillette," said the painter, falling on his knees. "I'd rather be loved than famous. For me you're more beautiful than wealth and honors. Go, throw away my brushes, burn those sketches. I was wrong. My calling is to love you. I'm not a painter, I'm a lover. Art and all its secrets can go hang!"

She admired him, she was happy, delighted! She ruled supreme, she felt instinctively that the arts were forgotten for her sake and cast at her feet like a grain of incense.

"And yet he's only an old man," Poussin continued. "He'll only be able to see the woman in you. You're so perfect!"

"I've got to love you!" she cried, prepared to sacrifice her romantic scruples to reward her lover for all the sacrifices he made for her. "But," she went on, "it would mean ruining me. Ah, to ruin myself for you! Yes, it's a beautiful thing, but you'll forget me. Oh, what a terrible idea you've come up with!"

"I've come up with it, and I love you," he said with a kind of contrition, "but it makes me a scoundrel."

"Shall we consult Father Hardouin?" she asked.

"Oh, no. Let it be a secret between the two of us."

"All right, I'll go; but you mustn't be there," she said. "Remain outside the door, armed with your dagger; if I scream, come in and kill the painter."

No longer seeing anything but his art, Poussin crushed Gillette in his arms.

"He doesn't love me anymore!" Gillette thought when she was alone.

She already regretted her decision. But she soon fell prey to a fear that was even crueler than her regret; she did her best to drive away an awful thought that was taking shape in her heart. She was thinking that she already loved the painter less, suspecting him of being less estimable than before.

2. Catherine Lescault

Three months after Poussin and Pourbus first met, Pourbus paid a visit to Master Frenhofer. The old man was at the time a prey to one of those spontaneous fits of deep discouragement, the cause of which, if one is to believe the firm opinions of traditional doctors, is indigestion, the wind, heat, or some bloating of the hypochondriac regions; but, according to psychologists, is really the imperfection of our moral nature. The man was suffering from fatigue, pure and simple, after trying to finish his mysterious painting. He was seated languidly in an enormous chair of carved oak trimmed with black leather; and, without abandoning his melancholy attitude, he darted at Pourbus the glance of a man who had settled firmly into his distress.

"Well, master," Pourbus said, "was the ultramarine you went to Bruges for bad? Weren't you able to grind your new white? Is your oil defective, or your brushes stiff?"

"Alas!" exclaimed the old man, "for a moment I thought my picture was finished; but now I'm sure I was wrong about a few details, and I won't be calm until I've dispelled my doubts. I've decided to take a trip to Turkey, Greece, and Asia to look for a model and compare my picture to different types of natural beauties. Maybe," he went on, with a smile of satisfaction, "I've got nature herself upstairs. Sometimes I'm almost afraid that a breath of air might wake up that woman and she might disappear."

Then he suddenly rose, as if to depart.

"Oh, oh," Pourbus replied, "I've come just in time to save you the expense and fatigue of the journey."

"How so?" asked Frenhofer in surprise.

"Young Poussin has a sweetheart whose incomparable beauty is totally flawless. But, dear master, if he agrees to lend her to you, at the very least you'll have to show us your canvas."

The old man just stood there, motionless, in a state of complete stupefaction.

"What!" he finally cried in sorrow. "Show my creation, my wife? Rend the veil with which I've chastely covered my happiness? But that would be a terrible prostitution! For ten years now I've been living with this woman; she's mine, only mine, she loves me. Hasn't she smiled at me at each brushstroke I've given her? She has a soul, the soul that I endowed her with. She would blush if anyone's eyes but mine were fixed on her. Show her! But where is the husband or lover so vile as to lead his wife to dishonor? When you paint a picture for the royal court, you don't put your whole soul into it; all you're selling to the courtiers is colored dummies. My kind of painting isn't painting, it's emotion, passion! She was born in my studio, she must remain there as a virgin, she can only leave when fully dressed. Poetry and women only surrender themselves naked to their lovers! Do we possess Raphael's model, Ariosto's Angelica, Dante's Beatrice? No, we only see their forms! Well, the picture I have under lock and key upstairs is something exceptional in our art. It isn't a canvas, it's a woman!—a woman with whom I weep, laugh, converse, and think. Do you want me suddenly to throw away ten years' happiness the way one throws off a coat? Do you want me suddenly to leave off being a father, a lover, God? That woman isn't a single creature, she's all of creation. Let your young man come; I'll give him my treasures, I'll give him pictures by Correggio, Michelangelo, Titian; I'll kiss the print of his feet in the dust; but make him my rival? Shame upon me! Ha, ha, I'm even more of a lover than I am a painter. Yes, I'll have the strength to burn my *Quarrelsome Beauty* with my dying breath; but to expose her to the eyes of a man, a young man, a painter? No, no! If anyone sullied her with a glance, I'd kill him the next day! I'd kill you on the spot, you, my friend, if you didn't salute her on your knees! Now do you want me to submit my idol to the cold eyes and stupid criticisms of imbeciles? Oh, love is a mystery, it lives only in the depths of our heart, and everything is ruined when a man says, even to his friend, 'This is the woman I love!'"

The old man seemed to have become young again; his eyes shone and were full of life; his pale cheeks were mottled with a vivid red, and his hands were trembling. Pourbus, astonished at the passionate vehemence with which those words were uttered, had nothing to say in reply to a sentiment that was as novel as it was profound. Was Frenhofer in his right mind or mad? Was he under the spell of some artistic fancy, or were the ideas he had expressed the result of that indescribable fanaticism produced in us by the long gestation of a great work? Could one ever hope to come to terms with that odd passion?

A prey to all these thoughts, Pourbus said to the old man:

"But isn't it one woman for another? Isn't Poussin exposing his sweetheart to your eyes?"

"Some sweetheart!" Frenhofer replied. "She'll betray him sooner or later. Mine will always be faithful to me!"

"All right," Pourbus continued, "let's drop the subject. But before you find, even in Asia, a woman as beautiful and perfect as the one I'm talking about, you may die without finishing your picture."

"Oh, it's finished," said Frenhofer. "Anyone who looked at it would imagine he saw a woman lying on a velvet bed beneath curtains. Near her, a golden tripod emits incense. You'd be tempted to take hold of the tassel of the cords that hold back the curtains, and you'd think you saw the bosom of Catherine Lescault, a beautiful courtesan nicknamed the Quarrelsome Beauty, heaving with her breath. And yet, I'd like to be sure . . ."

"Well, go to Asia," Pourbus replied, detecting a sort of hesitation in Frenhofer's eyes.

And Pourbus took a few steps toward the door of the room.

At that moment, Gillette and Nicolas Poussin had arrived near Frenhofer's dwelling. As the girl was about to go in, she freed herself from the painter's arm and recoiled as if gripped by some sudden presentiment.

"But what am I coming here for?" she asked her lover in deep tones, staring at him.

"Gillette, I've left it all up to you, and I want to obey you in all ways. You are my conscience and my glory. Go back to our room; I'll be happier, maybe, than if you . . ."

"Am I my own mistress when you speak to me that way? Oh, no, I'm only a child. — Let's go," she added, seeming to make a violent effort; "if our love dies and I'm laying in long days of regret for myself, won't your fame be the reward for my obedience to your wishes? Let's go in; being a kind of eternal memory on your palette will be like being still alive."

On opening the door to the house, the two lovers came upon Pourbus; amazed at the beauty of Gillette, whose eyes were full of tears at the moment, he took hold of her as she stood there trembling and, leading her in to the old man, said:

"Now, isn't she worth all the masterpieces in the world?"

Frenhofer gave a start. There was Gillette, in the naïve, simple attitude of an innocent, frightened girl of Caucasian Georgia who has been kidnapped and is being presented by brigands to a slave dealer. A modest blush gave color to her face, she lowered her eyes, her hands hung at her sides, her strength seemed to desert her, and tears protested against the violence being done to her modesty. At that moment, Poussin, in despair at having let that beautiful treasure out of his garret, cursed himself. He became a lover foremost and an artist next; a thousand scruples tortured his heart when he saw the rejuvenated eyes of the old man, who, as painters do, was mentally undressing the girl, divining her most secret forms. Then he reverted to the fierce jealousy of true love.

"Gillette, let's go!" he cried.

At that tone, at that cry, his joyful sweetheart raised her eyes in his direction, saw him, and rushed into his arms.

"Oh, you do love me!" she replied, bursting into tears.

After having had the energy to be silent about her suffering, she had no more strength left to conceal her happiness.

"Oh, leave her with me for just a while," said the old painter, "and you'll compare her to my Catherine. Yes, I consent."

There was still love in Frenhofer's cry. He seemed to have a lover's vanity for his painted woman and to be enjoying in advance the victory that his virgin's beauty would win over that of a real girl.

"Don't let him go back on his word!" cried Pourbus, tapping Poussin on the shoulder. "The fruits of love are quickly gone, those of art are immortal."

Looking hard at Poussin and Pourbus, Gillette replied, "Am I nothing more than a woman to him?" She raised her head proudly; but when, after darting a fierce glance at Frenhofer, she saw her lover busy contemplating once again the portrait he had recently taken for a Giorgione, she said:

"Ah! Let's go upstairs! He's never looked at me that way."

"Old man," Poussin resumed, torn from his meditation by Gillette's voice, "do you see this blade? I'll thrust it into your heart at the first word of complaint this girl utters; I'll set fire to your house, and no one will get out alive. Understand?"

Nicolas Poussin was somber, and his words were awesome. This attitude, and especially the young painter's gesture, consoled Gillette, who almost forgave him for sacrificing her to the art of painting and his glorious future. Pourbus and Poussin remained at the studio door, looking at each other in silence. If at first the painter of *St. Mary of Egypt* permitted himself a few exclamations—"Ah, she's getting undressed, he's asking her to stand in the daylight! He's comparing her!"—soon he fell silent at the sight of Poussin, whose face showed deep sadness. And, even though elderly painters no longer feel such petty scruples in the presence of art, he admired them for being so naïve and charming. The young man kept his hand on his dagger's hilt and his ear almost glued to the door. The two of them, standing there in the darkness, they looked like two conspirators awaiting the moment when they would strike down a tyrant.

"Come in, come in," called the old man, beaming with happiness. "My picture is perfect, and now I can show it with pride. Never will a painter, brushes, paints, canvas, or light create any rival to Catherine Lescault, the beautiful courtesan."

Prey to a keen curiosity, Pourbus and Poussin rushed into the midst of a vast studio covered with dust, in which everything was in disorder, in which they saw here and there pictures hung on the walls. They first stopped in front of a life-size woman's figure, half draped, for which they were overcome with admiration.

"Oh, don't bother about that," said Frenhofer, "it's a canvas I daubed over to study a pose, it's a worthless picture. Here are my mistakes," he went on, showing them captivating compositions hanging on the walls all around them.

At these words, Pourbus and Poussin, dumbfounded at this contempt for works of that merit, looked for the portrait they had been told about, but failed to catch sight of it.

"Well, here it is!" said the old man, whose hair was mussed, whose face was inflamed with a preternatural excitement, whose eyes sparkled, and who was panting like a young man drunk with love. "Ah, ha!" he cried. "You weren't expecting so much perfection! You're standing in front of a woman, and looking for a picture. There's such great depth to this canvas, the air in it is so real, that you can no longer distinguish it from the air that surrounds us. Where is art? Lost, vanished! Here are the very forms of a girl. Haven't I really captured her coloring, the lifelikeness of the line that seems to bound her body? Isn't it the same phenomenon that's offered to us by objects that exist within the atmosphere just as fish live in water? Don't you admire the way the contours stand out from the background? Don't you imagine that you could run your hand down that back? Thus, for seven years, I studied the effects of the mating of daylight and objects. And that hair, doesn't the light inundate it? . . . But she drew a breath, I think! . . . That bosom, see? Oh, who wouldn't want to worship her on his knees? The flesh is throbbing. She's going to stand up, just wait."

"Can you make out anything?" Poussin asked Pourbus.

"No. What about you?"

"Not a thing."

The two painters left the old man to his ecstasy, and looked to see whether the light, falling vertically onto the canvas he was showing them, wasn't neutralizing all its effects. Then they examined the painting, placing themselves to the right, to the left, straight in front of it, stooping down and getting up again in turns.

"Yes, yes, it's really a canvas," Frenhofer said to them, misunderstanding the purpose of that careful scrutiny. "Look, here's the stretcher, the easel; finally, here are my paints, my brushes."

And he took hold of a brush that he showed them in a naïve gesture.

"The sly old fox is having a joke with us," said Poussin, coming back in front of the so-called painting. All I see there is colors in a jumbled heap, contained within a multitude of peculiar lines that form a wall of paint."

"We're wrong. See?" Pourbus said.

Coming closer, they could discern in a corner of the canvas the tip of a bare foot emerging from that chaos of colors, tints, and vague nuances, a sort of shapeless mist; but a delicious foot, a living foot! They stood awestruck with admiration before that fragment which had escaped from an unbelievable, slow, and progressive destruction. That foot appeared there like the torso of some Parisian marble Venus rising up out of the ruins of a city that had been burned to the ground.

"There's a woman underneath all this!" cried Pourbus, indicating to Poussin the layers of paint that the old painter had set down one over the other, in the belief that he was making his painting perfect.

The two painters spontaneously turned toward Frenhofer, beginning to understand, though only vaguely, the state of ecstasy in which he existed.

"He's speaking in good faith," said Pourbus.

"Yes, my friend," replied the old man, awakening, "one must have faith, faith in art, and one must live with one's work for a long time in order to produce a creation like this. Some of these shadows cost me many labors. Look, on the cheek, beneath the eyes, there's a light penumbra that, if you observe it in nature, will seem all but uncapturable to you. Well, do you think that that effect didn't cost me unheard-of pains to reproduce? But also, dear Pourbus, look at my piece attentively and you'll understand more fully what I was telling you about the way to handle modeling and contours. Look at the light on the bosom and see how, by a series of strokes and highlights done in heavy impasto, I succeeded in catching true daylight and combining it with the gleaming whiteness of the illuminated areas; and how, to achieve the converse effect, eliminating the ridges and grain of the paint, I was able, by dint of caressing the figure's contour, which is submerged in demitints, to remove the very notion of a drawn line and such artificial procedures, and to give it the very look and solidity of nature. Come close, you'll see better how I worked. From a distance, it can't be seen. There! In this spot, I think, it's highly remarkable."

And with the tip of his brush he pointed out a blob of bright paint to the two artists.

Pourbus tapped the old man on the shoulder, turning toward Poussin. "Do you know that we have a very great painter in him?" he said.

"He's even more of a poet than a painter," Poussin replied gravely.

"This," continued Pourbus, touching the canvas, "is the extreme limit of our art on earth."

"And from there it gets lost in the skies," said Poussin.

"How many pleasures in this bit of canvas!" exclaimed Pourbus.

The old man, absorbed, wasn't listening to them but was smiling at that imaginary woman.

"But sooner or later he'll notice that there's nothing on his canvas!" cried Poussin.

"Nothing on my canvas!" said Frenhofer, looking by turns at the two painters and at his so-called picture.

"What have you done?" Pourbus replied to Poussin.

The old man gripped the young man's arm violently, saying: "You see nothing, vagabond, good-for-nothing, cad, catamite! Why did you come up here, anyway?—My dear Pourbus," he went on, turning to that painter, "could you too be making fun of me? Answer me! I'm your friend; tell me, have I really spoiled my picture?"

Pourbus, undecided, didn't dare say a thing; but the anxiety depicted on the old man's pallid face was so cruel that he pointed to the canvas and said: "Just look!"

Frenhofer studied his picture for a moment and tottered.

"Nothing, nothing! And after working ten years on it!"

He sat down and began weeping.

"So I'm just an imbecile, a lunatic! So I have no talent, no ability; I'm just a rich man who, when he does something, merely does it! So I haven't created anything!"

He studied his canvas through his tears. Suddenly he stood up with pride, and darted a furious glance at the two painters.

"By the blood, body, and head of Christ, you are envious men trying to make me believe that she's ruined, so you can steal her from me! *I* can see her!" he cried. "She's wonderfully beautiful."

At that moment, Poussin heard the weeping of Gillette, who had been forgotten in a corner.

"What's wrong, angel?" the painter asked her, suddenly becoming a lover again.

"Kill me!" she said. "I'd be a low creature if I still loved you, because I have contempt for you. I admire you, and you horrify me. I love you, and I think I hate you already."

While Poussin was listening to Gillette, Frenhofer was covering up his Catherine with a green serge, as gravely calm as a jeweler locking up his drawers because he thinks that skillful thieves are present. He threw the two painters a profoundly crafty look, full of scorn and suspicion, and silently turned them out of his studio, with convulsive haste. Then, on the threshold of his home, he said to them: "Farewell, my little friends."

That leavetaking chilled the heart of the two painters. The next day, Pourbus, worried, came to see Frenhofer again, and was informed that he had died during the night after burning his canvases.

Paris, February 1832.

Emile Zola

THE ATTACK ON THE MILL

L'Attaque du Moulin

I

Old Merlier's mill, that fine summer evening, was extremely festive. In the courtyard three tables had been laid, placed end to end, and were awaiting the guests. Everyone in the vicinity knew that on that day Merlier's daughter Françoise was to be betrothed to Dominique, a young man who was reproached for laziness, but whom the women for three leagues around looked upon with a gleam in their eyes, he was so handsome.

This mill of old Merlier's was a real treat. It was located right in the center of Rocreuse, in the spot where the highway makes a bend. The village has only one street, two rows of cottages, one row on each side of the road; but there, at the bend, meadows open out, and tall trees, following the course of the Morelle, cover the bottom of the valley with magnificent shade. In all of Lorraine, there isn't a more charming corner of nature. To the right and to the left, dense forests and centuries-old woods climb gentle slopes, filling the horizon with an ocean of greenery; while, toward the south, the plain stretches, wonderfully fertile, unfurling to infinity plots of ground divided by quickset hedges. But the charm of Rocreuse is chiefly due to the coolness of this pocket of greenery on the hottest days of July and August. The Morelle comes down from the forests, beneath which it flows for leagues; it brings along the murmuring sounds, the chilly and meditative shade of the woods. And that stream isn't the only source of coolness; all sorts of running streams sing beneath the trees; at each step, springs gush forth; when you follow the narrow paths, you feel as if underground lakes are penetrating the moss and taking advantage of the slightest cracks, at the foot of the trees, between the rocks, to pour out in crystal fountains. The whispering voices of these brooks are raised so loud and in such numbers that they drown out the song of the bullfinches. You'd think you were in some enchanted park, with cascades falling everywhere.

Farther down, the grasslands are soaked. Gigantic chestnut trees cast black shadows. Along the edges of the meadows, long curtains of poplars align their rustling tapestries. There are two avenues of enormous plane trees that cross the fields as they ascend to the old Château de Gagny, today in ruins. In this continually watered land, the grass grows luxuriantly. It forms a sort of garden plot between the two wooded hills, but a natural garden, with the meadows for lawns and the giant trees constituting the colossal flower beds. When the noonday sun beams down vertically, the shadows grow blue and the illuminated grass sleeps in the heat, while a chilly shudder runs through the foliage.

And it was there that old Merlier's mill brightened a corner of that wild greenery with its click-clack. The building, made of plaster and boards, seemed as old as the world. Half of it dipped into the Morelle, which at that spot rounds out into a clear pool. A sluice had been installed, with the water dropping several meters onto the mill wheel, which creaked as it turned with the asthmatic cough of a loyal servant who had grown old in the household. When people advised old Merlier to replace it, he shook his head, saying that a young wheel would be lazier and wouldn't know its job so well; and he used to patch up the old one with anything that came to hand, barrel staves, rusty scraps of iron, zinc, lead. The wheel seemed all the merrier for it, with its profile that had become strange, with its tufts of grass and moss all over. When the water struck it with its silvery current, it was covered with pearls, and its strange framework seemed to be adorned with a shining set of mother-of-pearl necklaces.

The part of the mill that dipped into the Morelle that way looked like a barbarian ark that had washed up there. A good half of the dwelling was built on piles. The water came in under the floor, there were deep places well known in the vicinity for the eels and enormous crayfish that were caught there. Downstream from the water drop, the pool was as limpid as a mirror, and when the wheel wasn't disturbing it with its foam, you could see schools of large fish swimming as slowly as a naval squadron. A broken staircase led down to the stream, near a piling to which a boat was tied up. A wooden gallery passed over the street. The mill had irregularly spaced windows. It was a hodgepodge of angles, small walls, belatedly added constructions, beams, and roof levels, which made it look like an old citadel that had been dismantled. But ivy had grown on it, and all sorts of climbing plants stopped up the cracks that were too big and threw a green mantle over the old dwelling. The well-born young ladies who passed that way used to draw old Merlier's mill in their sketchbooks.

On the side facing the road, the house was more solid. A stone gate led into the large courtyard, which was bordered on the right and left with sheds and stables. Near a well, an immense elm covered half the courtyard with its shade. At the far end of the yard, the house aligned the four windows of its second story, surmounted by a dovecote. Old Merlier's only concession to finery was to have that house front white-washed every ten years. It had just been repainted, and it dazzled the village when the sun lit it up at midday.

For twenty years, old Merlier had been mayor of Rocreuse. He was esteemed for the fortune he had been able to earn. People thought he was worth about eighty thousand francs, accumulated one sou at a time. When he married Madeleine Guillard, who brought him the mill as dowry, he barely owned more than his two arms. But Madeleine had never regretted her choice, because he had carried on the business of the couple so vigorously. Now his wife was dead and he remained a widower with his daughter Françoise. No doubt, he could have retired and let his mill wheel sleep in the moss; but he would have been too bored, and the house would have seemed dead to him. He kept on working for the pleasure of it. At the time, old Merlier was a tall old man, with a long, taciturn face; he never laughed, but all the same he was very jolly inside. He had been elected mayor on account of his money, and also for the fine appearance he made when officiating at a wedding.

Françoise Merlier had just turned eighteen. She wasn't considered one of the real beauties of the vicinity, because she was puny. Up to the age of fifteen she had even been homely. People in Rocreuse couldn't understand why the daughter of Mr. and Mrs. Merlier, both so sturdy, grew up so unsatisfactorily, as if regretfully. But at fifteen, though she remained frail, she developed a little face that was the prettiest in the world. She had black hair and dark eyes, and yet was very pink; her lips were always laughing, her cheeks were dimpled, and there seemed to be a wreath of sunlight on her clear brow. Although underdeveloped for local tastes, she wasn't scrawny, far from it; what they really meant to say was that she wouldn't have been able to lift a sack of wheat; but, as she grew older, she was becoming quite chubby, and in time she would be as round and luscious as a quail. Only, her father's long periods of silence had made her sensible while still quite young. If she was constantly laughing, that was to give pleasure to others. Deep down, she was serious.

Naturally, every local lad wooed her, even more for her money than for her pleasant personality. And she had finally made a choice that had just shocked the countryside. Across the Morelle lived a tall young fellow called Dominique Penquer. He wasn't from Rocreuse. Ten years earlier, he had come from Belgium to take over an inheritance from an uncle; this small property was located at the very edge of the Forest of Gagny, just opposite the mill, at a few rifle shots' distance. He said he had come merely to sell that property and go back home, but it seems that the area delighted him, because he never moved away. He was seen cultivating his little field and harvesting a few vegetables, which he lived on. He used to fish and hunt; several times the gamekeepers almost caught him and reported him to the police. This free-wheeling existence, which the peasants couldn't rightly see how he could afford, had finally given him a bad reputation. They vaguely called him a poacher. At any rate, he was lazy, because he was often found asleep on the grass at hours when he should have been working. The cottage he lived in, underneath the outermost trees in the forest, didn't resemble an honest fellow's home, either. If he had had dealings with the wolves in the ruins of Gagny, that wouldn't have surprised the old women one bit. And yet at times the girls ventured to defend him, because he was splendid-looking, that suspicious character, supple and tall as a poplar, with a very white skin and blond beard and hair that looked like gold in the sunlight. Now, one fine morning Françoise had announced to old Merlier that she loved Dominique and would never consent to marry any other man.

Just imagine what a cudgel blow old Merlier received that day! As was his custom, he said nothing. He was wearing his meditative expression, but his inner jollity was no longer gleaming from his eyes. They both sulked for a week. Françoise, too, was quite solemn. What was tormenting old Merlier was his failure to understand how that rascally poacher had been able to bewitch his daughter. Dominique had never come to the mill. The miller kept a lookout, and observed the wooer on the other side of the Morelle lying on the grass and pretending to be asleep. From her room Françoise could see him. The matter was clear; they must have fallen in love making eyes at each other over the mill wheel.

Meanwhile, another week went by. Françoise was becoming more and more solemn. Old Merlier still wasn't saying anything. Then, one evening, silently, he himself brought in Dominique. Françoise was just laying the table. She didn't appear surprised; all she did was add another setting; but the little dimples in her cheeks had just appeared again, and her laughter had returned. That morning, old Merlier had gone to see Dominique in his cottage on the edge of the woods. There the two men had talked for three hours, with doors and windows shut. No one ever found out what it was they said to each other. What is certain is that, when he came out, old Merlier was already treating Dominique like his son. No doubt the old man had found the lad he had gone looking for, an upstanding lad, in that lazybones who stretched out on the grass to get the girls to love him.

All Rocreuse talked. The women, in their doorways, couldn't say enough about the folly of old Merlier, who was taking a scoundrel into his house that way. He let them talk. Perhaps he had recalled his own wedding. He hadn't owned a red cent, either, when he had married Madeleine and her mill, but that hadn't prevented him from being a good husband. Besides, Dominique put an end to the gossip by beginning to work so hard that the locals were amazed. The mill hand had just been drafted into the army, and Dominique wouldn't hear of their hiring anyone else. He carried the sacks, drove the cart, and struggled with the ancient wheel when it needed to be coaxed to turn—all this so cheerfully that people came to watch him for their pleasure. Old Merlier wore his taciturn smile. He was very proud of having realized what that lad had in him. There's nothing like love to put heart into young men.

Amid all this heavy labor, Françoise and Dominique adored each other. They rarely spoke to each other, but they looked at each other with a smiling tenderness. Up to then old Merlier hadn't said a word about the wedding; and both of them respected that silence, awaiting the old man's pleasure. Finally, one day toward the middle of July, he had had three tables laid in the courtyard, under the big elm, inviting his friends from Rocreuse to come that evening for a drink with him. When the courtyard was full and everyone had his glass in his hand, old Merlier raised his very high and said:

"It's to have the pleasure of announcing to you that Françoise will marry that strapping fellow there in a month, on Saint Louis's Day."

Then they clinked glasses noisily. Everyone was laughing. But old Merlier, raising his voice, went on to say:

"Dominique, kiss your betrothed. It's the thing to do."

And they kissed, their faces red, while the guests laughed even louder. It was a real celebration. They emptied a small cask. Then, when only close friends were left, they chatted tranquilly. Night had fallen, a starry, very bright night. Dominique and Françoise, seated on a bench one next to the other, said nothing. An old peasant was talking about the war that the Emperor had declared on Prussia. All the village boys had already left. The day before, troops had gone by again. The fight was going to be a tough one.

"Bah!" said old Merlier, with the egotism of a happy man. "Dominique is a foreigner, he won't have to go . . ." And if the Prussians came, he'd be there to defend his wife.

The idea that the Prussians might come seemed like a good joke. They were going to get a real drubbing, and all would soon be over.

"I've already seen them, I've already seen them," the old peasant repeated in a hollow voice.

There was a silence. Then they clinked glasses again. Françoise and

Dominique hadn't heard any of this; they had taken each other's hand gently, behind the bench so that they couldn't be seen doing it, and they felt so good that way that they just sat there, their eyes lost in the depths of the darkness.

What a warm, splendid night! The village was falling asleep on the two sides of the white highway, as untroubled as a child. All that was still heard, at long intervals, was the crowing of some rooster that had awakened too early. From the great forests nearby, long exhalations descended and passed over the rooftops like caresses. The meadows, with their dark shade trees, took on a mysterious, reflective majesty, while all the springs, all the running waters that gushed forth in the dark, seemed to be the cool, rhythmic breathing of the sleeping countryside. At moments, the old mill wheel, in slumber, seemed to be having dreams, like those old watchdogs that bark as they snore; it creaked, it spoke to itself, rocked by the water drop in the Morelle; that sheet of water emitted a steady musical sound like an organ pipe. Never had such extensive peace been spread over a more fortunate corner of nature.

II

One month later to the day, precisely on the eve of Saint Louis's Day, Rocreuse was living in terror. The Prussians had beaten the Emperor, and were advancing toward the village in forced marches. For a week, people passing along the road had been announcing the Prussians: "They're at Lormières, they're at Novelles"; and, hearing these reports that they were drawing near so quickly, every morning the people of Rocreuse thought they saw them coming down through the Forest of Gagny. But they didn't come, and that frightened people even more. They would surely fall upon the village at night and slaughter everyone.

On the night before, a little before daybreak, there had been an alarm. The inhabitants had awakened, hearing a loud noise of men on the road. The women were already falling on their knees and crossing themselves, when some people recognized red trousers through their cautiously half-opened windows. It was a French detachment. Their captain had immediately asked for the local mayor, and he had remained at the mill after talking with old Merlier.

The sun was rising cheerfully that day. It would be hot at noon. A golden brightness hovered over the woods, while down below, above the meadows, white mists were rising. The village, clean and pretty, was waking up in the cool air, and the countryside, with its stream and fountains, had the moist charms of a bunch of flowers. But that beautiful day didn't make anyone smile. They had just seen the captain walking to and fro around the mill, looking at the neighboring houses, crossing the Morelle, and, from there, studying the region with binoculars. Old Merlier, who accompanied him, seemed to be giving him explanations. Next, the captain had stationed soldiers behind walls, behind trees, in hollows. The bulk of the detachment was camping in the courtyard of the mill. Was there going to be a battle, then? And when old Merlier got back, he was questioned. He gave a long nod but didn't speak. Yes, there was going to be a battle.

Françoise and Dominique were there in the courtyard looking at him. Finally he took his pipe out of his mouth, and spoke this simple sentence:

"Ah, my poor children, it's not tomorrow that I'll marry you!"

Dominique, his lips taut, with an angry wrinkle on his brow, raised himself up at times, keeping his eyes fixed on the Forest of Gagny, as if he wanted to see the Prussians arrive. Françoise, very pale and solemn, was coming and going, supplying the soldiers' needs. They were cooking soup in a corner of the courtyard and were joking while awaiting their food.

Meanwhile, the captain seemed delighted. He had inspected the bedrooms and main parlor of the mill that faced the stream. Now, seated near the well, he was talking with old Merlier.

"It's a real fortress you've got there," he was saying. "We'll hold out until this evening . . . The bandits are late. They should have been here by now."

The miller remained solemn. He pictured his mill blazing like a torch. But he wasn't lamenting, since he considered that futile. He only opened his mouth to say:

"You ought to have the boat hidden behind the wheel. There's a space there where it fits . . . It might come in handy."

The captain issued an order. This captain was a fine-looking man of about forty, tall, with a pleasant face. The sight of Françoise and Dominique seemed to gladden him. He was paying attention to them as if he had forgotten about the coming fight. His eyes followed Françoise's movements, and his expression made it clear that he found her charming. Then, turning toward Dominique, he asked him, point-blank:

"You aren't in the army, son?"

"I'm a foreigner," the young man replied.

The captain seemed to find this reason less than satisfactory. He blinked his eyes and smiled. Françoise was more pleasant to be around than cannons. Then, seeing him smile, Dominique added:

"I'm a foreigner; but I can put a bullet in an apple at five hundred meters . . . Look, my hunting rifle is there behind you."

"You may find use for it," was the captain's simple reply.

Françoise had come up to them, trembling slightly. And without caring about the people around, Dominique took the two hands she reached out to him, as if putting herself under his protection, and held them tightly in his own. The captain had smiled again, but didn't add a word. He remained seated, his sword between his legs, his eyes far away as if he were dreaming.

It was already ten o'clock. It was beginning to get very hot. A heavy silence ensued. In the courtyard, in the shade of the sheds, the soldiers had begun eating their soup. No sound was coming from the village; the inhabitants had all barricaded their houses, doors, and windows. A dog, left alone on the road, was howling. From the woods and the nearby meadows, which were fainting under the heat, came a distant, prolonged sound, comprised of all their scattered exhalations. A cuckoo called. Then the silence spread even further.

And in this sleeping air, all of a sudden, a shot rang out. The captain rose briskly, and the soldiers abandoned their plates of soup, which were still half-full. In a few seconds, they were all at their battle stations; the mill was occupied from top to bottom. Meanwhile, the captain, who had gone out to the road, couldn't see a thing; to his right, to his left, the road stretched into the distance, empty and all white. A second shot was heard, and still nothing, not even a shadow. But, turning around, between two trees in the direction of Gagny, he espied a light wisp of smoke floating away like a thread of gossamer. The forest remained deep and gentle.

"The scoundrels have hidden in the forest," he muttered. "They know we're here."

Then the fusillade continued, getting heavier all the while, between the French soldiers stationed around the mill and the Prussians concealed behind the trees. The bullets were whistling across the Morelle, without resulting in casualties on either side. The shots were irregularly spaced, coming from every bush; and all that could be seen so far was little puffs of smoke gently shaking on the breeze. That lasted nearly two hours. The officer was humming nonchalantly. Françoise and Dominique, who had remained in the courtyard, were raising their heads and looking over a low wall. They were especially interested in a little soldier stationed on the bank of the Morelle behind the skeleton of an old boat; lying on his stomach, he would observe, fire, then lower himself into a ditch a little behind him to reload his rifle; and his movements were so comical, so sly, so nimble, that they allowed themselves a smile as they watched him. He must have caught sight of some Prussian's head, because he stood up briskly and took aim; but before he could fire, he uttered a cry, spun around, and rolled into the ditch, where for a moment his legs underwent a convulsive stiffening like the feet of a chicken being slaughtered. The little soldier had just received a bullet full in the chest. He was the first fatality. Instinctively Françoise had gripped Dominique's hand and was seizing it in a nervous reaction.

"Don't stay here," said the captain. "The bullets are reaching this area."

Indeed, a little dry thud had been heard in the old elm, and the tip of a branch was rocking as it fell. But the two young people didn't budge; they were riveted there by their anguish at what they saw. At the edge of the woods, a Prussian had suddenly emerged from behind a tree as if from behind a stage flat, beating the air with his arms and falling over backwards. And nothing else stirred; the two dead men seemed to be sleeping in the broad daylight; even now no one was to be seen in the dull countryside. Even the crackling of the fusillade ceased. The only sound was the bright whispering of the Morelle.

Old Merlier looked at the captain with an air of surprise, as if to ask him whether it was all over.

"Here comes the main attack," the captain muttered. "Watch out! Don't stay here."

Before he had finished speaking, a terrifying volley was fired. The big elm had its foliage virtually mowed; a bunch of leaves were whirling in the air. Luckily the Prussians had fired too high. Dominique dragged away Françoise—nearly carried her away—while old Merlier was following them, shouting:

"Go into the little cellar; the walls are solid."

But they didn't listen to him; they went into the main parlor, where some ten soldiers were waiting silently, the shutters closed, looking out through cracks. The captain had remained alone in the courtyard, crouching behind the little wall, while furious volleys continued. Beyond the wall the soldiers he had stationed were only yielding ground a foot at a time. And yet they would creep back to cover one by one when the enemy had dislodged them from their hiding places. Their orders were to gain time and not to show themselves, so that the Prussians couldn't learn the strength of the unit that was facing them. Another hour went by. And when a sergeant came to report that there were only two or three men left outside, the officer pulled out his watch, muttering:

"Two-thirty . . . Look, we've got to hold out for four hours."

He had the big gate to the courtyard closed, and everything was put in readiness for an energetic resistance. Since the Prussians were on the other side of the Morelle, an immediate attack wasn't to be feared. True, there was a bridge two kilometers away, but they were no doubt unaware of its existence, and it was very hard to believe that they would try to ford the stream. And so the officer merely had the road watched. Their entire effort would be centered on the side facing the open country.

The fusillade had ceased again. The mill seemed dead in the strong sunlight. Not one shutter was open, no sound came from inside. Meanwhile, the Prussians were gradually showing themselves at the edge of the Forest of Gagny. They were sticking out their heads, they were growing bolder. In the mill several soldiers were already taking aim, but the captain shouted.

"No, no, wait! . . . Let them come closer."

They were very cautious doing so, looking at the mill distrustfully. That old dwelling, silent and gloomy, with its curtains of ivy, worried them. Still, they were moving forward. When there were about fifty of them in the meadow opposite, the officer said a single word:

"Go!"

A lacerating volley was to be heard; isolated shots followed. Françoise, shaking all over, had put her hands to her ears in spite of herself. Dominique, standing behind the soldiers, was watching; and when the smoke had cleared away a bit, he saw three Prussians lying on their backs in the middle of the meadow. The others had taken cover behind the willows and the poplars. And the siege began.

For over an hour the mill was riddled with bullets. They whipped its old walls like hail. When they struck stone, they could be heard squashing and bouncing off into the water. They penetrated wood with a muffled sound. At times a creaking indicated that the wheel had just been hit. The soldiers inside economized their shots, firing only when they could take proper aim. From time to time the captain consulted his watch. And, when a bullet split a shutter and lodged in the ceiling, he muttered:

"Four o'clock. We'll never make it."

In fact, that terrible fusillade was gradually shaking the old mill to pieces. A shutter fell into the water, riddled like a piece of lace, and had to be replaced by a mattress. Every minute old Merlier was leaving cover to check on the damage to his poor wheel, whose creaking made his heart ache. This time it was really finished off; he'd never be able to patch it up. Dominique had implored Françoise to go to her room, but she insisted on staying with him; she had taken a seat behind a big oak armoire that protected her. And yet a bullet struck the armoire, whose sides emitted a deep sound. Then Dominique took a stand in front of Françoise. He had not yet fired; he was holding his rifle in his hand, being unable to get near the windows, the full breadth of which was occupied by the soldiers. At each volley the floor shook.

"Watch out! Watch out!" the captain suddenly cried.

He had just seen a large dark mass emerging from the woods. Immediately a formidable volley firing began. It was like a whirlwind passing over the mill. Another shutter was blown away and bullets came in through the gaping window opening. Two soldiers rolled on the floor tiles. One stopped moving; they shoved him against the wall because he was in the way. The other writhed, asking to be finished off; but he wasn't listened to; the bullets were still coming in; everyone was getting out of their way and trying to find a loophole in order to return the fire. A third soldier was wounded; this one didn't say a word, but sank down beside a table with wildly staring eyes. Seeing these dead men, Françoise, horror-stricken, had automatically pushed away her chair; she sat down on the floor against the wall, believing she'd be a smaller target there, and in less danger. Meanwhile, all the mattresses in the house had been collected, and the gap in the window had been half-filled again. The room was filling up with debris, shattered weapons, and ripped-open furniture.

"Five o'clock," said the captain. "Hold tight . . . they're going to try to cross the stream."

At that moment Françoise uttered a cry. A bullet that had ricocheted had just grazed her forehead. A few drops of blood appeared. Dominique looked at her; then, going up to the window, he fired his first shot and didn't stop after that. He would load and fire, unconcerned with what was going on around him; only, from time to time, he would glance at Françoise. Moreover, he wasn't in a hurry, he took careful aim. The Prussians, moving along the poplars, were trying to cross the Morelle, as the captain had foreseen; but as soon as one of them ventured to do so, he fell, with one of Dominique's bullets in his head. The captain, who was observing this course of events, was amazed. He complimented the young man, saying that he'd be glad to have many marksmen of that quality. Dominique wasn't paying attention to him. A bullet cut into his shoulder, another bruised his arm. And he was still firing.

There were two more dead men. The mattresses, cut to ribbons, were no longing filling up the window spaces. A final volley seemed as if it would carry off the mill. Their position could no longer be held. And yet, the officer kept repeating:

"Hold tight . . . Another half-hour."

By now he was counting the minutes. He had promised his superiors to pin the enemy down there until evening, and he hadn't taken a step backward before the hour he had determined on for his retreat. He maintained his likable attitude, smiling at Françoise to reassure her. He himself had just picked up a dead soldier's rifle and was firing.

Only four soldiers were now left in the room.

The Prussians appeared en masse on the far bank of the Morelle, and they were obviously going to cross the stream at any moment. A few more minutes went by. The captain was still stubbornly refusing to give the order to retreat when a sergeant ran up and said:

"They're on the road, they're going to take us from behind."

The Prussians must have found the bridge. The captain pulled out his watch.

"Five more minutes," he said. "They won't be here for five minutes."

Then, at six o'clock precisely, he finally consented to have his men leave through a little door that opened onto an alleyway. From there they took cover in a ditch and reached the Forest of Sauval. Before going, the captain had taken very polite leave of old Merlier, apologizing for what had happened. And he had even added:

"Keep them entertained . . . We'll be back."

Meanwhile Dominique had remained alone in the parlor. He was still firing, paying attention to nothing, comprehending nothing. All he felt was the need to defend Françoise. The soldiers had left without his being aware of it in the least. He kept on aiming and killing a man with each shot. Suddenly there was a loud noise. From behind, the Prussians had just invaded the courtyard. He fired one last shot before they fell upon him, while his rifle was still smoking.

Four men held him fast. Others were shouting all around him in a terrifying language. They almost slaughtered him on the spot. Françoise had thrown herself in front of him imploringly. But an officer entered and had the prisoner handed over to himself. After exchanging a few sentences with the soldiers in German, he turned to Dominique and said to him roughly, in very good French:

"You'll be shot in two hours."

III

It was a regulation issued by the German general staff: any Frenchman, not belonging to the regular army, captured with weapon in hand, was to be shot. Even the companies of partisans weren't recognized as belligerents. By thus making terrible examples of the peasants who were defending their homes, the Germans were trying to prevent a universal call to arms, which they dreaded.

The officer, a tall, lean man about fifty, subjected Dominique to a brief interrogation. Even though he spoke French very correctly, he had a thoroughly Prussian severity.

"You're from this area?"

"No, I'm Belgian."

"Why did you take up arms? . . . All this should be no concern of yours."

Dominique didn't reply. At that moment the officer caught sight of

Françoise standing, very pale, and listening; on her white forehead her light wound made a red streak. He looked at the young couple one at a time, seemed to understand the situation, and merely added:

"You don't deny that you fired?"

"I fired as much as I could," Dominique calmly replied.

That confession was needless, because he was black with powder, drenched in sweat, and stained with a few drops of blood that had flowed from the scratch on his shoulder.

"Very well," the officer repeated. "You'll be shot in two hours."

Françoise didn't cry out. She joined her hands and raised them in a gesture of wordless despair. The officer noticed that gesture. Two soldiers had taken Dominique into an adjoining room, where they were to keep watch over him. The girl had dropped onto a chair, her legs giving way under her; she was unable to cry, she was stifling. Meanwhile the officer kept observing her. Finally he spoke to her:

"Is that boy your brother?" he asked.

She shook her head "no." He remained stiff and unsmiling. Then, after a silence:

"Has he lived in the area very long?"

She said "yes" with a nod.

"So he must be very familiar with the forests around here?"

This time she spoke.

"Yes, sir," she said, looking at him in some surprise.

He said nothing further, but turned on his heels, asking that the village mayor be brought to him. But Françoise had stood up, her face slightly red, believing she had grasped the intention of his questions, and feeling some hope again. She herself ran to find her father.

Old Merlier, the moment the firing had ceased, had briskly gone down by way of the wooden gallery to inspect his wheel. He adored his daughter, and had a staunch friendly feeling toward Dominique, his future son-in-law; but his wheel also had a big place in his heart. Since the two children, as he called them, had come out of the scrape safe and sound, he was thinking about his other love—and that one had really suffered. Leaning over the big wooden framework, he was studying its wounds brokenheartedly. Five paddles were in smithereens, and the central timberwork was riddled. He thrust his fingers into the bullet holes to measure their depth; he was wondering how he could repair all that damage. Françoise found him already plugging up cracks with debris and moss.

"Father," she said, "they're asking for you."

And finally she was able to cry, telling him what she had just heard. Old Merlier shook his head. People weren't shot like that. They had to wait and see. And he went back inside the mill in his taciturn, peaceful way. When the officer asked him for provisions for his men, he replied that the inhabitants of Rocreuse weren't accustomed to be bullied, and that he'd get nothing out of them if he used force. He would take care of everything, but only if he was allowed to act independently. At first the officer seemed angry at that calm tone; then he gave in to the old man's short, clear terms. He even called him back, to ask him:

"What do you call those woods opposite?"

"The Forest of Sauval."

"And how far do they extend?"

The miller stared at him.

"I don't know," he answered.

And he left. An hour later, the forced contribution of provisions and money that the officer had requested was in the courtyard of the mill. Night was approaching; Françoise observed the movements of the soldiers in anguish. She didn't go far from the room in which Dominique was locked up. About seven o'clock, she had a strong emotional shock; she saw the officer enter the prisoner's room, and for fifteen minutes she heard their voices raised. For a moment the officer reappeared on the threshold to give an order in German that she didn't understand; but when twelve men had taken up positions in the courtyard carrying rifles, a tremor seized her and she thought she would die. And so it was a sure thing; the execution was going to take place. The twelve men stayed there ten minutes; Dominique's voice was constantly raised in a tone of decided refusal. Finally the officer came out, slamming the door violently and saying:

"Very well, think it over . . . I give you till tomorrow morning."

And with a gesture he had the twelve men fall out. Françoise remained numb. Old Merlier, who had continued to smoke his pipe, looking at the platoon with a merely curious expression, came and took her by the arm with a father's gentleness. He took her to her room.

"Stay calm," he said, "try to sleep . . . Tomorrow it will be daylight, and we'll see."

As he went out, he locked her in out of caution. He believed firmly that women are totally incapable and spoil everything when they meddle in a serious matter. But Françoise didn't go to sleep. For a long time she remained seated on her bed, listening to the noises in the house. The German soldiers, who were camping in the courtyard, were singing and laughing; they must have been eating and drinking until eleven, because the racket didn't stop for a minute. Even inside the mill, heavy steps resounded from time to time, no doubt sentries being relieved. But what were especially interesting to her were the sounds she could make out in the room below her bedroom. Several times she stretched out on the floor, putting her ear down to it. That room was the very one in which Dominique had been locked up. He must be walking from the wall to the window, because for some time she heard the regular cadence of his footsteps; then came a long silence; he had probably sat down. In addition, all the noises ceased, everything was falling asleep. When she thought that the house was at rest, she opened her window as quietly as possible and leaned out.

Outside, the night was warm and clear. The narrow crescent of the moon, setting behind the Forest of Sauval, was illuminating the countryside as if with a night light. The long shadows of the tall trees made black lines across the meadows, while the grass in the open places took on the softness of greenish velvet. But Françoise was scarcely detained by the mysterious charm of the night. She was observing the countryside, looking for the sentries that the Germans must have stationed in that direction. She clearly saw their shadows spaced out along the Morelle. A single one was located in front of the mill, across the stream, near a willow whose branches dipped into the water. Françoise could make him out clearly. He was a tall lad who was standing still, his face turned skyward with the dreamy expression of a shepherd.

Then, after carefully inspecting the terrain in this manner, she returned to her bed and sat down again. She stayed there for an hour, deeply absorbed. Then she listened again: there was no longer a breath in the house. She returned to the window and glanced outside; but one tip of the moon that was still visible behind the trees must have seemed like an impediment to her, because she started waiting again. Finally, she thought the right time had come. The night was completely black; she could no longer see the sentry opposite her; the countryside stretched out like a sea of ink. She listened hard for a moment and made up her mind. Extending past the window, and near it, there was an iron ladder, bars sealed into the wall, running from the wheel to the attic. It had formerly been used by the millers to inspect certain gears; later on, the wheel works had been altered, and for a long time the ladder had been hidden beneath the dense ivy which covered that side of the mill.

Françoise bravely straddled the railing of her window, seized one of the iron bars, and found herself completely out in the open. She started to climb down. Her petticoats were a great nuisance to her. Suddenly a stone was dislodged from the wall and fell into the Morelle with a loud splash. She had stopped in her tracks, shivering with fright. But she realized that the water drop, with its unceasing drone, drowned out for distant ears any noise she could make, and then she descended more boldly, feeling the ivy with her foot and making sure of each rung. When she was level with the bedroom that was serving as Dominique's prison, she stopped. An unforeseen difficulty almost made her lose all her courage; the window of the lower room didn't open directly below her own bedroom window; it was at some distance from the ladder, and when she reached out her hand she felt only the wall. Would she have to climb back up, then, without carrying out her plan? Her arms were getting tired; the murmuring of the Morelle, below her, was beginning to make her dizzy. Then she detached little bits of plaster from the wall and threw them into Dominique's window. He didn't hear them; perhaps he was asleep. She crumbled more of the wall, skinning her fingers. And her strength was deserting her, she felt herself falling backward, when Dominique finally opened his window quietly.

"It's me," she murmured. "Catch me fast, I'm falling."

It was the first time she had ever used a familiar verb form in addressing him. He grabbed her, leaning out, and brought her into the room. Once inside, she had a crying fit, stifling her sobs so that she wouldn't be heard. Then, making a supreme effort, she calmed down.

"Are you being guarded?" she asked in a low voice.

Dominique, still amazed at seeing her arrive that way, merely nodded, pointing to his door. On the other side of it they could hear snoring; the sentry, succumbing to his weariness, must have lain down on the floor, up against the door, certain that, in that way, the prisoner would be unable to get out.

"You must run away," she continued briskly. "I've come to beg you to run away and to say good-bye to you."

But he didn't seem to hear her. He kept repeating:

"What! It's you, it's you . . . Oh, how you scared me! You could have been killed."

He took her hands and kissed them.

"How I love you, Françoise! . . . You're as brave as you're beautiful. I had only one fear: dying without seeing you again . . . But here you are, and now they can shoot me. After spending a quarter of an hour with you, I'll be ready."

Gradually he had drawn her close to him, and she was resting her head on his shoulder. Their danger brought them closer together. They forgot everything else while embracing that way.

"Oh, Françoise," Dominique went on in a caressing voice, "today is Saint Louis's Day, our wedding day that we waited for so long. Nothing has been able to separate us, since here we are alone together, faithful to the appointed date . . . Isn't that so? Right now it's our wedding morning."

"Yes, yes," she repeated, "our wedding morning."

They exchanged a kiss tremblingly. But all at once she pulled away from him; the awful reality loomed up before her.

"You must flee, you must flee," she stammered. "Don't waste a minute."

And as he reached out his arms in the darkness to take hold of her again, she addressed him as *tu* once more:

"Oh, please, listen to me . . . If *you* die, *I'll* die. In an hour it will be daylight. I want you to leave at once."

Then, rapidly, she detailed her plan. The iron ladder went all the way down to the wheel; there, he could use the wheel paddles and get into the boat that was located in a recess. Then he could easily reach the far bank of the stream and get away.

"But there must be sentries there," he said.

"Just one, directly opposite, at the foot of the nearest willow."

"And what if he notices me, what if he calls out?"

Françoise shuddered. She placed in his hands a knife she had brought down with her. There was a silence.

"And your father? And you?" Dominique went on. "No, no, I can't run away . . . After I'm gone, these soldiers might murder you . . . You don't know them. They offered to spare me if I agreed to guide them through the Forest of Sauval. When they find that I'm gone, they're capable of anything."

The girl wasted no time arguing. To every reason he gave she merely replied:

"Out of love for me, run away . . . If you love me, Dominique, don't stay here a minute longer."

Then she promised she would go back up to her room. No one would know she had helped him. Finally she took him in her arms, to kiss him, to persuade him, in an unusual burst of passion. He was vanquished. He didn't ask another question.

"Swear to me that your father knows what you're doing and that he advises me to run away."

"It was my father who sent me," Françoise boldly replied.

She was lying. At that moment she felt only one overpowering need, to know he was safe, to rid herself of the abominable thought that sunrise would be the signal for his death. Once he was far away, any misfortune could befall her; it would seem sweet to her, provided he was alive. The egotism of her affection wanted him alive, above all else.

"All right," said Dominique, "I'll do as you wish."

After that, they spoke no more. Dominique went and opened the window again. But suddenly a sound chilled them with fright. The door was shaken, and they thought it was being opened. Obviously, soldiers making their rounds had heard their voices. And the two of them, standing there close together, waited in unspeakable anguish. The door was rattled again, but it didn't open. Both of them stifled a sigh; they had just realized it must be the soldier sleeping on the threshold, who had turned over. In fact, silence ensued and the snoring resumed.

Dominique absolutely insisted that Françoise must first climb back up to her room. He took her in his arms, and took leave of her wordlessly. Then he helped her take hold of the ladder and clung to it himself. But he wouldn't go down a single rung before he was sure she was in her room. When Françoise was back in, she called down in a voice as light as a breath:

"Good-bye, I love you!"

She remained leaning out, trying to follow Dominique's movements. The night was still very dark. She looked for the sentry but couldn't see him; only the willow created a pale spot amid the darkness. For a moment she heard Dominique's body brushing against the ivy. Then the wheel creaked and there was a light lapping of water that indicated that the young man had just found the boat. In fact, a minute later, she made out the dark silhouette of the boat on the gray surface of the Morelle. Then a terrible anguish seized her by the throat again. Any moment she expected to hear the sentry's shout of alarm; the slightest sounds, scattered in the darkness, seemed to her like the hurried steps of soldiers, the clatter of weapons, the sound of rifles being cocked. And yet the seconds were passing, and the countryside retained its prevailing peace. Dominique must be reaching the far bank. Françoise could no longer see a thing. The silence was majestic. And she heard a stamping of feet, a hoarse cry, the fall of a body. Next, the silence became deeper. Then, as if she felt death passing by, she remained there, completely chilled, looking out onto the dense night.

IV

As soon as day broke, shouts rocked the mill. Old Merlier had come to unlock Françoise's door. She went down into the courtyard, pale and very calm. But, once there, she was unable to repress a shudder at the sight of the corpse of a Prussian soldier stretched out near the well on an outspread cloak.

Around the body soldiers were gesticulating and shouting in rage. Several of them were shaking their fists at the village. Meanwhile, the captain had just had old Merlier summoned, as mayor of the parish.

"Here," he said to him in a voice choked with anger, "is one of our men who has been found murdered on the bank of the stream . . . We must make a conspicuous example, and I'm counting on you to help us locate the killer."

"I'll do anything you want," the miller replied with his customary nonchalance. "But it won't be easy."

The officer had stooped down to remove a corner of the cloak that was concealing the dead man's face. A terrible wound was thus revealed. The sentry had been struck in the throat, and the weapon had remained in the wound. It was a kitchen knife with a black handle.

"Look at this knife," the officer said to old Merlier. "Maybe it will help us in our investigation."

The old man had given a start. But he controlled himself at once; he replied, without moving a muscle in his face:

"Everyone in our area has knives like this . . . Maybe your man was tired of fighting and polished himself off. Things like that happen."

"Be still!" the officer shouted furiously. "I don't know what's keeping me from setting fire to the entire village."

Fortunately his anger prevented him from noticing the strong emotions in Françoise's face. She had felt it necessary to sit down on the stone bench near the well. In spite of herself, she couldn't take her eyes off that corpse stretched out on the ground almost at her feet. He was a tall, good-looking young fellow, who resembled Dominique, with blond hair and blue eyes. That resemblance made her heartsick. She was thinking that the dead man might have left behind, there in Germany, some sweetheart who was going to mourn for him. And she recognized her knife in the dead man's throat. She had killed him.

Meanwhile, the officer was speaking of taking awful measures against Rocreuse, when some soldiers ran up to him. Only now had they noticed that Dominique had escaped. That caused an enormous row. The officer went to the scene of the deed, looked out of the window, which had been left open, understood the whole thing, and returned, exasperated.

Old Merlier seemed quite annoyed at Dominique's flight.

"The fool!" he muttered. "He's ruining everything."

Françoise, who heard him, was anguish-stricken. But her father didn't suspect her complicity. He shook his head, saying to her quietly:

"Now we're in for it!"

"It's that scoundrel! It's that scoundrel!" the officer was shouting. "He probably made it into the woods . . . But we've got to find him again, or else the village will pay for what he did."

And, addressing the miller:

"Come on now, you must know where he's hiding."

Old Merlier gave one of his silent laughs, pointing to the wide extent of the wooded hills.

"How do you expect to find a man in there?" he said.

"Oh, there must be hiding places there that you know. I'll give you ten men. You'll guide them."

"I'm perfectly willing. But it'll take us a week to comb through all the woods in the vicinity."

The old man's calmness infuriated the officer. Of course he understood how ridiculous such a search would be. It was then that he noticed Françoise, pale and trembling on the bench. He was struck by the anxiety in the girl's appearance. He kept silent for a moment, examining now the miller, now Françoise.

Finally he asked the old man harshly, "Isn't that man your daughter's lover?"

Old Merlier turned livid, and looked as if he was going to pounce on the officer and choke him. He stiffened up and didn't reply. Françoise had put her hands to her face.

"Yes, that's it," the Prussian continued; "you or your daughter helped him get away. You're his accomplice . . . For the last time, will you turn him over to us?"

The miller didn't reply. He had turned aside and was looking into the distance with an unconcerned expression, as if the officer weren't taking to him. That raised the captain's anger to the highest pitch.

"Very well," he announced, "you'll be shot in his place."

And once again he called out a firing squad. Old Merlier kept calm. He merely shrugged his shoulders slightly; all this drama struck him as being in poor taste. Most likely, he didn't believe that they would shoot a man so readily. Then, when the firing squad was there, he said earnestly:

"So you're serious? . . . I'm willing. If you must absolutely have somebody, it may as well be me as anyone else."

But Françoise had risen, mad with fright, stammering:

"Mercy, sir, don't hurt my father! Kill me instead . . . I'm the one who helped Dominique get away. I'm the only guilty party."

"Quiet, daughter!" old Merlier exclaimed. "Why are you lying? . . . She spent the night locked up in her room, sir. She's lying, I assure you."

"No, I'm not lying," the girl went on ardently. "I climbed down through the window, I urged Dominique to run away . . . It's the truth, that and nothing else . . ."

The old man had become very pale. He could see from her eyes that she wasn't lying, and the whole affair frightened him. Oh, these children, with their emotions, how they ruined everything! Then he got angry.

"She's crazy, don't listen to her. She's telling you stupid stories . . . Come, let's get it over with."

She tried to protest again. She knelt down, she joined her hands. The officer was a calm spectator of that painful struggle.

"By God!" he finally said. "I'm taking your father because I no longer have the other man . . . Try to locate the other one, and your father will be free."

For a moment she looked at him, her eyes wide open at the atrociousness of that proposition.

"It's awful," she muttered. "Where do you expect me to find Dominique by this time? He's gone, I don't know where."

"Well, choose. He or your father."

"Oh, God, am I able to choose? Even if I knew where Dominique is, I couldn't choose! . . . You're breaking my heart . . . I'd rather die on the spot. Yes, that would be an end of it. Kill me, I beg you, kill me . . ."

This scene of tearful despair finally made the officer impatient. He exclaimed:

"Enough of this! I want to be kind; I consent to give you two hours . . . If your sweetheart isn't here in two hours, your father will pay the price for him."

And he had old Merlier led to the room that had served as Dominique's prison. The old man asked for tobacco and started smoking. No emotion could be read on his impassive face. But when he was alone, smoking, he shed two fat tears that slowly trickled down his cheeks. How his poor, dear child was suffering!

Françoise had remained in the middle of the courtyard. Prussian soldiers passed by laughing. Some of them flung remarks at her, jokes she didn't understand. She was looking at the door through which her father had just disappeared. And, in a slow gesture, she raised her hand to her forehead, as if to keep it from bursting.

The officer turned on his heels, repeating:

"You have two hours. Try to make good use of them."

She had two hours. That sentence kept buzzing in her head. Then, like an automaton, she left the courtyard and walked straight ahead. Where to go? What to do? She wasn't even attempting to make a decision, because she was well aware how futile her efforts would be. And yet, she would have liked to see Dominique. They would have reached an understanding together, they might have found a way out of their difficulties. And, amid the confusion of her thoughts, she went down to the bank of the Morelle, which she crossed downstream from the sluice in a spot where there were big stepping stones. Her feet led her to the nearest willow, at the corner of the meadow. As she bent down, she saw a pool of blood that made her turn pale. That must have been the spot. And she followed Dominique's trail in the trodden grass; he must have run; you could see a line of widely spaced steps cutting across the meadow obliquely. Then, beyond that, she lost the trail. But in a nearby meadow she thought she picked it up again. That led her to the edge of the forest, where all signs were obliterated.

All the same, Françoise plunged in beneath the trees. It was a relief to her to be alone. She sat down for a while. Then, recalling that time was slipping away, she stood up again. How long was it since she had left the mill? Five minutes? A half-hour? She was no longer aware of the time. Maybe Dominique had gone to hide in a thicket she knew, where they had eaten hazelnuts together one afternoon. She went to the thicket and inspected it. A single blackbird flew out, whistling its sweet, sad phrase. Then it occurred to her that he might have hidden out in a rocky hollow where he sometimes lay in ambush for game; but the rocky hollow was empty. What was the good of looking for him? She wouldn't find him. And gradually the desire to discover him excited her, and she walked more quickly. Suddenly she got the idea that he must have climbed a tree. From then on she walked with her eyes raised, and, so that he would know she was near him, she called him every fifteen or twenty paces. Cuckoos answered her; a breeze blowing through the branches made her think he was there and climbing down. Once she even imagined she saw him; she stopped, choking and feeling an urge to run away. What would she tell him? Had she really come to take him back and get him shot? Oh, no, she wouldn't talk about those things at all. She would call to him to escape, not to remain in the vicinity. Then, the thought of her father, who was awaiting her, caused her a burning grief. She fell onto the grass, weeping, and repeating out loud:

"My God! My God! Why am I here?"

It was mad of her to have come. And, as if terror-stricken, she ran, trying to get out of the forest. Three times she took a wrong turn, and she was thinking that she'd never find the mill again, when she emerged onto a meadow directly opposite Rocreuse. As soon as she saw the village, she halted. Was she going to go back alone?

She was still standing there when a voice softly called her:

"Françoise! Françoise!"

And she saw Dominique raising his head over the rim of a ditch. Good God! She had found him! Did heaven, then, want him to die? She held back a cry, and slid into the ditch.

"You were looking for me?" he asked.

"Yes," she answered, her head buzzing, not knowing what she was saying.

"Ah! What's been going on?"

"Nothing, I was worried, I wanted to see you."

Then, feeling calmer, he explained to her that he hadn't wanted to go far away. He was afraid for them. Those scoundrelly Prussians were quite capable of taking revenge on women and old men. But after all, everything was going well; and he added, laughing:

"Our wedding will be postponed for a week, that's all."

Then, since she was still obviously upset, he became serious again.

"But what's the matter? You're hiding something from me."

"No, I swear I'm not. I had to run to get here."

He kissed her, saying that it would be imprudent for her and for him to talk any longer; and he made a move to climb out of the ditch so as to reenter the forest. She held him back. She was trembling.

"Listen, maybe it would be better all the same if you stayed here . . . No one is looking for you, you have nothing to fear."

"Françoise, you're hiding something from me," he repeated.

Again she swore that she wasn't hiding anything from him. It was just that she preferred knowing he wasn't far away from her. And she stammered out other excuses. She seemed to him to be acting so oddly that now he himself would have refused to go far away. Besides, he firmly believed that the French would return. Troops had been sighted in the direction of Sauval.

"Oh, make them hurry, let them be here as soon as possible!" she murmured fervently.

At that moment the church bell of Rocreuse struck eleven. The ringing reached them clearly and distinctly. She stood up, frightened; it was two hours since she had left the mill.

"Listen," she said swiftly, "if we should have need of you, I'll go up to my room and wave my handkerchief."

And she left at a run, while Dominique, very worried, stretched out on the rim of the ditch to survey the mill. As she was about to enter Rocreuse, Françoise met an elderly beggar, old Bontemps, who was familiar with the whole region. He greeted her; he had just seen the miller in the midst of the Prussians; then, crossing himself repeatedly and muttering broken phrases, he continued on his way.

"The two hours have passed," said the officer when Françoise appeared. Old Merlier was there, sitting on the bench near the well, and still smoking. Once again the girl begged, wept, knelt. She wanted to gain time. The hope of seeing the French return had grown stronger in her mind, and while she was lamenting she thought she could hear far off the regular steps of an army on the march. Oh, if they would only appear, if they would only set them all free!

"Listen, sir, an hour, just one more hour . . . You surely can grant us an hour!"

But the officer remained unbending. He even ordered two men to seize her and take her away, so they could proceed calmly with the execution of the old man. Then, a fearful combat took place in Françoise's heart. She couldn't let her father be murdered that way. No, no, rather than that, she would die along with Dominique; and she was dashing toward her room when Dominique himself entered the courtyard.

The officer and the soldiers uttered a cry of triumph. But as for him, as if no one were around but Françoise, he walked over to her calmly and a little sternly.

"This is bad," he said. "Why didn't you bring me back with you? I had to hear about everything from old Bontemps . . . Anyway, here I am."

V

It was three o'clock. Big black clouds had slowly filled the sky, the tip of some nearby storm. That yellow sky, those coppery shreds, changed the valley of Rocreuse, so cheerful in the sunlight, into a lair of assassins filled with suspicious shadows. The Prussian officer had simply had Dominique locked up, without making a declaration about the fate he had in store for him. Since noon, Françoise had felt the agonies of an unspeakable anguish. She didn't want to leave the courtyard in spite of her father's urging. She was waiting for the French to come. But the hours went by, night was on the way, and she was suffering all the more because it didn't seem as if all that time gained could change the awful ending.

Meanwhile, about three, the Prussians made their preparations to withdraw. For a while, as on the day before, the officer had closeted himself with Dominique. Françoise had understood that the young man's future was being decided. Then she joined her hands in prayer. Old Merlier, beside her, maintained his wordless, rigid bearing, that of an old peasant who doesn't fight against the inevitability of facts.

"Oh, God! Oh, God!" Françoise stammered. "They're going to kill him . . ."

The miller drew her near him and took her on his knees like a child.

At that moment the officer came out, while, behind him, two men were bringing Dominique.

"Never! Never!" the young man was shouting. "I'm ready to die."

"Think it over carefully," the officer replied. "This service you refuse to do for me will be done for us by someone else. I offer you your life, I'm generous . . . All you need to do is guide us to Montredon across the woods. There must be paths there."

Dominique no longer answered.

"So you remain obstinate?"

"Kill me and get it over with," he replied.

Françoise, her hands joined, was beseeching him from a distance. She forgot everything else, she would have advised him to be a coward. But old Merlier took hold of her hands, so that the Prussians wouldn't see her gesture, like that of a maddened woman.

"He's right," he murmured, "it's better to die."

The firing squad was there. The officer was waiting for Dominique to weaken. He still expected to convince him. There was a silence. Far off violent thunderclaps were heard. An oppressive heat crushed the countryside. It was during that silence that a shout resounded:

"The French! The French!"

It was, in fact, they. On the Sauval road, at the edge of the forest, the line of red trousers could be discerned. There was an unusual bustle in the mill. The Prussian soldiers were running, with guttural exclamations. Still, not a shot had yet been fired.

"The French! The French!" cried Françoise, clapping her hands.

She acted like a lunatic. She had wrenched herself from her father's grasp, and she laughed, arms in the air. So they had finally come, and had come in time, because Dominique was still there, standing!

A terrible volley of shots, which exploded in her ears like a thunderclap, made her turn around. The officer had just muttered:

"Before anything else, let's finish off this business."

And, he himself shoving Dominique against the wall of a shed, he had given the order to fire. When Françoise turned, Dominique was on the ground with twelve bullet holes in his chest.

She didn't weep, she stood there in a stupor. Her eyes became fixed, and she went and sat down below the shed, a few steps from the body. She was watching; at moments she made a vague, childish gesture with her hand. The Prussians had seized old Merlier as a hostage.

It was a fine fight. The officer had rapidly stationed his men, realizing he couldn't beat a retreat without being overpowered. His best bet was to sell his life dearly. Now it was the Prussians who were defending the mill and the French who were attacking it. The fusillade began with unheard-of violence. It didn't stop for a half-hour. Then, a muffled explosion was heard and a cannonball broke one of the biggest boughs of the centuries-old elm. The French had artillery. A battery, located right above the ditch in which Dominique had hidden, was sweeping the main street of Rocreuse. The battle couldn't last long, after that.

Ah, the poor mill! Cannonballs were piercing it through and through. Half the roofing was blown away. Two walls collapsed. But it was especially on the Morelle side that the disaster became lamentable. The ivy, torn away from the shaken walls, was hanging like ragged clothing; the stream was carrying off debris of all sorts, and through a breach in the wall could be seen Françoise's bedroom, with its bed, whose white curtains were carefully drawn. One after another, the old wheel was hit by two cannonballs, and emitted one last moan: the wheel paddles were carried away in the current, and the framework crashed. The soul of the jolly mill had just been breathed away.

Then the French moved in for the attack. There was a furious combat with swords. Beneath the rust-colored sky, the assassins' lair of the valley filled up with dead men. The wide meadows seemed fierce, with their tall, isolated trees and their curtains of poplars casting blotches of darkness. To the right and to the left, the forests were like the walls of an amphitheater that enclosed the combatants; while the springs, fountains, and running waters began to sound like sobbing, in the panic of the countryside.

Below the shed, Françoise hadn't stirred, crouched there opposite Dominique's body. Old Merlier had just been killed outright by a stray bullet. Then, when the Prussians were wiped out and the mill was burning, the French captain was the first to enter the courtyard. Since the beginning of the campaign, this had been his only success. And so, at the height of excitement, straightening up his tall body to the utmost, he was laughing with his affable air of a dashing cavalier. And, catching sight of Françoise insensible between the bodies of her husband and her father, amid the smoking ruins of the mill, he saluted her gallantly with his sword, crying:

"Victory! Victory!"

Prosper Mérimée

MATEO FALCONE

Leaving Porto-Vecchio and heading northwest, toward the interior of the island, you see the terrain rising quite rapidly; and after walking three hours along twisting paths, obstructed by large boulders and sometimes intersected by ravines, you find yourself at the edge of a very extensive area of brushwood. This brush is the home of the Corsican shepherds and of anyone who has fallen afoul of the law. You must know that the Corsican farmer, to save himself the trouble of manuring his field, sets fire to a certain stretch of forest: it's just too bad if the flames spread farther than necessary—let things take their course!— he'll be sure to have a good crop if he sows on that soil fertilized by the ashes of the trees that once grew on it. After the ears of grain are removed—they leave the stalks, which would be bothersome to gather—the roots that have remained in the soil without being burned put out shoots the following spring, very thick clusters that in a very few years reach a height of seven or eight feet. It is this type of dense under-brush that is called *maquis*. It is made up of various species of trees and bushes, mingled and confused as God wishes. A man can only open a passage through it with an axe in his hands, and you can find areas of brush so thick and close that even the wild sheep can't penetrate them.

If you've killed a man, go to the Porto-Vecchio *maquis*, and you'll be safe there with a good rifle, powder, and bullets; don't forget a brown cape furnished with a hood,[1] which serves as a blanket and a mattress. The shepherds will give you milk, cheese, and chestnuts, and you'll have nothing to fear from the law or the dead man's relatives, except when you have to go down to the town to get more ammunition there.

When I was in Corsica in 18—, Mateo Falcone's house was located half a league from this *maquis*. He was rather wealthy for that vicinity, living like a nobleman—that is, he did no work himself, but lived off the produce of his flocks, which shepherds of a nomadic type led out to graze here and there in the mountains. When I saw him, two years after the event I'm about to narrate, he seemed to me to be fifty at the

---

[1] Pilone.

very most. Picture a short but robust man with frizzy hair as black as jet, an aquiline nose, thin lips, large, alert eyes, and a complexion the color of boot tops. His skill with a rifle was deemed extraordinary, even in his country, where there are so many good shots. For example, Mateo would never have fired at a wild sheep with buckshot, but, at a hundred twenty paces, he would bring it down with a bullet in the head or shoulder, just as he chose. He used his weapons at night as easily as by day, and I've been told about a feat of his that may seem incredible to those who haven't visited Corsica. At eighty paces, a lighted candle was placed behind a sheet of translucent paper the width of a plate. He took aim, then the candle was extinguished, and after a minute in the most total darkness, he would fire, hitting the paper three times out of four.

With such transcendent merit, Mateo Falcone had acquired a great reputation. He was said to be as good to have as a friend as he was dangerous to have as an enemy: helpful and charitable besides, he lived at peace with everyone in the Porto-Vecchio district. But the story was told of him that, in Corte, where he had taken a wife, he had most vigorously gotten rid of a rival said to be as formidable in war as in love: at least, Mateo was credited with a certain rifle shot that took this rival by surprise as he was shaving in front of a small mirror hanging in his window. When the matter had quieted down, Mateo married. His wife, Giuseppa, had at first given him three daughters (which made him furious), but finally a son, whom he named Fortunato: he was the hope of the family, the heir to his name. The girls had made good marriages: their father could count on the daggers and blunderbusses of his sons-in-law in an emergency. The son was only ten, but he already gave promise of gratifying natural gifts.

On a certain autumn day, Mateo went out early with his wife to visit one of his flocks in a clearing in the *maquis*. Little Fortunato wanted to accompany him, but the clearing was too far; besides, it was necessary for someone to stay and guard the house; thus, his father refused: we shall see whether he didn't have occasion to regret it.

He had been gone for several hours, and little Fortunato was peacefully stretched out in the sun, looking at the blue mountains and thinking that, on the following Sunday, he would go and dine in town at the home of his uncle the *caporale*,[2] when he was suddenly interrupted

---

[2] The *caporali* were formerly the chiefs appointed by the Corsican commoners when they revolted against their feudal lords. Today, this name is still sometimes given to a man who, through his property and his connections by marriage and in business, exerts an influence and a sort of *de facto* magistracy over a *pieve* or a canton. By ancient custom, Corsicans are divided into five castes: gentlemen (of whom some are *magnifici*, others *signori*), *caporali*, citizens, plebeians, and foreigners.

in his meditations by the report of a firearm. He got up and turned toward the direction in the plain from which that sound had come. Other rifle shots followed, fired at unequal intervals, and coming nearer and nearer all the time; at last, on the path that led from the plain to Mateo's house, there appeared a man wearing a pointed cap like those worn by mountaineers; he was bearded, covered with rags, and dragging himself along painfully, using his rifle for support. He had just been shot in the thigh.

This man was a bandit[3] who had set out at night to get gunpowder in town and, on the way, had fallen into an ambush laid by Corsican light infantrymen.[4] After defending himself vigorously, he had managed to beat a retreat, eagerly pursued and taking pot shots from one boulder to another. But he wasn't far ahead of the soldiers, and his wound made him incapable of reaching the *maquis* before they caught up with him.

He approached Fortunato and said:

"You're the son of Mateo Falcone?"

"Yes."

"I'm Gianetto Sanpiero. I'm being pursued by the yellow collars.[5] Hide me, because I can't go any farther."

"And what will my father say if I hide you without his permission?"

"He'll say you did the right thing."

"Who knows?"

"Hide me fast; they're coming."

"Wait for my father to get back."

"Wait? Damnation! They'll be here in five minutes. Come on, hide me, or I'll kill you."

Fortunato replied with the greatest coolness:

"Your rifle is unloaded and there are no more cartridges in your *carchera*."[6]

"I have my stiletto."

"But will you run as fast as me?"

He made a jump, placing himself out of reach.

"You're not the son of Mateo Falcone! So you'll let me be arrested in front of your house?"

The child seemed to be affected by this.

"What'll you give me if I hide you?" he asked, coming closer.

---

[3] Here this word is synonymous with "outlaw."

[4] This is a corps formed by the government only a few years ago; it polices the countryside concurrently with the gendarmerie.

[5] At the time the uniform of these *voltigeurs* was a brown outfit with a yellow collar.

[6] A leather belt that serves as a cartridge pouch and wallet.

The bandit groped through a leather pouch that hung from his belt, and pulled out a five-franc piece that he had no doubt kept to buy powder with. Fortunato smiled when he saw the silver coin; he seized it, saying to Gianetto:

"Don't worry about a thing."

At once he made a large hole in a haystack located near the house. Gianetto huddled in it, and the child covered him up in such a way that he left him a little air to breathe, but it was nevertheless impossible to suspect that the hay concealed a man. On top of that, he thought of a primitive ruse that was quite ingenious. He went and got a cat and her kittens and placed them on the haystack to give the impression that it hadn't been touched recently. Next, noticing traces of blood on the path near the house, he carefully covered them with dust; after that, he lay down in the sun again as calmly as could be.

A few minutes later, six men in brown uniforms with yellow collars, commanded by a sergeant-major, stood in front of Mateo's door. This sergeant was very slightly related to Falcone. (As is well known, in Corsica degrees of kinship are traced much further than elsewhere.) His name was Tiodoro Gamba; he was an active man, much dreaded by the bandits, several of whom he had already tracked down.

"Hello, little cousin," he said to Fortunato, coming up to him. "My, but you've grown! Did you see a man go by a little while ago?"

"Oh! I'm still not as big as you, cousin," the child replied, playing the simpleton.

"You'll get there. But, tell me, didn't you see a man go by?"

"Did I see a man go by?"

"Yes, a man with a black-velvet pointed cap and a jacket embroidered in red and yellow."

"A man with a pointed cap and a jacket embroidered in red and yellow?"

"Yes, answer fast, and don't repeat my questions."

"This morning the parish priest passed by our door on his horse Piero. He asked me how Papa was feeling, and I told him . . ."

"Ah, you little scamp, you're trying to be smart! Tell me quickly which way Gianetto went—he's the one we're looking for—and I'm sure he took this path."

"Who knows?"

"Who knows? I know that you saw him."

"Do you see people pass by when you're sleeping?"

"You weren't sleeping, you scamp; the rifle shots woke you up."

"Cousin, do you really think your rifles make so much noise? My father's blunderbuss makes much more."

"The devil take you, you damned brat! I'm sure you saw Gianetto.

Maybe you even hid him. Come on, men, go into this house and see if our man isn't there. He was walking on only one leg and he has too much good sense, the rogue, to have tried to reach the *maquis* hobbling along. Besides, the trail of blood stops here."

"And what will Papa say?" Fortunato asked, snickering. "What will he say if he finds out his house has been entered while he was out?"

"Rascal!" said Sergeant Gamba, taking him by the ear. "Do you real-ize it's only up to me to make you change your tune? Maybe if I give you twenty blows with the flat of my saber, you'll finally talk."

And Fortunato kept on snickering.

"My father is Mateo Falcone!" he said, significantly.

"Little scamp, do you realize that I can take you to Corte or Bastia? I'll stretch you out in a dungeon, on straw, with irons on your feet, and I'll have you guillotined if you don't tell me where Gianetto Sanpiero is."

The child burst out laughing at that ridiculous threat. He repeated: "My father is Mateo Falcone!"

"Sergeant," one of the infantrymen said quietly, "let's not get on the wrong side of Mateo."

Gamba looked obviously embarrassed. He chatted in a low voice with his soldiers, who had already inspected the whole house. This wasn't a very long procedure, because a Corsican's hut consists of a sin-gle square room. The furniture is comprised of a table, benches, chests, and hunting and household utensils. Meanwhile, little Fortunato was petting his cat, seeming to take malicious satisfaction in the embarrass-ment of the infantrymen and his cousin.

A soldier approached the haystack. He saw the cat, and negligently stabbed the hay with his bayonet, shrugging his shoulders as if he felt his precaution was laughable. Nothing stirred: and the child's face betrayed not the slightest emotion.

The sergeant and his troop were in despair: by this time they were looking seriously in the direction of the plain, as if disposed to go back where they had come from—when their leader, convinced that threats would have no effect on Falcone's son, decided to make one last effort and try out the power of blandishments and presents.

"Little cousin," he said, "you look to me like a really sharp fellow! You'll go places. But the game you're playing with me is a nasty one; and if I weren't afraid of hurting my cousin Mateo, devil take me if I didn't lead you away with me."

"Bah!"

"But when my cousin is back, I'll tell him what happened, and to punish you for lying, he'll whip you till he draws blood."

"How's that?"

"You'll see . . . But wait . . . Be a good boy and I'll give you something."

"As for me, cousin, I'll give you a piece of advice: if you wait any longer, Gianetto will be in the *maquis*, and then it'll take more than one strapping fellow like you to go get him there."

The sergeant drew from his pocket a silver watch that was worth at least thirty francs; and, observing that little Fortunato's eyes sparkled when he looked at it, he dangled the watch from the end of its steel chain, saying:

"Scalawag! You'd surely like to have a watch like this hanging from your neck while you promenaded through the streets of Porto-Vecchio, proud as a peacock, with people asking you, 'What time is it?' and you saying, 'Look at my watch and see.'"

"When I grow up, my uncle the *caporale* will give me a watch."

"Yes, but your uncle's son already has one . . . not as beautiful as this one, it's true . . . But he's younger than you."

The child sighed.

"Well, little cousin, do you want this watch?"

Fortunato, stealing sidelong glances at the watch from the corner of his eye, looked like a cat that was being offered a whole chicken. Since it feels it is being made fun of, it doesn't dare put its claws on it, and from time to time it turns away its eyes to avoid succumbing to the temptation; but every moment it licks its chops, seeming to say to its master:

"How cruel your joke is!"

And yet Sergeant Gamba appeared to be acting in good faith in offering his watch. Fortunato didn't reach out for it, but he said with a bitter smile:

"Why are you ribbing me?"[7]

"By God, I'm not ribbing you. Just tell me where Gianetto is, and this watch is yours."

Fortunato emitted a sigh of disbelief, and, with his dark eyes staring directly into the sergeant's, he strove to see how much trust he ought to repose in his words.

"May I lose my epaulets," the sergeant exclaimed, "if I don't give you the watch on those terms! My comrades are witnesses, and I can't go back on my word."

While saying this, he kept moving the watch nearer until it almost touched the child's pale cheek. The boy's face clearly showed the struggle being waged in his soul between greed and respect for the laws of hospitality. His bare chest was heaving mightily, and he seemed close to choking. Meanwhile the watch was swinging, turning, and at times

---

[7] *Perchè me c . . .?*

striking the tip of his nose. Finally, little by little, his right hand rose in the direction of the watch; he touched it with his fingertips; and it was resting in his hand with its full weight, although the sergeant didn't release the end of the chain . . . The dial was blue . . . the case newly polished . . . in the sunlight, it seemed to be all ablaze . . . The temptation was too strong.

Fortunato raised his left hand, too, and with his thumb pointed over his shoulder at the haystack on which he was leaning. The sergeant understood him at once. He let go of the end of the chain; Fortunato realized he was sole possessor of the watch. He rose with the agility of a deer and moved ten paces away from the haystack, which the infantrymen immediately began to knock over.

Before long they saw the hay moving, and a bleeding man, dagger in hand, came out; but, when he tried to stand up, his stiffened wound made it impossible to keep his feet any longer. He fell. The sergeant pounced on him and tore his stiletto from him. At once he was tightly bound hand and foot despite his resistance.

Gianetto, lying on the ground, trussed up like a bundle of firewood, turned his head toward Fortunato, who had come up to him.

"Son of a . . .!" he said, with more contempt than anger.

The child threw at him the silver coin he had received from him, feeling that he no longer deserved it; but the outlaw seemed to pay no heed to that action. As calmly as possible he said to the sergeant:

"My friend Gamba, I can't walk; you're going to have to carry me to town."

"Just a while ago you were running faster than a roebuck," the cruel victor retorted; "but relax: I'm so happy over catching you that I'd carry you a league on my back without getting tired. Anyway, comrade, we're going to make you a litter out of branches and your cloak, and at the Crespoli farm we'll find horses."

"Good," said the prisoner, "and put a little straw on your litter so I'll be more comfortable."

While the infantrymen were busy, some making a sort of stretcher out of chestnut branches, and the others dressing Gianetto's wound, Mateo Falcone and his wife suddenly appeared at the bend of a path that led into the *maquis*. His wife was walking, painfully stooped under the weight of an enormous sack of chestnuts, while her husband was strutting at his ease, carrying nothing but a rifle in his hand and another slung across his back: because it's beneath a man's dignity to carry any burden other than his weapons.

At sight of the soldiers, Mateo's first thought was that they had come to arrest him. But why did he have that idea? Had Mateo had any run-ins with the law, after all? No. He enjoyed a good reputation.

He was what is called "an individual of good repute"; but he was a Corsican and a mountaineer, and there are few Corsican mountaineers who, if they racked their memory, wouldn't discover some little peccadillo, in the nature of rifle shots, stiletto stabs, and other trifles. More than many another, Mateo had a clear conscience, because for over ten years he hadn't pointed his rifle at a man; but nevertheless he was cautious, and he now prepared to defend himself bravely if it should prove necessary.

"Wife," he said to Giuseppa, "put down your sack and be prepared."

She obeyed at once. He gave her the rifle he had been carrying on his back; it might have hampered his movements. He cocked the one he had in his hands and proceeded slowly toward his house, keeping close to the trees that lined the road and ready, at the least sign of hostility, to dash behind the thickest trunk and thus be able to fire from a position of cover. His wife was following at his heels, holding his spare rifle and his cartridge pouch. The duty of a good housewife, in times of combat, is to load her husband's guns.

On the other side, the sergeant was most distressed to see Mateo advancing that way, with measured tread, his rifle pointed forward and his finger on the trigger.

"If by chance," he thought, "Mateo was a relative of Gianetto, or if he was his friend, and wanted to defend him, the wads of his two rifles would reach two of us, just as sure as a letter in the mail, and if he aimed at me, despite our relationship . . . !"

In that perplexity, he made a very courageous decision: he advanced alone toward Mateo to tell him what was going on, greeting him like an old acquaintance; but the short space separating him from Mateo seemed terribly long to him.

"Hi there, old comrade!" he shouted. "How's it going, friend? It's me, it's Gamba, your cousin."

Without a word in reply, Mateo had stopped, and, while the other man was speaking, he gently raised the barrel of his rifle, so that, by the time the sergeant reached him, it was pointing to the sky.

"Hello, brother!"[8] the sergeant said, offering his hand. "I haven't seen you for quite a while."

"Hello, brother!"

"I had come to say hello to you as I passed by, and to my cousin Pepa. We've covered a lot of ground today; but you mustn't feel sorry for our being tired, because we've made a wonderful catch. We've just laid hands on Gianetto Sanpiero."

---

[8] *Buon giorno, fratello,* the customary greeting in Corsica.

"God be praised!" exclaimed Giuseppa. "He stole a milk goat from us last week."

Those words delighted Gamba.

"Poor devil!" said Mateo. "He was hungry."

"The scamp defended himself like a lion," continued the sergeant, a little mortified. "He killed one of my infantrymen, and, as if that wasn't enough, he broke Corporal Chardon's arm; but there's no great harm in that, he was only a Frenchman . . . After that, he hid so well that the devil couldn't have detected him. Without my little cousin Fortunato, I would never have been able to find him."

"Fortunato!" Mateo exclaimed.

"Fortunato!" Giuseppa repeated.

"Yes, Gianetto had concealed himself in that haystack over there; but my little cousin pointed out the trick to me. I'm also going to tell his uncle the *caporale* about it, so he'll send him a fine gift for his trouble. And his name and yours will be in the report I'll send to the public prosecutor."

"Damnation!" said Mateo quietly.

They had come up to the detachment. Gianetto was already lying on his litter and ready to leave. When he saw Mateo in company with Gamba, he smiled a strange smile; then, turning toward the door to the house, he spat on the threshold, saying:

"House of a betrayer!"

Only a man determined to die would have dared pronounce the word "betrayer" with reference to Falcone. A firm stiletto stab, which wouldn't need to be repeated, would have immediately repaid the insult. And yet Mateo made no other gesture than to raise his hand to his forehead like a man overwhelmed.

Fortunato had gone into the house on seeing his father arrive. He soon reappeared with a bowl of milk, which he offered to Gianetto with eyes cast down.

"Get away from me!" the outlaw shouted with a crushing voice.

Then, turning to one of the infantrymen, he said:

"Comrade, give me a drink."

The soldier put his canteen in his hands, and the bandit drank the water given to him by a man with whom he had just been exchanging rifle shots. Then he requested to have his hands tied so that they would be crossed over his chest instead of having them tied behind his back.

"I like to lie comfortably," he said.

They hastened to satisfy him; then the sergeant gave the signal for departure, said good-bye to Mateo, who didn't reply, and descended to the plain in quick time.

Nearly ten minutes went by before Mateo opened his mouth. With nervous eyes, the child was looking now at his mother and now at his father, who, leaning on his rifle, was observing him with an expression of concentrated anger.

"You're making a fine beginning!" Mateo finally said in a voice that was calm but frightening for anyone who knew him well.

"Father!" exclaimed the child, stepping forward with tears in his eyes, as if intending to go down on his knees to him.

But Mateo shouted to him:

"Stand back!"

And the child stopped, sobbing motionlessly a few paces away from his father.

Giuseppa approached. She had just caught sight of the watch chain, one end of which was protruding from Fortunato's shirt.

"Who gave you that watch?" she asked with a severe expression.

"My cousin the sergeant."

Falcone seized the watch and, hurling it violently against a rock, shattered it into bits.

"Wife," he said, "is this child mine?"

Giuseppa's brown cheeks turned brick-red.

"What are you saying, Mateo? And do you realize who you're talking to?"

"Well, then, this child is the first of his line to betray anyone."

Fortunato's sobs and hiccups redoubled, and Falcone kept his lynx eyes fixed on him. Finally he struck the ground with his rifle butt, then threw the rifle over his shoulder, and went back onto the road to the *maquis*, calling to Fortunato to follow him. The child obeyed.

Giuseppa ran after Mateo and took hold of his arm.

"He's your son," she said, her voice trembling and her dark eyes staring into her husband's, as if to detect what was going on in his soul.

"Let me go," Mateo replied. "I'm his father."

Giuseppa kissed her son and entered her hut, weeping. She fell on her knees in front of a statuette of the Virgin and prayed fervently. Meanwhile, Falcone walked some two hundred paces along the path, not stopping until he reached a small ravine, into which he descended. He tested the soil with his rifle butt and found it soft and easy to dig. The spot seemed suitable for his purpose.

"Fortunato, go over to that big rock."

The child did what he was ordered to, then knelt down.

"Say your prayers."

"Father, father, don't kill me!"

"Say your prayers!" Mateo repeated in fearsome tones.

The child, stammering and sobbing, recited the Lord's Prayer and the Apostles' Creed. His father loudly replied "Amen!" at the end of each prayer.

"Are those all the prayers you know?"

"Father, I also know the 'Hail, Mary' and the litany my aunt taught me."

"It's pretty long, but go ahead."

The child completed the litany in a toneless voice.

"Are you done?"

"Oh, father, mercy! Forgive me! I'll never do it again! I'll keep on begging my cousin the *caporale* until Gianetto is pardoned!"

He was still speaking; Mateo had cocked his rifle and was taking aim, saying:

"May God forgive you!"

The child made a desperate effort to get up and clasp his father's knees, but he didn't have the time. Mateo fired, and Fortunato fell down dead.

Without even glancing at the corpse, Mateo went back along the road to his house to fetch a spade so he could bury his son. He had scarcely taken a few steps when he met Giuseppa, who was running up, alarmed at the shot.

"What have you done?" she exclaimed.

"I've dealt out justice."

"Where is he?"

"In the ravine. I'm going to bury him. He died like a Christian; I'll have a Mass sung for him. Have my son-in-law Tiodoro Bianchi told to come and move in with us."

André Gide

THE RETURN OF THE PRODIGAL SON

Le Retour de l'Enfant Prodigue

As was done in old triptychs, I have painted here, for my secret pleasure, the parable told to us by Our Lord Jesus Christ. Leaving scattered
and indistinct the double inspiration which moves me, I have not tried
to prove the victory of any god over me—or my victory. And yet, if the
reader demands of me some expression of piety, he will not perhaps
look for it in vain in my painting, where, like a donor in the corner of
the picture, I am kneeling, a pendant to the prodigal son, smiling like
him and also like him, my face soaked with tears.

The Prodigal Son

When, after a long absence, tired of his fancies and as if fallen out of
love with himself, the prodigal son, from the depths of that destitution
he sought, thinks of his father's face; of that not too small room where
his mother used to bend over his bed; of that garden, watered with a
running stream but enclosed and from which he had always wanted to
escape; of his thrifty older brother whom he never loved, but who still
holds, in the expectation of his return, that part of his fortune which,
as a prodigal, he was not able to squander—the boy confesses to himself that he did not find happiness, nor even succeed in prolonging very
much that disorderly excitement which he sought in place of happiness. "Ah!" he thinks, "if my father, after first being angry with me,
believed me dead, perhaps, in spite of my sins, he would rejoice at seeing me again. Ah, if I go back to him very humbly, my head bowed and
covered with ashes, and if, bending down before him and saying to
him: 'Father, I have sinned against heaven, and before you,' what shall
I do if, raising me with his hand, he says, 'Come into the house, my
son'?" And already the boy is piously on his way.

When from the top of the hill he sees at last the smoking roofs of the
house, it is evening. But he waits for the shadows of night in order to
veil somewhat his poverty. In the distance he hears his father's voice.

His knees give way. He falls and covers his face with his hands because he is ashamed of his shame, and yet he knows that he is the lawful son. He is hungry. In a fold of his tattered cloak he has only one handful of those sweet acorns which were his food, as they were the food of the swine he herded. He sees the preparations for supper. He makes out his mother coming on to the doorstep. . . . He can hold back no longer. He runs down the hill and comes into the courtyard where his dog, failing to recognize him, barks. He tries to speak to the servants. But they are suspicious and move away in order to warn the master. Here he is!

Doubtless he was expecting his prodigal son, because he recognizes him immediately. He opens his arms. The boy then kneels before him, and hiding his forehead with one arm, he raises his right hand for pardon:

"Father! Father! I have gravely sinned against heaven and against you. I am not worthy to be called. But at least, like one of your servants, the humblest, let me live in a corner of our house."

The father raises him and embraces him.

"My son, blessed is this day when you come back to me!" And his joy weeps as it overflows his heart. He raises his head from his son's brow which he was kissing, and turns toward his servants:

"Bring forth the best robe. Put shoes on his feet, and a precious ring on his finger. Look in our stables for the fattest calf and kill it. Prepare a joyful feast, for my son whom I thought dead is alive."

And as the news spreads rapidly, he hastens. He does not want another to say:

"Mother, the son we wept for has returned to us."

Everyone's joy mounting up like a hymn troubles the older son. He sits down at the common table because his father invites him and urges him forcibly. Alone, among all the guests, for even the humblest servant is invited, he shows an angry expression. To the repentant sinner why is there more honor than to himself, who has never sinned? He esteems order more than love. If he consents to appear at the feast, it is because by giving credit to his brother, he can lend him joy for one evening. It is also because his father and mother have promised him to rebuke the prodigal tomorrow, and because he himself is preparing to admonish him seriously.

The torches send up their smoke toward heaven. The meal is over. The servants have cleared the tables. Now, in the night, when not a breath is stirring, soul after soul, in the weary house, goes to sleep. And yet, in the room next to the prodigal's, I know a boy, his younger brother, who throughout the night until dawn will try in vain to sleep.

The Father's Reprimand

Lord, like a child I kneel before You today, my face soaked with tears. If I remember and transcribe here your compelling parable, it is because I know who your prodigal child was. I see myself in him. At times I hear in myself and repeat in secret those words which, from the depth of his great distress, You have him cry:

"How many hirelings of my father have bread enough and to spare, and I perish with hunger!"

I imagine the father's embrace, and in the warmth of such love my heart melts. I imagine an earlier distress, and even,—ah! I imagine all kinds of things. This I believe: I am the very one whose hearts beats when, from the top of the hill, he sees again the blue roofs of the house he left. What keeps me then from running toward my home and going in?—I am expected. I can see the fatted calf they are preparing . . . Stop! Do not set up the feast too quickly!—Prodigal son, I am thinking of you. Tell me first what your Father said to you the next day, after the feast of welcome. Ah! even if the elder son prompts you, Father, let me hear your voice sometimes through his words!

"My son, why did you leave me?"

"Did I really leave you? Father, are you not everywhere? Never did I cease loving you."

"Let us not split hairs. I had a house which kept you in. It was built for you. Generations worked so that in it your soul could find shelter, luxury worthy of it, comfort and occupation. Why did you, the heir, the son, escape from the House?"

"Because the House shut me in. The House is not You, Father."

"It is I who built it, and for you."

"Ah! you did not say that, my brother did. You built the whole world, the House and what is not the House. The House was built by others. In your name, I know, but by others."

"Man needs a roof under which he can lay his head. Proud boy! Do you think you can sleep in the open?"

"Do you need pride to do that? Some poorer than I have done so."

"They are poor. You are not poor. No one can give up his wealth. I had made you rich above all men."

"Father, you know that when I left, I took with me all the riches I could. What do I care about goods that cannot be carried away?"

"All that fortune you took away, you have spent recklessly."

"I changed your gold into pleasures, your precepts into fantasy, my chastity into poetry, and my austerity into desires."

"Was it for that our thrifty parents strove to instil into you so much virtue?"

"So that I should burn with a brighter flame perhaps, being kindled by a new fervor."

"Think of that pure flame Moses saw on the sacred bush. It shone, but without consuming."

"I have known love which consumes."

"The love which I want to teach you, refreshes. After a short time, what did you have left, prodigal son?"

"The memory of those pleasures."

"And the destitution which comes after them."

"In that destitution, I felt close to you, Father."

"Was poverty needed to drive you back to me?"

"I do not know. I do not know. It was in the dryness of the desert that I loved my thirst more."

"Your poverty made you feel more deeply the value of riches."

"No, not that! Can't you understand me, Father? My heart, emptied of everything, became filled with love. At the cost of all my goods, I bought fervor."

"Were you happy, then, far from me?"

"I did not feel far from you."

"Then, what made you come back? Tell me."

"I don't know. Laziness perhaps."

"Laziness, my son? What! Wasn't it love?"

"Father, I have told you. I never loved you better than in the desert. But each morning I was tired of looking for my subsistence. In the House, at least there is food to eat."

"Yes, servants look after that. So, what brought you back was hunger."

"Cowardice also perhaps, and sickness. . . . In the end, that food I was never sure of finding weakened me. Because I fed on wild fruit and locusts and honey. I grew less and less able to stand the discomfort which at first quickened my fervor. At night, when I was cold, I thought of my tucked-in bed in my father's house. When I fasted, I thought of my father's home where the abundance of food served always exceeded my hunger. I weakened; I didn't feel enough courage, enough strength to struggle much longer and yet . . ."

"So yesterday's fatted calf seemed good to you?"

The prodigal son throws himself down sobbing, with his face against the ground.

"Father! Father! The wild taste of sweet acorns is still in my mouth, in spite of everything. Nothing could blot out their savor."

"Poor child!" says the father as he raises him up. "I spoke to you perhaps too harshly. Your brother wanted me to. Here it is he who makes the law. It is he who charged me to say to you: 'Outside of the House, there is no salvation for you.' But listen. It was I who made you. I know what is in you. I know what sent you out on your wanderings. I was waiting for you at the end of the road. If you had called me . . . I was there."

"Father! might I then have found you without coming back?"

"If you felt weak, you did well to come back. Go now. Go back to the room I had prepared for you. Enough for today. Rest. Tomorrow you will speak with your brother."

The Elder Brother's Reprimand

The prodigal son first tries to bluster.

"Big brother," he begins, "we aren't very much alike. Brother, we aren't alike at all."

The elder brother says:

"It's your fault."

"Why mine?"

"Because I live by order. Whatever differs from it is the fruit or the seed of pride."

"Am I different only in my faults?"

"Only call quality what brings you back to order, and curtail all the rest."

"It is that mutilation I fear. What you plan to suppress comes also from the Father."

"Not suppress—curtail, I said."

"I understand. All the same, that is how I curtailed my virtues."

"And that is also why now I still see them in you. You must exaggerate them. Understand me. It is not a diminution of yourself, but an exaltation I propose, in which the most diverse, the most unruly elements of your flesh and your spirit must join together harmoniously, in which the worst in you must nourish the best, in which the best must submit to . . ."

"It was exaltation which I also sought and found in the desert—and perhaps not very different from the one you propose to me."

"To tell the truth, I wanted to impose it on you."

"Our Father did not speak so harshly."

"I know what the Father said to you. It was vague. He no longer expresses himself very clearly, so that he can be made to say what one wants. But I understand his thought very well. With the servants, I am the one interpreter, and who wants to understand the Father must listen to me."

"I understand him quite easily without you."

"You thought you did. But you understood incorrectly. There are not several ways of understanding the Father. There are not several ways of listening to him. There are not several ways of loving him, so that we may be united in his love."

"In his House."

"This love brings one back here. You see this, for you have come back. Tell me now, what impelled you to leave?"

"I felt too clearly that the House is not the entire universe. I myself am not completely in the boy you wanted me to be. I could not help imagining other cultures, other lands, and roads by which to reach them, roads not yet raced. I imagined in my self the new being which I felt rushing down those roads. I ran away."

"Think what could have happened if, like you, I had deserted our Father's House. Servants and thieves would have pillaged all our goods."

"That would not have mattered to me, since I was catching sight of other goods . . ."

"Which your pride exaggerated. My brother, indiscipline is over. You will learn, if you don't yet know it, out of what chaos man has emerged. He has just barely emerged. With all of his artless weight, he falls back into it as soon as the Spirit no longer supports him above it. Do not learn this at your own expense. The well-ordered elements which make up your being wait only for an acquiescence, a weakening on your part in order to return to anarchy . . . But what you will never know is the length of time it was needed for man to elaborate man. Now that we have the model, let us keep it. 'Hold that fast which thou hast,' says the Spirit to the Angel of the Church, and He adds, 'that no man take thy crown.' *That which thou hast* is your crown, that royalty over others and over yourself. The usurper lies in wait for your crown. He is everywhere. He prowls around you and in you. *Hold fast*, my brother! Hold fast."

"Too long ago I let go my hold. And now I cannot close my hand over my own wealth."

"Yes, you can. I will help you. I have watched over your wealth during your absence."

"And moreover, I know those words of the Spirit. You did not quote them all."

"You are right. It goes on: 'Him that overcometh will I make a pillar in the temple of my God, and he shall go no more out.'"

"'And he shall go no more out.' That is precisely what terrifies me."

"If it is for his happiness."

"Oh! I understand. But I had been in that temple . . ."

"You found you were wrong to have left, since you wanted to return."

"I know, I know. I am back now. I agree."

"What good can you look for elsewhere, which here you do not find in abundance? Or better—here alone your wealth is to be found."

"I know that you kept my riches for me."

"The part of your fortune which you did not squander, namely that part which is common to all of us: the property."

"Then do I personally own nothing else?"

"Yes. That special allotment of gifts which perhaps our Father will still consent to grant you."

"That is all I want. I agree to own only that."

"How proud you are! You will not only be consulted. Between you and me, that portion is risky. I would advise your giving it up. It was that allotment of personal gifts which already brought on your downfall. That was the wealth you squandered immediately."

"The other kind I couldn't take with me."

"Therefore you will find it intact. Enough for today. Find rest now in the House."

"That suits me well, for I am tired."

"Then blessed be your fatigue! Now go and sleep. Tomorrow your mother will speak to you."

The Mother

Prodigal son, whose mind still rebels against the words of your brother, let your heart now speak. How sweet it is, as you lie at the feet of your mother, with your head hidden on her lap, to feel her caressing hand bow your stubborn neck!

"Why did you leave me for so long a time?"

And since you answer only with tears:

"Why weep now, my son? You have been given back to me. In waiting for you, I have shed all my tears."

"Were you still waiting for me?"

"Never did I give up hoping for you. Before going to sleep, every evening I would think: if he returns tonight, will he be able to open the door? And it took me a long time to fall asleep. Every morning, before I was totally awake, I would think: Isn't it today he will come back? Then I prayed. I prayed so hard that it was not possible for you not to come back."

"Your prayers forced me to come back."

"Don't smile because of me, my child."

"Oh mother, I have come back to you very humble. See how I place my forehead lower than your heart! There is not one of my thoughts of yesterday which does not become empty today. When close to you, I can hardly understand why I left the house."

"You will not leave it again?"

"I cannot leave it again."

"What then attracted you outside?"

"I don't want to think of it any more. Nothing . . . Myself . . ."

"Did you think then that you would be happy away from us?"

"I was not looking for happiness."

"What were you looking for?"

"I was looking for . . . who I was."

"Oh! son of your parents, and brother among your brothers."

"I was not like my brothers. Let's not talk any more about it. I have come back now."

"Yes, let's talk of it further. Do not believe that your brothers are so unlike you."

"Henceforth my one care is to be like all of you."

"You say that as if with resignation."

"Nothing is more fatiguing than to realize one's difference. Finally my wandering tired me out."

"You have aged, that's true."

"I have suffered."

"My poor child! Doubtless your bed was not made every evening, nor the table set for all your meals?"

"I ate what I found and often it was green or spoiled fruit which my hunger made into food."

"At least did you suffer only from hunger?"

"The sun at mid-day, the cold wind in the heart of the night, the shifting sand of the desert, the thorns which made my feet bloody, nothing of all that stopped me, but—I didn't tell this to my brother—I had to serve . . ."

"Why did you conceal it?"

"Bad masters who harmed me bodily, exasperated my pride, and gave me barely enough to eat. That is when I thought: 'Serving for the sake of serving! . . .' In dreams I saw my house, and I came home."

The prodigal son again lowers his head and his mother caresses it tenderly.

"What are you going to do now?"

"I have told you. Try to become like my big brother, look after our property, like him choose a wife . . ."

"You have doubtless someone in mind, as you say that."

"Oh, anyone at all will be my first preference, as soon as you have chosen her. Do as you did for my brother."

"I should have preferred someone you love."

"What does that matter? My heart had made a choice. I renounce the pride which took me far away from you. Help me in my choice. I submit, I tell you. And I will have my children submit also. In that way, my adventure will not seem pointless to me."

"Listen to me. There is at this moment a child you could take on already as a charge."

"What do you mean and of whom are you speaking?"

"Of your younger brother who was not ten when you left, whom you hardly recognized, but who . . ."

"Go on, mother! What are you worried about now?"

"In whom you might well have recognized yourself because he is like what you were when you left."

"Like me?"

"Like what you were, I said, not yet, alas, what you have become."

"What he will become."

"What you must make him become immediately. Speak to him. He will listen to you, doubtless, you the prodigal. Tell him what disappointment you met on your way. Spare him . . ."

"But what causes you such alarm about my brother? Perhaps simply a resemblance of features . . ."

"No, no! the resemblance between you two is deeper. I worry now for him about what first did not worry me enough for you. He reads too much, and doesn't always prefer good books."

"Is that all it is?"

"He is often perched on the highest part of the garden, from where, as you know, you can see the countryside over the walls."

"I remember. Is that all?"

"He spends less time with us than in the farm."

"Ah! what does he do there?"

"Nothing wrong. But it is not the farmers he stays with, it is the farm hands who are as different from us as possible and those who are not from this country. There is one in particular, who comes from some distance, and who tells him stories."

"Ah! the swineherd."

"Yes. Did you know him? . . . Your brother each evening in order to listen to him, follows him into the pigsties. He comes back only for dinner, but with no appetite, and his clothes reeking. Remonstrances have no effect. He stiffens under constraint. On certain mornings, at dawn, before any of us are up, he runs off to accompany that swineherd to the gate when he is leading off his herd to graze."

"He knows he must not leave."

"You knew also! One day he will escape from me, I am sure. One day he will leave . . ."

"No, I will speak to him, mother. Don't be alarmed."

"I know he will listen to a great deal from you. Did you see how he watched you that first evening, with what prestige your rags were covered, and the purple robe your father put on you! I was afraid that in his mind he will confuse one with the other, and that he is attracted first by the rags. But now this idea seems ridiculous to me. For if you, my child, had been able to foresee such unhappiness, you would not have left us, would you?"

"I don't know now how I was able to leave you, you who are my mother."

"Well, tell him all that."

"I will tell him that tomorrow evening. Now kiss me on my forehead as you used to when I was small and you watched me fall asleep. I am sleepy."

"Go to bed. I am going to pray for all of you."

Dialogue with the Younger Brother

Beside the prodigal's, there is a room not too small, with bare walls. The prodigal, a lamp in his hand, comes close to the bed where his younger brother is lying, his face toward the wall. He begins in a low voice, so as not to disturb him if the boy is sleeping.

"I would like to talk to you, brother."

"What is stopping you?"

"I thought you were sleeping."

"I don't have to sleep in order to dream."

"You were dreaming? Of what?"

"What do you care? If I can't understand my dreams, I don't think you will be able to explain them to me."

"Are they that subtle, then? If you told them to me, I would try."

"Do you choose your dreams? Mine are what they want to be, and are freer than I . . . What have you come here for? Why are you disturbing me in my sleep?"

"You aren't sleeping, and I'm here to speak gently to you."

"What have you to say to me?"

"Nothing, if that is the tone you take."

"Then goodbye."

The prodigal goes toward the door, but puts the lamp on the floor so that the room is barely lighted. Then, coming back, he sits on the edge of the bed and in the dark strokes for a long time the boy's forehead which is kept turned away.

"You answer me more gruffly than I ever did your brother. Yet I too rebelled against him."

The stubborn boy suddenly sat up.

"Tell me, is it my brother that sent you?"

"No, not him, but our mother."

"So, you wouldn't have come of your own accord."

"But I came as a friend."

Half sitting up on his bed, the boy looks straight at the prodigal.

"How could one of my family be my friend?"

"You are mistaken about our brother . . ."

"Don't speak to me about him! I hate him! My whole heart cries out against him. He's the reason for my answering you gruffly."

"Explain why."

"You wouldn't understand."

"Tell me just the same."

The prodigal rocks his brother in his arms and already the boy begins to yield.

"The evening you returned, I couldn't sleep. All night I kept thinking: I had another brother, and I didn't know it . . . That is why my heart beat so hard when, in the courtyard of our house, I saw you come covered with glory."

"Alas, I was covered then with rags."

"Yes, I saw you. You were already glorious. And I saw what our father did. He put a ring on your finger, a ring the like of which our brother does not have. I did not want to question anyone about you. All that I knew was that you had come from very far away, and that your eyes, at table . . ."

"Were you at the feast?"

"Oh! I know you did not see me. During the whole meal you looked far off without seeing anything. And it was all right when on the second evening you spoke with our father, but on the third . . ."

"Go on."

"Ah! you could have said to me at least one word of love!"

"You were expecting me then?"

"Impatiently! Do you think I would hate our brother so much if you had not gone to talk with him that evening and for so long? What did you find to say to each other? You certainly know, if you are like me, that you can have nothing in common with him."

"I had behaved very wrong toward him."

"Is that possible?"

"At any rate toward our father and mother. You know that I ran away from home."

"Yes, I know. A long time ago, wasn't it?"

"When I was about your age."

"Ah! And that's what you call behaving wrong?"

"Yes, it was wrong, it was my sin."

"When you left, did you feel you were doing wrong?"

"No, I felt duty-bound to leave."

"What has happened since then to change your first truth into an error?"

"I suffered."

"And is that what makes you say: I did wrong?"

"No, not exactly. That is what made me reflect."

"Then, before, you didn't reflect?"

"Yes, but my weak reason let itself be conquered by my desires."

"As later by your suffering. So that today you have come back . . . conquered."

"No, not exactly,—resigned."

"At any rate, you have given up being what you wanted to be."

"What my pride persuaded me to be."

The boy remains silent a moment, then suddenly cries with a sob:

"Brother! I am the boy you were when you left. Tell me. Did you find nothing but disappointments on your wanderings? Is all that I imagine outside and different from here, only an illusion? All the newness I feel in me, is that madness? Tell me, what did you meet on your way that seemed so tragic? Oh! what made you come back?"

"The freedom I was looking for, I lost. When captive, I had to serve."

"I am captive here."

"Yes, but I mean serving bad masters. Here you are serving your parents."

"Ah! serving for the sake of serving! At least don't we have the freedom of choosing our bondage?"

"I had hoped for that. As far as my feet carried me, I walked, like Saul in search of his she-asses, in search of my desire. But there where a kingdom was waiting for him, I found wretchedness. And yet . . ."

"Didn't you mistake the road?"

"I walked straight ahead."

"Are you sure? And yet there are still other kingdoms, and lands without kings, to discover."

"Who told you?"

"I know it, I feel it. I have already the impression of being the lord over them."

"Proud boy!"

"Ah! ah! that's something our brother said to you. Why do you repeat it to me now? Why didn't you keep that pride? You would not have come back."

"Then I would never have known you."

"Yes, yes, out there where I would have joined you, you would have recognized me as your brother. It seems to me even that I am leaving in order to find you."

"That you are leaving?"

"Haven't you understood? Aren't you yourself encouraging me to leave?"

"I wanted to spare your returning, but by sparing your departure."

"No, no, don't tell me that. No, you don't mean that. You yourself left like a conqueror, didn't you?"

"And that is what made my bondage seem harder to me."

"Then, why did you give in to it? Were you already so tired?"

"No, not then. But I had doubts."

"What do you mean?"

"Doubts about everything, about myself. I wanted to stop and settle down somewhere. The comfort which this master promised me was a temptation . . . Yes, I feel it clearly now. I failed."

The prodigal bows his head and hides his face in his hands.

"But at first?"

"I had walked for a long time through large tracts of wild country."

"The desert?"

"It wasn't always the desert."

"What were you looking for there?"

"I myself do not understand now."

"Get up from my bed. Look, on the table beside it, there, near that torn book."

"I see a pomegranate split open."

"The swineherd brought it to me the other evening, after he had not been back for three days."

"Yes, it is a wild pomegranate."

"I know. It is almost unbearably bitter. And yet I feel, if I were sufficiently thirsty, I would bite into it."

"Ah! now I can tell you. That is the thirst I was looking for in the desert."

"A thirst which that sour fruit alone can quench . . ."

"No, but it makes you love that thirst."

"Do you know where it can be picked?"

"In a small deserted orchard you reach before evening. No longer does any wall separate it from the desert. A stream flowed through it. Some half-ripe fruit hung from the branches."

"What fruit?"

"The same which grows in our garden, but wild. It had been very hot all day."

"Listen. Do you know why I was expecting you this evening? I am leaving before the end of the night. Tonight, this night, as soon as it grows pale . . . I have girded my loins. Tonight I have kept on my sandals."

"So, what I was not able to do, you will do?"

"You opened the way for me, and it will help me to think of you."

"It is for me to admire you, and for you to forget me, on the contrary. What are you taking with you?"

"You know that as the youngest, I have no share in the inheritance. I am taking nothing."

"That is better."

"What are you looking at through the window?"

"The garden where our dead forefathers are sleeping."

"Brother . . ." (and the boy who has gotten out of bed, puts, around the prodigal's neck, his arm which has become as tender as his voice)— "Come with me."

"Leave me! leave me! I am staying to console our mother. Without me you will be braver. It is time now. The sky turns pale. Go without making any noise. Come! kiss me, my young brother, you are taking with you all my hopes. Be strong. Forget us. Forget me. May you never come back . . . Go down quietly. I am holding the lamp . . ."

"Ah! give me your hand as far as the door."

"Be careful of the steps as you go down."

Jules Renard

THE DARK LANTERN

La Lanterne Sourde

I. Crazy Tiennette

CHRIST PUNISHED

As she passes the foot of the cross set outside the village, apparently to protect it from surprises, crazy Tiennette notices that the Christ has fallen down.

No doubt, that night, a heavy wind has weakened the nails and thrown him to the ground.

Tiennette blesses herself and rights the Christ with many precautions, as she would a person still alive. She cannot set him back upon the tall cross; she cannot leave him all alone, at the side of the path.

What is more, he has hurt himself in the fall and some of his fingers are off.

"I must bring the Christ to the carpenter," she says, "and he will mend them."

She hugs him reverently around the middle and bears him off, not running. But he is so heavy he slips through her arms, and she must often hoist him up again with a rough jolt.

And when she does, the nails that pierce the Christ's feet hook to Tiennette's skirt and raise it a little and uncover her legs.

"Will you stop that now, Lord!" she says to him.

And Tiennette, simple, gives the Christ's cheeks a few light slaps, but delicately, with all respect.

THE SNOWCHILD

Snow is falling, and through the streets, bareheaded, crazy Tiennette is running like a crazy woman. She plays all alone, catches the white flies as they fall in her violet hands, sticks out her tongue to dissolve the light candy she can just taste, and, with the tip of her finger, draws sticks and rings on the bright sheet.

Farther on she guesses that this little star print has fallen from a bird, this big one from a goose, and this other strange one from the sky maybe.

Then the shoes that made her as tall as the roof thatch and dizzied her so come loose. She topples and stays on the ground a long while, making a cross, being good, until her portrait sinks in.

Then she makes herself a snowchild.

His limbs are twisted and shrunken from the cold. His eyes have been gouged out, his nose has one hole to take the place of two, his mouth has no teeth, and his skull has no hair, because hair and teeth are too hard.

"The poor little thing!" says Tiennette.

She clasps him to her heart and whistles a lullaby, then, once he starts to melt, she changes him quickly and give him a maternal roll in the fresh snow so the bed that envelops him will be clean.

Tiennette Lost

Tiennette goes out at her pleasure, walks where she will; and her innocence protects her. She walks hurriedly, never strolls, always seems in flight.

This morning, having left home one hour ago by the clock, she stops and says:

"Oh God! I've lost myself!"

She searches, reflects, worried, hunting for herself.

The countryside has vanished under snow. It fills the tree branches; this one seems to have dressed as a traveler waiting for the coach.

But Tiennette spies her own tracks, still fresh, in the snow, and the idea comes to her: she will follow and find herself again.

Sometimes she softly sets her feet inside the deep prints, and if other tracks cross hers she stoops and sets them right. Sometimes she runs, losing her breath, as if there were wolves at her back.

When she reaches the village and recognizes her house among the crouching shapes:

"I probably went back home," she thinks.

She stops hurrying. She takes a breath, drops her anxiety from her shoulders like a shawl grown too heavy, pushes open the door, and says calmly:

"I knew it; there I am!"

The Stick

Tiennette rolls a stick between her fingers, scratches it with her nails, bites it with the tips of her teeth, strips its bark off. She moves on down the road and says to the trees:

"You must have heard that this is my wedding day. I'm serious, I mean it. He loves me, I expect him soon."

She gives them smiles left and right, already rehearsing the ceremony. But a voice from among the trees gives her an order:

"Take off your cap, Tiennette."

She pauses, looks at the trees, hears breathing among them, and asks, trembling:

"Is it really you this time?"

"Yes, Tiennette; take off your cap."

Reassured, she throws away her cap, just as she threw away the leaves she pulled from her stick.

"Take off your jacket, Tiennette."

She obeys, throws away her jacket just as she threw away the thin branches she pulled from her stick.

"Take off your skirt, Tiennette."

She reaches a hand around to undo the knotted strings, but she sees the stick in her other hand, naked, its bark pulled off, and, abruptly waking up, Tiennette shamefacedly picks up her cap and jacket and runs away, far from the libertine who wanted to trap her again and who stays there, behind the trees, laughing.

II. Tiennot

THE CHERRY MAN

Tiennot, walking through the market place, sees baskets filled with cherries so fat and red they cannot be real. He says to the owner:

"Let me eat as many cherries as I want, and we'll settle for ten pennies."

The owner agrees, sure of a profit, because cherries aren't scarce this year and he could afford to give away a barrowful for ten pennies, at the price they bring in.

Tiennot lies down on his right side among the baskets.

Not hurrying, he chooses the finest cherries and eats them one by one. Slowly he empties the first basket, then the second.

The owner smiles. Now and then some market people come to watch. The druggist shows up, then the café owner. Everyone gives Tiennot encouragement.

He carefully keeps from answering. Without moving he methodically opens and closes his mouth. At times, when a passing cherry is more juicy than the others, he seems to be asleep.

The owner, already uneasy, thinks:

"I may not lose anything on this, but I won't gain much by it."

And the ten-cent piece clenched between his teeth shrinks in value. Suddenly reviving, he says:

"Well?"

Tiennot stirs, tries to lift himself, but the effort seems painful. In the end he only changes position, rolls over on his left side, gropes for another basket.

But he has worked up an appetite, and now he begins to devour the cherry stones as well.

The Spring and the Sugar

Tiennot is quenching his thirst with spring water. His hand serves as a cup at first; later he prefers a straight drink and he lies down over the spring, wetting his chin and nose. When he stops to breathe, he looks around at the animals and the water's white plume as it rises.

"It tastes good," he says, "but I know it would taste better with sugar."

He runs to the village, buys a piece of sugar, and steals back at nightfall to drop it into the spring.

"Tomorrow morning," he says just for himself, "I will have a feast."

All the people are still asleep when Tiennot leaves his bed and hurries to the spring.

Before he tastes the water, he says, sucking with his lips:

"Oh! What a fine taste!"

He bends down, tastes, and says, letting his lips relax:

"Yes. No. There's no more sugar in it than there was yesterday."

He is baffled, he fixes his eyes on his crestfallen reflection.

"My God! What a fool I am!" he shouts. "A child would know: water runs, and my melted sugar ran along with it. It left the spring behind and ran away across the field; it can't be going fast, I can catch it."

And Tiennot departs, walking beside the brook. He carefully counts out twenty paces and then stops. He takes a mouthful of water and savors it. But then he tosses his head, suddenly, and departs again in pursuit of his sugar.

The Fist of God

In a short smock and a shaggy top hat Tiennot is coming home from the fair. All he had to sell is sold, his pig, his cheese, and his two old hens, but the hens were sold for pullets, after he gave them wine and made them drunk.

They were full of life, their eyes glittered, they had fever in their wings and claws, they deceived a trusting woman who may be weighing them again, surprised and angry to see them dangling, cold, broken. Tiennot smiles; he feels no remorse; he has put it over many times. He zigzags, his legs give, he wanders all over the road, for while the hens were picking up drops of wine out of a bowl, he was drinking the rest of the bottle.

Then a cyclist shouts, a bell sounds, a horn trumpets right behind him. He hears nothing. He goes back and forth across the road, waving his arms, gesticulating, feeling compassion, as if he were selling his hens a second time.

And suddenly a fist blow crushes down his shaggy top hat.

Tiennot stops, bends double, his head a prisoner, surrounded by night down to the ears. He tries to lift his hat off; he tries for some time; but his head is caught, the circle around his skull hurts him. Tiennot struggles, heaves, bellows, finally frees himself.

He looks around: nobody on the road, nobody ahead, nobody behind. He looks over the hedge, first left, then right.

He sees nothing.

And Tiennot, who got his hens drunk and sold them, mechanically makes the sign of the cross.

The Fine Corn

On the dry road, under the burning sun, Tiennot and Baptiste are driving back home in their donkey cart. They pass near a field of ripe corn, and Baptiste, who knows all about corn, says:

"What fine corn!"

Tiennot is driving and says nothing; he bows his back. Baptiste bows his own in imitation, and their necks, exposed, tough, slowly broil, shine like copper pans.

Like a machine, Tiennot pulls or shakes the reins. Sometimes he raises a stick and aims a lively blow at the donkey's buttocks, as if they were a bespattered pair of breeches. The donkey never changes pace; he bends his head, probably to watch the play of his hoofs as they move in and out, one after another, never mistaking. The cart follows along after him as best it can; a roundish shadow drags after; Tiennot and Baptiste bend down still farther.

They pass through villages that look deserted because of the heat. They meet a few scarce people who give only a single sign. They close their eyes against the road's white glare.

And yet they arrive that night, very late. In the end one always arrives. The donkey halts before the door, perks its ears. Baptiste and Tiennot, sluggish, stir themselves, and Tiennot answers Baptiste:

"Yes, it is fine corn."

Gérard de Nerval

EMILIE

"No one really knows the story of Lieutenant Desroches, who was killed last year at the battle of Hambergen, two months after his wedding. If it was suicide, may God forgive him! But surely a man who died defending his country deserves to have his actions given a better name than that, whatever his intentions."

"Which brings us back," said the doctor, "to the question of compromising with conscience. Desroches was a philosopher who had had enough of life. He didn't want to die a useless death, so he plunged bravely into battle and killed as many Germans as he could, saying, 'This is the best I can do. Now I'm content to die.' And as he took the blow that killed him he shouted, 'Vive l'Empereur!' Ten soldiers from his company will tell you the same thing."

"It was no less a suicide for that," said Arthur. "Still, it wouldn't have been right to deny him church burial."

"In that case, you underrate the self-sacrifice of Curtius. That young Roman knight may have been ruined by gambling, unlucky in love, and tired of living, who knows? But there must be something fine about a man who when he has made up his mind to leave this world, makes his death useful to others. So you can't call Desroches a suicide, for suicide is no less than the supreme act of egoism, which is the only reason men condemn it. . . . What are you thinking about, Arthur?"

"About what you were just saying—that Desroches killed as many Germans as he could before he died."

"Well?"

"Well, those fine fellows will give a pretty poor accounting of the lieutenant's glorious death before God. And you must admit, this *suicide* looks very much like *homicide*."

"Oh, but who would think of that? The Germans are our enemies."

"But does a man who has made up his mind to die have enemies? At that moment, all feelings of nationality disappear, and I doubt if one thinks of any country but the next world, or of any emperor but God. But here's the abbé, listening to us without a word. Still, I hope he approves of what I'm saying. Come now, Father, give us your opinion, and try to reconcile us. It's a knotty question, and the story of Desroches, or rather

126

what the doctor and I think we know of it, appears to be every bit as involved as our discussion."

"Yes," said the doctor, "I've heard that Desroches was greatly distressed by his last wound—the one that disfigured him so badly—and that perhaps he surprised his young bride wincing or making fun of him. Philosophers are easily offended. At any rate, he died, and willingly."

"Willingly, if you must, but don't call death in battle suicide. It only adds to the confusion. You die in battle because someone kills you, not because you want to die."

"Then . . . do you suppose it's fate?"

"My turn," said the priest, who had been collecting his thoughts during this discussion. "Perhaps you will think it strange of me to object to your paradoxes and suppositions. . . ."

"Go right ahead, by all means. You probably know more about it than we do. You've been living at Bitche for a long time now, and we've been told that Desroches knew you. Perhaps you were even his confessor."

"In that case, I should have to keep silent. Unfortunately, I wasn't, but I assure you, he died like a Christian, and I shall tell you how and why, so that you will think of him as a gentleman and a soldier who died a timely death for humanity and for himself, according to the will of God.

"Desroches joined a regiment when he was only fourteen, at a time when most of our men were getting killed on the frontier, and our Army of the Republic was drafting children. He was as weak and slender as a girl, and it distressed his comrades to see his young shoulders sink under the weight of his gun. You must have heard the story of how permission was obtained from the captain to have it cut down six inches. With his weapon thus suited to his strength, Desroches did splendidly in Flanders; later on, he was sent to Hagenau, where we, or rather you, had been fighting for so long.

"At the time of which I am going to speak, Desroches was at the height of his powers, and as regimental ensign-bearer, he served far in advance of his rank, for he was practically the only man to survive two reinforcements. He had just been made a lieutenant when, twenty-seven months ago, at Bergheim, he led a bayonet charge and received a Prussian saber cut straight across the face. The wound was ghastly. The field surgeons, who had often joked with him because he had come through thirty battles without a scratch, frowned when he was brought in. 'If he lives,' they said, 'he'll lose his wits or go mad.'

"The lieutenant was sent to Metz to recover, and many miles went by before he regained consciousness. It took five or six months in a decent bed, with the best of care, before he could sit up, and another hundred days before he could open one eye and see. Soon tonics were prescribed, then sunlight and movement, and finally, short walks. One morning, supported by two companions, he set out all giddy and trembling for the Quai St. Vincent, which adjoins the military hospital, and there they sat him in the noonday sun, under the lime trees, at the edge of the promenade: the poor fellow thought he was seeing the light of day for the very first time.

"Soon he could walk by himself, and every morning he came to sit on the same bench. His head was a mass of black taffeta bandages that all but covered his face, and as he passed, he could always count on a friendly greeting from the men, and a gesture of deep sympathy from the women. From this, however, he derived little comfort.

"But once seated on his bench, he forgot his misfortune and thought only of how lucky he was to be alive after such a shock, and in such pleasant surroundings. Before him, the old fortress—a ruin since the time of Louis XVI—spread its dilapidated ramparts, the flowering lime trees cast shadows on his head, and at his feet, in the valley that dipped away from the promenade, the Moselle, overflowing its banks, kept the meadows of St. Symphorien green and fertile between its two arms. Then came the isle of St. Saulcy, with its powder magazine, and its shady trees and cottages, and finally, the foamy white falls of the Moselle, its course sparkling in the sunlight. Then, as far as he could see, the Vosges Mountains rose up bluish and misty in broad daylight, and he gazed at them with ever-increasing delight, his heart gladdened by the thought that there lay his country—not conquered land, but true French soil, while these rich new provinces he had fought for were fickle beauties, like those of a love won yesterday, and gone tomorrow.

"In the early days of June, the heat was intense, and as the bench Desroches had chosen was well in the shade, one day two women came and sat down beside him. He greeted them calmly and continued to gaze at the horizon, but his appearance inspired so much interest they could not resist the temptation to ply him with sympathetic questions. One of the two was well advanced in age, and proved to be the aunt of the other, whose name was Emilie. The older woman earned her living by doing gilt embroidery on silk or velvet. When Desroches replied to their questions with questions of his own, the aunt informed him that Emilie had left Hagenau to keep her company, that she embroidered for churches, and that she had been an orphan for some time.

"The next day, the bench was similarly occupied, and by the end of the week, its three occupants were fast friends. Desroches, in spite of his weakness and humiliation at the attentions the girl lavished on him as if he were a harmless old man, felt lighthearted, and more like rejoicing at his good fortune than being distressed by it. Then, on his return to the hospital, he remembered his ghastly wound, and his scarecrow appearance, which caused him many hours of despair, though he had become almost used to it.

"Desroches had not dared remove the useless bandages, or look at himself in a mirror. Now the thought of doing so frightened him more than ever. Nevertheless, he ventured to lift up one corner of the dressing, and found beneath it a scar that was slightly pink, but by no means too repulsive. On further examination, he found that the various parts of his face had been sewn together fairly well, and that his eyes were as healthy and clear as ever. Of course, a few scraps of eyebrow were missing, but that was nothing! The slanting scar across his face, from forehead to ear was . . . well, it was a sword cut received at Bergheim, and nothing could be finer, as many a song has said.

"Desroches was astonished to find that he was so presentable after the long months during which he seemed a virtual stranger to himself. He cleverly concealed the hair that had turned gray on the wounded side under the abundant black on the left, drew his mustache out as far as it would go over the line of the scar, and on the following day, put on his new uniform and set out triumphantly for the park. Those who passed him on the way failed to recognize this sprightly young officer with tilted shako and a sword that jauntily slapped his thigh.

"He was the first to arrive at the bench by the lime trees, and sat down with his customary deliberation, although he was profoundly agitated and much paler than usual, despite the approval of his mirror.

"The two ladies were not long in arriving, but they suddenly turned and walked away at the sight of the smart-looking officer sitting on their accustomed bench. Desroches was deeply moved.

"'What!' he cried. 'Don't you recognize me?'

"You mustn't think this is the prelude to a tale of pity turned to love, like the plot of some contemporary opera. The lieutenant now had serious intentions. Glad to find himself once more considered eligible, he hastened to reassure the two ladies, who seemed disposed to continue their friendship. Their reserve gave way before his forthright declarations. Besides, the match was suitable from every point of view: Desroches had a little property near Épinal, while Emilie's parents had left her a small house at Hagenau, which she rented as a restaurant, and received an income of five or six hundred francs, half of which she gave to her brother Wilhelm, chief clerk to the notary at Schennberg.

"When the arrangements had been completed, it was decided that the wedding should take place at Hagenau, which was Emilie's real home, for she had come to Metz only to be with her aunt, and it was agreed that she should return there afterward. Emilie was delighted at the prospect of seeing her brother again, and more than once Desroches's astonishment was aroused by the fact that the young man was not in uniform, like his contemporaries. He was told he had been excused on account of poor health, and Desroches was full of sympathy for him.

"So one day the prospective bride and groom and the aunt set out together for Hagenau. They took places in the public carriage that changes horses at Bitche. In those days, it was simply a ramshackle stagecoach made of leather and wickerwork. As you know, the road leads through beautiful country. Desroches, who had only been along it in uniform, sword in hand, with three or four thousand other men, was now able to enjoy the solitude, the hills in their mantle of dark green foliage, and the fantastic shape of rocks that cut the skyline. The fertile uplands of St. Avold, the factories of Saarguemines, and the thickly wooded copses of Limblingue, where poplar, ash, and pine display their varying banks of foliage, ranging from gray to dark green . . . you know what delightful scenery it is.

"As soon as they arrived at Bitche, they stopped at the Dragon, and Desroches sent for me at the fort. I went at once to join him, met his new family, and complimented the young lady, whose rare beauty and charm impressed me greatly. It was easy to see that she was very much in love with her future husband. The three of them lunched with me right here, where we're sitting, and several officers who were old friends of Desroches came to the inn and begged him to dine with them at the restaurant near the fort, where the staff took their meals. So it was agreed that the ladies should retire early, and that the lieutenant should devote his last evening as a bachelor to his friends.

"The dinner was lively; everyone enjoyed his share of the happiness and gaiety Desroches had brought with him. They all spoke rapturously of Egypt and Italy, and complained bitterly of the hard luck that kept so many good soldiers cooped up on the frontier.

"'Yes,' grumbled some of the officers, 'the monotony is getting on our nerves. We're stifling here. We might as well be off on a ship somewhere as live without fighting or distractions of any kind, or any chance of promotion. *The fort is impregnable.* That's what Napoleon said when he passed through here to rejoin his forces in Germany. About all we have here is a chance to die of boredom.'

"'Alas, my friends,' replied Desroches, 'it was hardly more amusing in my time. When I was stationed here, I had the same complaints. I got my commission by tramping in army boots down highway and byway, and knew only three things: military drill, the direction of the wind, and the kind of grammar you learn from the village schoolmaster. So, when I was made second lieutenant and sent to Bitche with the second battalion of the Cher, I looked upon my stay here as an excellent opportunity for some real uninterrupted study. With this in mind, I assembled a collection of books, maps, and charts. I had studied tactics, and learned German without any trouble, for nothing else was spoken in this good French country. This way, the time—so tedious for you who have so much less to learn—seemed to pass all too quickly. At night I retired into a little stone room under the spiral of the main staircase. There I lit my lamp and worked, with all the loopholes carefully stopped, and on just such a night . . .'

"Here, Desroches paused a moment, drew his hand over his eyes, emptied his glass, and went on without finishing his sentence.

"'You all know,' he said, 'the little path that leads up here from the plain—the one they've made impassable by blowing up a huge rock and not filling up the pit. Well, it was always fatal to hostile troops attacking the fort. No sooner did the poor devils start climbing up than they were raked by four twenty-fours that swept the whole length of the path. I suppose they're still there.'

"'You must have distinguished yourself,' said one of the colonels. 'Wasn't that the place you won your promotion?'

"'Yes, Colonel, and that was where I killed the first and only man I ever struck down in hand-to-hand fighting. That's why it always distresses me to see this fort.'

"'What!' they cried. 'After twenty years in service, fifteen pitched battles, and perhaps fifty skirmishes, you expect us to believe you've killed only one man?'

"'I didn't say that, gentlemen; of the ten thousand cartridges I've rammed into my gun, for all I know, half may have missed the mark. But at Bitche, I give you my word, my hand was first stained with the blood of an enemy, and my arm first drove the cruel point of my sword into a human breast—till it quivered to the hilt.'

"'It's true,' interrupted one of the officers, 'a soldier does lots of killing, but hardly ever feels it. Gunfire isn't really execution; it's only the intention to kill. As for bayonets, they play only a small part in the most dangerous charges; ground is held or lost without close personal combat. Guns clash, then disengage when resistance gives way. Take the cavalry, for instance. They really fight hand to hand.'

"'And so,' replied Desroches, 'just as you never forget the last look of a man you kill in a duel, his death rattle, or the sound of his fall, so I bear with me, almost in remorse—yes, laugh at me if you will—the pale, dreadful sight of the Prussian sergeant I killed in the little powder magazine of this fort.'

"Everyone fell silent, and Desroches went on:

"'It was night, and as I just explained, I was working. At two o'clock everyone was asleep except the sentinels. They patrolled in complete silence, so that any sound was suspicious. However, I kept hearing some kind of protracted argument in the gallery below my room. Then

someone bumped against a door, and it creaked. I ran out into the corridor and listened. I called to the sentry in a low voice—no answer. I
hurried to alert the gunners, threw on my uniform, grabbed my naked
sword, and ran in the direction of the noise. About thirty of us arrived
at once at the place where the galleries converge, and in the dim
lantern light, we recognized the Prussians. A traitor had let them in
through the postern gate. They dashed forward in great confusion, and
catching sight of us, fired a few shots, which produced terrific detona-
tions under those low, shadowy ceilings.

"'So there we were, face to face, with more of us pouring in all the
time. We could hardly move, but a six- to eight-foot space still divided us.
We French were so surprised, and the Prussians so disappointed, that no
one thought of entering the lists. But this hesitation was only momentary.

"'Extra torches and lanterns lit the scene—some of the gunners had
hung theirs on the walls, and a kind of old-fashioned fighting took place.
I was in the front line, face to face with a tall Prussian sergeant covered
with stripes and decorations. He had a gun, but there was such a crush
he could hardly move it. Alas! How well I remember! I don't know if he
even intended to resist me; I lunged at him, and thrust my sword into
his noble heart, then his eyes opened horribly, he tried to clench his
fists, and he toppled backward into the arms of his comrades.

"'I don't remember what happened next; later, I found myself in the
courtyard, drenched with blood. The Prussians had retreated through the
postern gate, and our gunfire followed them back to their encampment!'

"When Desroches had finished speaking, there was a long silence,
and then they spoke of other things. The look of sadness worn by these
soldiers after hearing of this seemingly ordinary misfortune was very
curious, when you come to think of it—and you could tell just how
much a man's life is worth—even a German life, doctor—by examining the faces of those professional killers."

"I agree," replied the doctor, slightly taken aback, "bloodshed is a terrible thing, no matter what causes it. Still, Desroches did nothing
wrong—he was simply defending himself."

"Who knows?" muttered Arthur.

"A while ago, Doctor, you spoke of compromising with conscience.
Tell us now, wasn't this sergeant's death a bit like murder? Can we be
sure the Prussian would have killed Desroches?"

"But that's war. Who's to blame?"

"All right, that's war. But we kill men at three hundred paces in the
darkness—men we don't know and who can't see us; we face these men
we don't hate, and slaughter them with anger blazing in our eyes. Then
we pat ourselves on the back and feel proud. And we call ourselves hon-
orable, and Christians."

"It was time for bed, and Desroches himself was the first to forget his dismal story, for, from the little room he had been given, he could see a certain window through the trees, where a night lamp was burning. There lay his future happiness, and when, in the middle of the night, he was awakened by the watchman making his round, he was oppressed and a little frightened by the thought that in case of danger his courage would no longer electrify him into action. The next day, before the morning gun was fired, the captain of the guard opened a door for him and he found the two ladies waiting near the outer fortification. I accompanied them as far as Neunhoffen, and they went on to Hagenau to be married at the Registry Office, after which they were to return to Metz for the religious ceremony.

"Emilie's brother Wilhelm welcomed Desroches cordially enough, and the two brothers-in-law proceeded to take each other's measure. Wilhelm was of medium height, but well built. His blond hair was already very thin, as if he had been weakened by too much study or some great sorrow, and he wore blue glasses, for, as he said, his eyes were so weak that the least light pained him. Desroches had brought a bundle of papers with him, to which the young law student gave his careful attention, and then Wilhelm, in turn, produced the title deeds to his family property, insisting that Desroches should examine them. But he was dealing with a man who was trusting, unselfish, and in love, so the inspection did not last long. This attitude seemed to flatter Wilhelm somewhat, so he began taking Desroches's arm as they walked, offered him the use of one of his best pipes, and took him to see all his friends in Hagenau.

"This involved much smoking and drinking, and after ten introductions, Desroches begged for mercy. From then on he was allowed to spend his evenings alone with his fiancée.

"A few days later, the two lovers of the promenade bench were wed by the mayor of Hagenau. This worthy functionary, who must have been burgomaster before the French Revolution, had often held Emilie in his arms when she was a young child. He himself may even have registered her birth, and on the day before the wedding he had whispered to her, 'Why don't you marry a good German?'

"Emilie appeared to give little thought to such distinctions. Even Wilhelm had become reconciled to the lieutenant's mustache, for, to tell the truth, at first there had been a decided coolness between them. But Desroches had made great concessions—Wilhelm, a few, for his sister's sake—and with Emilie's good aunt to pacify and smooth things over at every interview, there was perfect agreement between them, and Wilhelm embraced his brother-in-law most cordially after the marriage contract had been signed. Before nine in the morning, everything was in order, so the four of them set out for Metz that same day. By six o'clock in the evening, the coach drew up before the Dragon at Bitche.

"Travel is none too easy in this country of woodland and interlacing streams; there are at least ten hills for every mile you go, and the coach shakes up its passengers pretty badly. This was probably the main reason for the young bride's discomfort on arriving at the inn. Her aunt and Desroches stayed in her room with her, while Wilhelm, who was famished, went down to the little dining room where the officers dined at eight.

"This time no one knew of Desroches's arrival, and the soldiers of the garrison had spent a field-day in the Huspoletden woods. Desroches was determined not to leave his wife that evening, and told the landlady not to mention his name to a soul. The three of them stood at the window, watching the soldiers go back into the fort, and later, as it grew darker, they saw the men, dressed in fatigues, lining up in front of the canteen for their army bread and goat's-milk cheese.

"Wilhelm, meanwhile, trying to pass the time and forget his hunger, had lit his pipe and was lolling near the doorway, where he could breathe in both the tobacco smoke and the smell of the cooking. At the sight of this middle-class traveler with his cap pulled down to his ears and his blue glasses fastened on the kitchen, the officers took it that he would dine with them and looked forward to meeting him. Perhaps he had come from a distance, was clever, or had some news. That would be a stroke of luck. On the other hand, if he came from the district, and maintained a stupid silence, they could enjoy poking fun at him.

"A second lieutenant from the military school approached Wilhelm and questioned him with exaggerated politeness.

"'Good evening, sir. Have you any news from Paris?'

"'No, sir, have you?' he replied quietly.

"'Good Lord, sir, we never leave Bitche. How would we ever get any?'

"'And I, sir, never leave my office.'

"'Are you in the Engineers?'

"This quip, aimed at Wilhelm's glasses, delighted the other officer.

"'I am clerk to a notary, sir.'

"'Really? That's odd, at your age.'

"'Do you wish to see my passport, sir?'

"'Of course not.'

"'Very well. Just tell me you're not trying to make a fool of me, and I'll answer all your questions.'

"The officers became more serious, and the lieutenant went on:

"'I asked you, with no ill intentions, if you were in the Engineers, because you wear glasses. Don't you know that the officers in that corps are the only ones who have the right to wear them?'

"'And I suppose that proves I'm in the army, as you say.'

"'But everyone's a soldier these days. You're not twenty-five yet; you must be in the army, or else you are rich, you have an income of fifteen or twenty thousand francs, and your parents have made sacrifices for you, in which case you wouldn't take the dinner at a place like this.'

"Wilhelm shook out his pipe and said, 'I don't know, sir, whether you have the right to question me like this, but I'll answer you explicitly. I have no income; I am simply a clerk to a notary, as I told you. I was excused from the service on account of my eyes. In short, I'm nearsighted.'

"This declaration was greeted by peals of laughter.

"'My dear fellow,' cried Captain Vallier, slapping him on the back. 'You're quite right. A the proverb says, *Better a live coward than a dead hero!*'

"Wilhelm turned crimson. 'I'm not a coward, Captain, and I'll prove it whenever you like. What's more, my papers are in order, and if you are a recruiting officer, I'll be glad to show them to you.'

"'Enough!' cried several of the officers, 'let him alone, Vallier; he's a peaceful fellow with a perfect right to eat here.'

"'Yes, of course,' said the captain, 'let's sit down and eat. I meant no harm, young man. Don't worry—I'm not the recruiting doctor and this isn't the recruiting room. And just to show you there are no hard feelings, how's about sharing a wing of this tough old bird they'd like us to think is a chicken?'

"'No, thank you,' said Wilhelm, whose appetite had vanished. 'One of those trout at the end of the table will be enough for me.' And he motioned to the servant girl to bring him the dish.

"'Are they trout, really?' said the captain to Wilhelm, who had taken off his glasses to eat. 'By God, you've got better eyesight than I have. Look here, frankly you could handle a gun as well as the next man . . . but you have influence, and know how to use it. Quite right, too. You love peace and quiet. And why not? But if I were you, it would make my blood boil to read the army bulletin and hear about young men my own age getting killed in Germany. Perhaps you aren't French?'

"'No,' said Wilhelm, with an effort that, however, brought him great satisfaction. 'I was born at Hagenau; I'm not French, I'm German.'

"'German? But Hagenau is on this side of the Rhine frontier. It's one of the finest villages in the French Empire, province of the Lower Rhine. Look at the map!'

"'I'm from Hagenau, I tell you. Ten years ago it was German; today it's French. But I shall always be German, just as you would always be French if your country ever belonged to Germany.'

"'Those are dangerous things you're saying, young man. Be careful.'

"'I may be wrong,' Wilhelm continued impetuously, 'and no doubt it would be wiser to keep them to myself, since I can't change them. But you yourself have carried things so far, that I must justify myself at all costs or be taken for a coward. And now you know the reason that, to my mind, warrants my eagerness to make use of a real infirmity, though perhaps it would not stand in the way of someone who really wanted to defend his country. I must admit, I feel no hatred for the people you are fighting. If I had been forced to march against them, I suppose I, too, might be helping to lay waste and burn German fields and cities, and slaughter my own countrymen—former countrymen, if you prefer. And who knows?—perhaps even slay my own flesh and blood, or some friend of my father's, in some group of pretended enemies. Surely you can see that it's far better for me to busy myself with documents in a notary's office at Hagenau. And besides, there's been enough bloodshed in my family. My father gave his to the last drop, you see, and I—'

"'Your father was a soldier?' interrupted Captain Vallier.

"'My father was a soldier in the Prussian army and for a long time he defended the territory you occupy today. He was killed in the last attack on the fort at Bitche.'

"At these words, everyone pricked up his ears, and lost interest in refuting the nonsense about Wilhelm's nationality.

"'Was it in '93?'

"'In '93, on the seventeenth of November. My father had left Sirmasen the day before to rejoin his company. I know he told my mother that by means of a daring plan the fort would be taken without firing a shot. Twenty-four hours later he was brought back to us, dying. He expired on the doorstep, after he made me swear to stay with my mother. She followed him two weeks later.

"'Afterward I learned that that night the sword of a young soldier had pierced his breast, and thus fell one of the finest grenadiers in Prince Hohenlohe's army.'

"'But we've heard about that,' said the major.

"'Yes,' said Captain Vallier, 'that's the story of the Prussian sergeant killed by Desroches.'

"'Desroches!' cried Wilhelm. 'Do you mean Lieutenant Desroches?'

"'Oh no, no,' replied one of the officers hastily, realizing they were on the brink of some terrible revelation, 'the Desroches we meant was a light infantryman from this garrison who was killed four years ago, the first time he went into action.'

"'Ah, he's dead,'' said Wilhelm, mopping the sweat from his brow.

"A few minutes later the officers saluted and withdrew. Desroches watched their departure from his window upstairs, and then came down to the dining room, where he found his brother-in-law sitting at the long table with his head in his hands.

"'Hmm . . . Asleep already? Well, I'd like some supper. My wife's finally got to sleep, and I'm famished. Let's have a glass of wine. It'll rouse us a bit, and you can keep me company.'

"'No, I have a headache,' said Wilhelm. 'I'm going up to my room. By the way, those gentlemen told me some interesting things about the fort. Why don't you take me up there tomorrow?'

"'Of course.'

"'Fine. I'll wake you in the morning.'

"After supper, Desroches went up to Wilhelm's room, where a bed had been prepared for him, for he would sleep alone until the religious ceremony had been performed. Wilhelm lay awake all night, sometimes weeping silently, and sometimes glaring furiously at Desroches, who smiled in his dreams.

"What we call presentiment is very much like the pilotfish that swim ahead of an enormous half-blind whale to bring it news of jagged rocks and sandy bottoms. We go through life so mechanically that some of our fellow beings, who are heedless by nature, would run afoul or be dashed to bits without a moment's thought of God, if nothing ever ruffled the surface of their happiness. Some take warning from the ravens' flight; others, for no apparent reason; and yet others proceed with the greatest care if they have had some sinister dream. Such is presentiment. 'You are going to be in danger,' says the dream. 'Watch out,' cries the raven. 'Be sad,' whispers the brain.

"Toward the end of the night, Desroches had a peculiar dream. He was in a cave beneath the earth. A white shadow was following him, and its garments kept brushing against his heels. When he turned upon it, the figure drew back. Finally, it retreated so far he could see nothing but a little white speck. Presently this speck began to grow. It became luminous and filled the whole grotto with light. Then it went out. A slight noise was heard, and Wilhelm entered the room, wearing his hat and a long blue cloak.

"Desroches woke up with a start. 'Good Lord! Have you been out already this morning?'

"'You must get up,' replied Wilhelm.

"'But will they let us in at the fort?'

"'Of course. Everyone but the guards is out drilling.'

"'Already? Very well. I'll be with you in a moment. Just give me time to say good morning to my wife.'

"'She's quite all right, I've seen her. Don't concern yourself.'

"Desroches was rather surprised at this reply, but he put it down to impatience and gave in once more to this fraternal authority that he would soon be able to shake off.

"On their way to the fort, he looked back at a window in the inn, and thought, 'Emilie is probably asleep.' But the curtain fluttered and was drawn across the window, and Desroches thought he saw someone step back into the room to avoid being seen.

"They had no trouble gaining entrance to the fort. A disabled captain, who had not dined at the inn the night before, was in command of the outpost. Desroches asked for a lantern and proceeded to guide his silent companion from room to room.

"After stopping at several points of interest to which Wilhelm paid little attention, he asked, 'Aren't you going to show me the underground passages?'

"'Certainly, if you like, I assure you it won't be very pleasant. The dampness down there is terrible. The gunpowder is stored under the left wing and we can't get in without a special pass. On the right, are the water mains and raw saltpeter, and in the center, the countermines and galleries. Do you know what a vault is like?'

"'Never mind. I'm curious to see where so many sinister encounters took place, and where you yourself, I am told, were once in mortal danger.'

"'He won't spare me a single vault,' thought Desroches. 'This way, then, Brother; this gallery leads to the postern.'

"The light from the lantern flickered dismally on the musty walls, and glinted here and there on rusty sword blades and gun barrels.

"'What weapons are these?' asked Wilhelm.

"'Spoils from the Prussians killed in the last attack. My friends hung them here as trophies.'

"'Then several Prussians were killed here?'

"'A great many, where these passages meet.'

"'Didn't you kill a sergeant here, a tall elderly man with a red mustache?'

"'Yes, did I tell you about it?'

"'No, but at dinner last night I was told of that exploit . . . you so modestly kept from us.'

"'What's the matter, Brother? Why are you so pale?'

"'Don't call me Brother, but enemy! Look, I am a Prussian! I am the son of the sergeant you murdered!'

"'Murdered!'

"'Or killed! Does it matter? See, here's where your sword went in.'

"Wilhelm threw back his cloak and pointed to a tear in his father's green uniform, which he had reverently kept and was now wearing.

"'You—the son of that sergeant! For God's sake, tell me you're only joking!'

"'Joking! Who would make jokes about a frightful deed like that? My father was killed here; his noble blood reddened these stones; perhaps this was his very sword! Come now, take another, and give me my revenge. . . . Come, this is no duel, it's German against Frenchman! *En garde!*'

"'My dear Wilhelm, have you lost your mind? Put down that rusty sword. You want to kill me—is it really my fault?'

"'You have a chance to kill me, too. Come on, defend yourself!'

"'Wilhelm! Kill me as I am, unarmed. I'm going mad; my head's spinning. Wilhelm! I did what every soldier has to do. Just think! And besides, I'm your sister's husband—she loves me. Oh no! It's impossible!'

"'My sister! . . . Yes, and that's the best reason there is why one of us has to die! My sister! She knows everything, and will never again set eyes on the man who made her an orphan. Your parting from her yesterday was final.'

"Desroches uttered a cry of rage and rushed at Wilhelm to disarm him; the struggle was a lengthy one; for the younger man answered Desroches's shaking with a strength born of fury and desperation.

"'Give me that saber, you idiot! Give it to me!' Desroches cried. 'I refuse to be killed by a madman!'

"'Go ahead,' Wilhelm retorted, choking with rage. 'Kill the son in the same gallery. And the son's a German too! A German!'

"At that moment footsteps were heard and Desroches let go. Wilhelm was at the end of his strength.

"Those footsteps were mine, gentlemen. Emilie had come to the presbytery and told me everything. The poor child wished to put herself under the protection of the Church. I kept back the words of pity that rose to my lips, and when she asked me whether she could continue to love her father's murderer, I said nothing. She understood, shook my hand, and left in tears. I had a hunch, and followed her to the inn, where she was told that her brother and husband had gone together to the fortress, and, suspecting the awful truth, I arrived in time to prevent these two men, maddened by rage and grief, from enacting a further tragedy.

"Although disarmed, Wilhelm refused to listen to Desroches's pleading; he was beaten, but his eyes still blazed with anger.

"I reproached him for his obstinacy. 'You alone,' I said, 'make the dead cry out for vengeance, and you alone would be the cause of this dreadful thing. Aren't you a Christian? Do you want to trespass on God's justice? Are you prepared to go through life with a murder on your hands? Atonement will be made, you may be sure of that, but it's not for us to force it.'

"Desroches shook my hand and said, 'Emilie knows everything. I will never see her again. But I know what I must do to give her her freedom."

"'What are you saying?' I cried. 'Do you mean suicide?'

"At this word, Wilhelm got up and took Desroches's hand.

"'No!' he said, 'I was wrong. I am the only offender. I should have borne my suffering in silence.'

"I shan't describe the agony we all went through on that fateful morning; I used every religious and philosophical argument I knew, but could find no way out of that cruel situation. A separation was inevitable, in any case, but what grounds for it could be stated in court? Not only would it be painful for all concerned, but there was a political danger in letting it be known.

"I devoted myself to the task of defeating Desroches's sinister intentions and creating in his mind a religious antipathy to the crime of suicide. As you know, the poor fellow had been schooled in eighteenth-century materialism. Since his wound, however, his ideas had changed considerably and he had become one of those half-skeptical Christians— we've seen so many—who have concluded a little religion can't do any harm, and even consult a priest in case there may be a God! It was a vague belief like this that enabled him to listen to my comforting words.

"A few days went by. Wilhelm and his sister had not left the inn, for Emilie's health had not withstood the shock. Desroches stayed at the presbytery with me and spent his days reading the pious books I lent him. One day he went alone to the fort, and spent several hours there; on his return he showed me a sheet of paper with his name on it—his appointment as captain in a regiment that was about to rejoin the Partouneaux division.

"In about a month's time we received news of his strange and glorious death. Whatever may be said of the mad frenzy that drove him into battle, one felt sure that his bravery was a splendid example to the whole battalion, which had sustained heavy losses in the first charge.'

When the story was over, the listeners remained silent, their minds absorbed by what they had heard of the life and death of this man. Then the priest rose from his seat and said, "If you have no objection to a change in the direction of our evening walk, gentlemen, we can follow this line of poplars glowing in the sunset, and I will take you to the Butte-aux-Lierres. From there we can see the cross of the convent where Madame Desroches withdrew."

Voltaire

MICROMEGAS

Micromégas

Philosophical Story

Chapter I

JOURNEY OF AN INHABITANT OF THE WORLD
OF THE STAR SIRIUS TO THE PLANET SATURN

On one of those planets which revolve around the star named Sirius,
there was a very witty young man whom I had the honor of knowing
during the last journey he made to our little anthill. He was called
Micromegas, a name which is most appropriate for all big men. He was
eight leagues high. By eight leagues I mean twenty-four thousand geo-
metrical paces of five feet each.

Some mathematicians, men constantly useful to the public, will
immediately take their pens and discover that, since Mr. Micromegas,
an inhabitant of the land of Sirius, measures from head to foot twenty-
four thousand royal feet, and since we citizens of earth barely measure
five feet, and since our globe has nine thousand leagues in circumference, they will discover, I say, that the globe which produced him
absolutely must have exactly twenty-one million six hundred thousand
times more circumference than our small earth. Nothing is more simple and more commonplace in nature. The states of a few sovereigns
in Germany or Italy, which can be crossed in half an hour, compared
with the empires of Turkey, Muscovy or China, are only a faint image
of the prodigious differences which nature has created in all beings.

His Excellency's size being the height I said, all our sculptors and all
our painters will easily agree that his waist measures fifty thousand royal
feet around and this makes him very well proportioned.

As for his mind, it is one of the most cultured we have. He knows
many things. He has invented some. He was not yet two hundred and
fifty years old, and was studying, according to custom, at the Jesuit col-
lege on his planet, when he solved, by the power of his brain, more

141

than fifty theorems of Euclid. That is eighteen more than Blaise Pascal, who, after solving thirty-two with ease, according to his sister, then became a rather mediocre geometrician and a very bad metaphysician. At the end of childhood, when he was about four hundred and fifty years old, he dissected many of those small insects which do not have a hundred feet in diameter and which escape ordinary microscopes. He wrote a very unusual book about them which brought him trouble. The mufti of his country, a very ignorant hair-splitter, found in his book statements that were suspect, foul, rash, heretical, and smacking of heresy. He prosecuted him actively. The problem was whether the bodies of the fleas of Sirius were of the same substance as slugs. Micromegas defended himself wittily and won the women to his side. The lawsuit lasted two hundred and twenty years. At the end, the mufti had the book condemned by jurists who had not read it and the author was ordered not to appear at court for eight hundred years.

He was only slightly upset at being banished from a court which was seething with vexations and pettinesses. He composed a very amusing song against the mufti who was unaffected by it. And he began to journey from planet to planet, in order to complete the development of "his mind and his heart," as people say. Those who travel only in post-chaise or coach will doubtless be amazed at the conveyances in the planet above, for we, on our little mud pile, cannot imagine anything other than what we use. Our traveler knew remarkably well the laws of gravitation, and all the forces of attraction and repulsion. He used them so skillfully that, at times with the help of a sunbeam, and at other times with the help of a comet, he and those with him went from globe to globe, as a bird flits from branch to branch. He crossed the Milky Way in a very short time, and I am obliged to confess that he never saw, through the stars with which it is sown, that beautiful empyrean sky which the famous Reverend Derham boasts of having seen at the end of his spyglass. It's not that I claim that Mr. Derham did not see properly. God forbid! But Micromegas was on the spot. After a long journey, Micromegas reached the globe of Saturn. Despite his being accustomed to seeing new things, he could not at first, on seeing the smallness of the globe and its inhabitants, keep from smiling in that superior fashion in which at times the wisest of men indulge. For Saturn, in a word, is scarcely nine hundred times larger than the earth, and the citizens of that land are dwarfs who are only a mere thousand fathoms tall. At first he and his friends laughed at them a bit, much as an Italian musician laughs at Lully's music when he comes to France. But since the Sirian was intelligent, he quickly understood that a thinking being may very well not be ridiculous because he is only six thousand feet tall. After amazing them, he became acquainted with the Saturnians.

He became an intimate friend of the secretary of the Academy of Saturn, a man of great wit who indeed had invented nothing, but who was well aware of the inventions of other men, and who produced quite good light verse and important computations. I shall relate here, for the benefit of the readers, an unusual conversation which Micromegas had one day with Mr. Secretary.

Chapter II

CONVERSATION OF THE INHABITANT OF SIRIUS
WITH THE INHABITANT OF SATURN

After his Excellency had gone to bed and the secretary had drawn near to his face, Micromegas said: "You must confess that there is much variety in nature."

"Yes," said the Saturnian, "nature is like a flower bed in which the flowers . . ."

"Oh!" said the other, "forget about your flower-bed."

The secretary continued, "It is like a gathering of blondes and brunettes whose dresses . . ."

"What do I care about your brunettes?" said the other.

"Then it is like a gallery of pictures whose features . . ."

"But no," said the traveler, "once more I tell you, nature is like nature. Why try to make comparisons?"

"To please you," answered the secretary.

"I don't want to be pleased," answered the traveler, "I want to be taught. First begin by telling me how many senses the men in your world have."

"We have seventy-two," said the academician, "and every day we complain of the small number. Our imagination surpasses our needs. We find that with our seventy-two senses, with our ring and our five moons, we are too limited. And despite all our curiosity and the fairly large number of passions which come from our seventy-two senses, we have all the time in the world to be bored."

"I believe you," said Micromegas, "for in our world we have almost a thousand senses, and we still have strange vague desires, a strange restlessness which keeps warning us that we are of little consequence, and that there are beings much more perfect. I have traveled a little. I have seen mortals much below us. I have seen others far superior to us. But I have not seen any who have not more desires than real needs, and more needs than satisfaction. Perhaps one day I shall reach the country where nothing is lacking. But up until now no one has given me any real news of that country."

The Saturnian and the Sirian then wore themselves out with conjectures. But after many very ingenious and very insecure arguments, they had to come back to facts. "How long do you live?" asked the Sirian.

"A very short time," answered the small man from Saturn.

"It is the same with us," said the Sirian. "We are always complaining about the short time. It must be a universal law of nature."

"Alas!" said the Saturnian, "we live only five hundred complete revolutions of the sun. (That comes to fifteen thousand years, or approximately, in our way of counting.) You can see that means dying almost at the moment of birth. Our existence is a point, our duration an instant, our globe an atom. We have just begun to learn a few things when death comes before we have any experience. As for me, I don't dare make any plans. I feel like a drop of water in a huge ocean. In front of you, especially, I am ashamed of the ridiculous figure I cut in this world."

Micromegas answered him, "If you were not a philosopher, I should fear to upset you by telling you that our life is seven hundred times longer than yours. But you know too well that when a man has to return his body to the elements, and to reanimate nature under another form—this is called dying—when that moment of metamorphosis has come, to have lived for an eternity or to have lived for a day, are precisely the same thing. I have been in countries where they live a thousand times longer than in my country, and there I discovered that people still complained. But everywhere there are intelligent people who know how to accept their fate and give thanks to the Creator. He spread over this universe abundant varieties with a kind of remarkable uniformity. For example, all thinking beings are different, and all fundamentally resemble one another in the gift of thought, and desires. Matter extends everywhere, but on each globe, it has different properties. How many of these various properties do you count in your matter?"

"If," said the Saturnian, "you are speaking of those properties without which we believe this globe could not exist as it is, we count three hundred, such as extension, impenetrability, mobility, gravitation, divisibility, and so on."

"It seems," replied the traveler, "that this small number sufficed for the plans which the Creator had for your small dwelling. I admire His wisdom in everything. Everywhere I see differences, but also everywhere a sense of proportion. Your globe is small and so are your inhabitants. You have few sensations. Your matter has few properties. All that is the work of Providence. What color is your sun when you examine it closely?"

"A very yellowish white," said the Saturnian. "And when we divide one of its rays, we find it contains seven colors."

"Our sun borders on red," said the Sirian, "and we have thirty-nine primary colors. Among all those I have approached, there is not one sun which resembles another, as on your world there is no face which is not different from all others."

After several questions of this nature, he asked how many essentially different substances they counted on Saturn. He learned that they counted only about thirty, such as God, space, matter, beings which have extension and feeling, beings which have extension, feeling and thought, beings which have thought and no extension, beings which understand themselves and those which do not, and so forth. The Sirian, in whose world they counted three hundred, and who had discovered three thousand others in his travels, amazed to a prodigious degree the philosopher from Saturn. At last, after communicating to one another a bit of what they knew and a great deal of what they did not know, after arguing throughout a revolution of the sun, they decided to make a little philosophical journey together.

Chapter III

Journey of the Two Inhabitants of Sirius and Saturn

Our two philosophers were ready to embark upon the atmosphere of Saturn, with a fine supply of mathematical instruments, when the mistress of the Saturnian, who had heard of this, came in tears to protest. She was an attractive small brunette who was only six hundred and sixty fathoms tall, but who made up for the smallness of her stature by many charms. "Ah! cruel man," she cried, "after resisting you for fifteen hundred years, when at last I was beginning to give in, you leave me to go on a journey with a giant from another world, when I had scarcely spent a hundred years in your arms. Off with you! Curiosity is your only passion; you have never been in love. If you were a real Saturnian, you would be faithful. Where are you trotting off to? What do you want? Our five moons are less mobile than you. Our ring is less variable. It is over now, I shall never love anyone else." The philosopher kissed her, wept with her, despite his being a philosopher, and the lady, after fainting, went off to find consolation with one of the fops of the land.

In the meantime, our two seekers after truth departed. First they jumped on to the ring, which they found rather flat, as a famous inhabitant of our small globe has very well guessed. From there they went from moon to moon. A comet passed very close to the last moon, and they threw themselves on it with their servants and instruments. When they had covered about a hundred and fifty million leagues, they came upon Jupiter's satellites. They went on to Jupiter itself and stayed there a year during which they learned some very fine secrets which would now be in the process of being printed save for the inquisitors who found a few of the propositions a bit harsh. But I read the manuscript in the library of the famous Archbishop of . . . , who, with a generosity and a kindness which cannot be sufficiently praised, let me see his books.

But let us come back to our travelers. After leaving Jupiter, they crossed a space of about one hundred million leagues and came alongside the planet of Mars, which, as you know, is five times smaller than our small globe. They saw two moons which serve this planet, and which have escaped the eyes of our astronomers. I know that Father Castel will deny, and even humorously, the existence of those two moons. But I rely on those who reason by analogy. Those good philosophers know how difficult it would be for Mars, which is so far from the sun, to do without at least two moons. Whatever the truth is, our friends found it so small that they were afraid of finding no sleeping quarters, and they continued on their way like two travelers who scorn a poor village inn and go on to the next town. But the Sirian and his companion soon repented. They continued for a long time and found nothing. At last they saw a faint glimmer. It was the earth. It aroused pity in people coming from Jupiter. Yet, through fear of repenting a second time, they decided to disembark. They passed along the tail of the comet, and finding an aurora borealis close at hand, they climbed into it and reached the earth on the northern coast of the Baltic Sea, the fifth of July, 1737, new style.

Chapter IV
What happened to them on Earth

After resting a while, they ate a breakfast of two mountains which their servants prepared for them quite well. Then they decided to reconnoiter the small country where they were. First they went from north to south. The ordinary steps of the Sirian and his men were about thirty thousand king's feet. The dwarf from Saturn followed at a distance, panting. He had to take about twelve steps to each stride of the other. Just imagine (if it is permissible to make such comparisons) a very small lap-dog following a captain of the guards of the Prussian king.

As those foreigners moved quite fast, they had circled the globe in thirty-six hours. It is true that the sun, or rather the earth, accomplishes a similar journey in a day. But you must remember that one travels more easily by turning on one's axis than when walking on foot. Here they are then back from where they left, after seeing that puddle, almost imperceptible to them, called the "Mediterranean," and that other little pond which under the name of "Great Ocean," encircles the molehill. The dwarf was never in deeper than the calves of his legs, and the other scarcely wet his heels. They did all they could, both going and coming back, above and below, to try to see whether this globe was inhabited or not. They stooped, they lay down, they felt everywhere with their hands. But their eyes and hands were not proportioned to the tiny beings which crawl here. They did not feel the slightest sensation which might cause them to suspect that we and our colleagues, the other inhabitants of this globe, have the honor to exist.

The dwarf, who at times judged a bit too hastily, decided first that there was no one on the earth. His first reason was that he had seen no one. Micromegas politely made him feel that this was bad reasoning. "For," he said, "you do not see with your small eyes certain stars of the fiftieth magnitude which I see very distinctly. Do you thereby conclude that those stars do not exist?"

"But," said the dwarf, "I carefully felt with my hands."

"But," answered the other, "you did a bad job."

"But," said the dwarf, "this globe is so badly constructed and so irregular and of a shape which seems so ridiculous to me! Everything seems in chaos here. Do you see those little brooks, no one of which goes in a straight line, and those ponds that are neither round nor square nor oval, nor in any regular form, and all those small pointed things with which this globe is studded and which took the skin off my feet? (He was referring to the mountains.) Look again at the shape of the entire globe, how flat it is at the poles, how awkwardly it turns around the sun, in such a way that necessarily the polar regions are waste lands. What really makes me believe that there is no one here, is that it seems to me that intelligent people would not want to live here."

"Well," said Micromegas, "perhaps those who live here are not intelligent people. But there is some indication that this was not made for nothing. You say that everything is laid out by rule and line in Saturn and in Jupiter. Well, it is perhaps for that very reason that here there is a bit of confusion. Haven't I told you that in my travels I have always noticed variety?" The Saturnian gave answer to all these arguments. The discussion would never have ended, if fortunately Micromegas, as he grew excited with talking, had not broken the string of his diamond necklace. The diamonds fell to the ground. They were attractive small stones, quite unequal, the heaviest of which weighed four hundred pounds, and the smallest fifty. The dwarf picked up a few of them and noticed when he put them to his eye, that these diamonds, because of the way they were cut, were excellent microscopes. He therefore took a small microscope of one hundred and sixty feet in diameter and put it to his eye. Micromegas chose one of two thousand five hundred feet. They were excellent. But at first nothing could be seen with their help. They had to be adjusted. Finally the inhabitant from Saturn saw something imperceptible moving under water in the Baltic Sea. It was a whale. He picked it up very skillfully with his little finger, and putting it on the nail of his thumb, he showed it to the Sirian who began to laugh at the extreme smallness of the inhabitants of our globe. The Saturnian, convinced that our world was inhabited, quickly imagined that it was inhabited solely by whales, and since he was a great reasoner, he wished to find out from where so small an atom drew its movement and whether it had ideas and a will and freedom. This discomfited Micromegas, who examined the animal very patiently. The result of the examination was that it was impossible to believe a soul was lodged there. The two travelers were therefore disposed to believe that there was no spirit on our earth, when with the help of the microscope they saw something bigger than a whale which was floating on the Baltic Sea. It is known that at that very time, a band of philosophers were returning from the Arctic Circle where they had gone to make observations of which no one up until then had taken any notice. The newspapers said that their ship sank off the coast of Bothnia and that they had difficulty in escaping. But in this world we never know the real story. I am going to tell with great simplicity what actually took place, without adding any word of my own. This is no small effort for an historian.

Chapter V

EXPERIENCES AND REASONINGS OF THE TWO TRAVELERS

Micromegas gently stretched out his hand to the spot where the object appeared, and putting out two fingers, and withdrawing them for fear of being mistaken, then opening them and closing them, he very skillfully picked up the ship carrying those gentlemen, and again placed it on his nail, without squeezing too much, for fear of crushing it. "This animal is very different from the first," said the dwarf from Saturn. The Sirian placed the supposed animal in the hollow of his hand. The passengers and the members of the crew who had thought a cyclone had lifted them up and believed they were on a kind of rock, all started to move about. The sailors took casks of wine, threw them on to the hand of Micromegas, and jumped down after them. The geometricians took their quadrants, their sectors and some Lapp girls, and climbed down to the fingers of the Sirian. They made such a bustle that at last he felt something moving which tickled his fingers. It was an iron-shod pole which they were driving a foot deep into his index finger. He judged, from this prickling sensation, that something had come out from the small animal he was holding. But at first he did not suspect anything more than that. The microscope, which could hardly distinguish a whale and a ship, had no power to see beings so imperceptible as men. I have no desire to offend the vanity of anyone, but I am obliged to ask the leading citizens to make a small observation with me. When we take on the size of men of about five feet, we do not cut on the earth a bigger figure than would an animal of approximately the six hundred thousandth part of an inch in height on a ball ten feet in circumference. Imagine a being which could hold the earth in its hand, and which had organs in proportion to ours. It is quite possible that there are a large number of these beings. Then I beg you to imagine what they would think of those battles which won for us two villages which later we had to give back.

I do not doubt that if some captain of the tall grenadiers ever reads this work, he will add two feet at least to the hats of his troop. But I warn him that this will be in vain, that he and his men will never be anything save infinitely small.

What marvellous skill did our philosopher from Sirius need then in order to see the atoms of which I have just spoken! When Leeuwenhoek and Hartsoeker were the first to see or believed they saw the germ from which we are formed, they did not make, not by a long way, such a surprising discovery. What pleasure Micromegas felt in seeing those little machines move, in examining all their tricks and in following them in all their operations! He shouted with glee. How joyfully he put one of his microscopes into the hands of his traveling companion! "I see them," they both said at the same time. "Don't you see them carrying bundles, bending down and standing up again?" As they said these words, their hands trembled, at the pleasure of seeing such new objects, and at the fear of losing them. The Saturnian, passing from an excess of doubt to an excess of belief, thought he saw them trying to propagate the species.

"Ah!" he said, "I have caught nature in the act." But he was deceived by appearances, which happens only too often whether microscopes are used or not.

Chapter VI

WHAT HAPPENED TO THEM WITH THE MEN

Micromegas, a much better observer than his dwarf, clearly saw that the atoms were talking to another. He called his companion's attention to this, who, ashamed of having been mistaken over the issue of pro-creation, was unwilling to believe that such species were able to com-municate ideas to one another. He had the gift of languages as well as the Sirian, but he did not hear our atoms speaking and he assumed they were not speaking. Moreover, how could those imperceptible beings have organs of speech and what would they have to say? In order to speak, you have to think, or almost; but if they thought, they would then have the equivalent of a soul. Now, to attribute the equivalent of a soul to that species seemed absurd to him. "But," said the Sirian, "you believed just now that they were making love. Do you think it possible to make love without thinking and without uttering some words, or at least without making oneself understood? Do you even suppose it is more difficult to produce an argument than a child?"

"To me they both seem great mysteries. I no longer dare believe or deny," said the dwarf. "I no longer have an opinion. We must try to examine these insects. We will argue afterwards."

"Well spoken," replied Micromegas. And immediately he pulled out a pair of scissors with which he cut his nails. With a paring from his thumb nail, he made on the spot a kind of large speaking trumpet, like a gigantic funnel, whose small end he placed in his ear. The circum-ference of the funnel surrounded the ship and all the crew. The weak-est voice entered the circular fibers of the nail, and in this way, thanks to his ingenuity, the philosopher from above heard perfectly the buzzing of our insects from below. In a short time, he was able to dis-tinguish words, and at last to hear French. The dwarf also, although with more difficulty. The amazement of the travelers grew with each moment. They heard mites talking quite good sense, and this trick of nature seemed inexplicable to them. You can well believe that the Sirian and his dwarf burned with impatience to enter into conversation with the atoms. The dwarf feared that his thunderous voice and espe-cially the voice of Micromegas would deafen the mites without being understood by them. They had to reduce the strength of the voice. They put in their mouths a kind of small toothpick of which the very fine end came close to the ship. The Sirian held the dwarf on his knees, and the ship with its crew on a nail. He bent his head and spoke in a low voice. At last, by means of all these precautions and many others still, he began to speak with these words:

"Invisible insects, whom it has pleased the hand of the Creator to have born in the abyss of the infinitely small, I thank Him for having deigned to reveal to me secrets which seemed unfathomable. Perhaps at my court people would not deign to look at you, but I scorn no one, and I offer you my protection."

If anyone was ever surprised, it was the people who heard these

words. They could not imagine from where they came. The ship's
chaplain recited prayers of exorcism, the sailors cursed, and the ship's
philosophers invented a system. But no matter what system they made,
they could never guess who was speaking to them. The dwarf from
Saturn, who had a softer voice than Micromegas, then told them in
very few words with what species they had to deal. He told them of the
journey from Saturn and made them aware what Mr. Micromegas was.
After sympathizing with them for being so small, he asked them if they
had always been in this miserable state so close to nonexistence, and
what they did on a globe which seemed to belong to whales, if they
were happy, if they multiplied, if they had a soul, and a hundred other
questions of this kind.

One reasoner in the group, bolder than the others, and shocked that
it was doubted he had a soul, looked at his interlocutor through the
eyelet holes on a quadrant, made two observations, and at the third,
spoke thus: "So you believe, Sir, because you are a thousand fathoms
tall, that you are a . . ."

"A thousand fathoms!" cried the dwarf. "Good heavens! how can he
know my height? A thousand fathoms! He is not an inch off. Why, this
atom has measured me! He is a geometrician and knows my height.
And I who can see him only through a microscope, don't yet know his!"

"Yes, I have measured you," said the physicist, "and I can also easily
measure your big friend." The proposition was accepted. His
Excellency stretched out full length, for if he had remained standing,
his head would have been too far above the clouds. Our philosophers
planted in him a big tree on a spot which Dr. Swift would name, but
which I shall refrain from calling by its name, because of my great
respect for the ladies. Then, by a series of triangles tied together, they
concluded that what they saw was in reality a young man one hundred
and twenty thousand royal feet long.

At that moment Micromegas said these words, "More than ever I see
that we must not judge anything by its apparent size. O Lord, who have
given intelligence to beings which seem so contemptible, the infinitely
small costs You as little as the infinitely great. If it is possible that there
are creatures smaller than these, they may still have minds superior to
those magnificent animals I have seen in the sky whose foot alone
would cover the globe to which I have come."

One of the philosophers answered him that he might indeed believe
there are intelligent beings much smaller than man. He related to him,
not all the fables Virgil said about bees, but what Swammerdam discovered, and what Réaumur dissected. He taught him, in a word, that
there are animals which are to bees what the bees are to man, what the

Sirian himself was to those tremendous animals he had mentioned,
and what those great animals are to other beings before which they
seem like mere atoms. Gradually the conversations became interesting,
and Micromegas spoke as follows.

Chapter VII

CONVERSATION WITH THE MEN

"O intelligent atoms, in whom the Almighty was pleased to manifest
His skill and His power, you must doubtless enjoy very pure pleasures
on your globe, for having so little body and seeing to be all spirit, you
must pass your lives in love and in thought, which is the true life of spirits. I have seen real happiness nowhere, but it is doubtless here."

At this speech all the philosophers shook their heads, and one of
them, more frank than the others, confessed with candor that apart
from a small number of inhabitants who were held in very little esteem,
all the rest were a crowd of fools, of wicked and unhappy men and
women. "We have more matter than we need," he said, "in order to do
much evil, if evil comes from matter; and too much spirit, if evil comes
from the spirit. Are you aware, for example, that at this moment when
I am speaking to you, there are one hundred thousand fools of our
species, wearing hats, who are killing or being killed by one hundred
thousand other animals wearing turbans, and that almost throughout
the entire earth this is how people have been behaving from time
immemorial?" The Sirian shuddered and asked what the reason could
be for those horrible disputes between such puny animals. "A few mudpiles as big as your heel," said the philosopher, "are the issue. It is not
that one of those millions of men who are slaughtering one another,
claims one straw on the mudpiles. The problem is to know whether it
will belong to a certain man called *Sultan* or to another called, I don't
know why, *Caesar.* Neither one has even seen or ever will see the bit of
earth in question. And almost none of those animals who are mutually
slaughtering one another, has ever seen the animal for which he is
slaughtered."

"Wretch!" cried the Sirian indignantly, "such an excess of mad rage
is inconceivable! I have the urge to take three steps and crush with
three blows of my foot this anthill of ludicrous assassins."

"Don't go to that trouble," the philosopher answered him, "they are
working well enough toward their own ruin. Know that after ten years,
no more than a hundredth part of those wretches are alive. Know that
even if they have not drawn their sword, hunger, fatigue or intemper-

ance kill almost all of them. Moreover, they aren't the ones to be punished, but those sedentary barbarians who in their private offices, when they are digesting their food, order the massacre of a million men, and then afterwards solemnly offer up thanks to God for the deed."

The traveler felt deep pity for the tiny human race in which he discovered such astonishing contrasts. "Since you belong to the small number of wise men," he said to these gentlemen, "and since apparently you kill no one for money, tell me, I beg you, how you spend your time."

"We dissect flies," said the philosopher, "we measure lines and gather numerical information. We agree upon two or three points which we understand, and we disagree on two or three thousand which we do not understand."

Immediately a whim took the Sirian and the Saturnian to question these thinking atoms, in order to learn the things on which they agreed. "What is the distance," asked the Saturnian, "between the Dog-star and Gemini?"

They all answered in chorus, "Thirty-two and a half degrees."

"What is the distance from here to the moon?"

"Sixty times the radius of the earth, in round numbers."

"What does your air weigh?" He thought he had caught them, but they all said to him that air weighs about nine hundred times less than a similar volume of the lightest water, and nineteen thousand times less than ducat gold. The little dwarf from Saturn, amazed at their answers, was tempted to take for sorcerers those same people to whom he had refused a soul a quarter of an hour previously.

Finally, Micromegas said to them," Since you are so well acquainted with what is outside of you, doubtless you know even better what is within. Tell me what your soul is and how you form your ideas." The philosophers all spoke at the same time as before, but they were all of different opinions. The oldest quoted Aristotle, another pronounced the name of Descartes, a third that of Malebranche, a fourth Leibnitz, and still another Locke. An aged Peripatetic said loudly and confidently, "The soul is an entelechy, and a proof of its power to be what it is. That is what Aristotle expressly states, on page 633 of the Louvre edition: Ἐντελεχεία ἐστι."

I don't understand Greek too well," said the giant.

"Nor do I," said the philosophical mite.

"Why then," the Sirian continued, "do you quote a certain Aristotle in Greek?"

"Because," answered the scholar, "one must quote what one doesn't understand at all in the language one understands the least."

The Cartesian began speaking and said, "The soul is a pure spirit which has received in its mother's womb all metaphysical ideas, and which, on leaving it, has to go to school and learn all over again what it knew so well and will never know again."

"There is no point then," answered the animal eight leagues long, "for your soul to be so learned in your mother's womb, if it is so ignorant when you have a beard on your chin. But what do you mean by spirit?"

"What kind of question is that?" said the reasoner. "I have no idea. They say it is not matter."

"But at least do you know what matter is?"

"Yes, I do," the man replied. "For example, this stone is gray and of a certain shape. It has three dimensions, is heavy and divisible."

"Well," said the Sirian, "will you tell me what this thing is which seems to you divisible, heavy and gray? You see a few attributes, but do you know basically what the thing is?"

"No!" said the other.

"Then you don't know what matter is."

Mr. Micromegas, then speaking to another wise man whom he held on his thumb, asked him what his soul was and what it did. "Nothing at all," answered the disciple of Malebranche. "God does everything for me. I see everything in Him and I do everything in Him. He does everything without my interfering."

"It would be as worth while not to exist," the sage from Sirius went on. "And you, my friend," he said to a disciple of Leibnitz who was there, "what is your soul?"

The Leibnitzian answered, "It is a hand which shows the hours while my body chimes. Or if you prefer, it is my soul which chimes while my body shows the hour. Or my soul is the mirror of the universe, and my body is the frame of the mirror. All that is clear."

A little partisan of Locke was quite nearby, and when they finally spoke to him, he said, "I do not know how I think, but I know that I have never had a thought save by means of my senses. That there are immaterial and intelligent beings I do not doubt, but that it is impossible for God to communicate thought to matter I strongly doubt. I revere the power of God. It is not my place to limit it. I affirm nothing and I am satisfied with believing there are more things possible than we think."

The animal from Sirius smiled. He did not find this last man the least wise, and the dwarf from Saturn would have embraced the follower of Locke if there hadn't been a vast difference in size. But unfortunately there was present a small animalcule in a clerical hat who interrupted all the philosophical animalcules. He said he knew the entire secret. It was in the *Summa* of Saint Thomas. He looked the two celestial inhabitants up and down, and asserted that their persons, their worlds, their suns, their stars, all were created solely for man. At this speech, our two travelers fell on each other, overcome with that inextinguishable laughter which, according to Homer, is the lot of the gods. Their shoulders and bellies shook, and in these convulsions, the ship which the Sirian had on his nail fell into a pocket of the Saturnian's trousers. These two good people looked for it a long time. At last, they recovered the ship and crew and set everything up again in excellent order. The Sirian picked up the mites again. He spoke to them again with much kindness although he was a bit angry in the bottom of his heart at seeing that infinitely small beings had an infinitely great pride. He promised to prepare a fine book of philosophy for them, written very small so that they could read it; and that in this book they would see the explanation of everything. To be sure, he did give them this volume before his departure. They took it to Paris, to the Academy of Sciences. But when the secretary opened it, he saw only a book with blank pages. "Ah!" he said, "I thought as much."

Alphonse Daudet

THE POPE'S MULE

La Mule du Pape

Of all the pretty sayings, proverbs, and adages with which our peasants in Provence lace their speech, I don't know any that are more picturesque or more unusual than this one. In a radius of fifteen leagues around my windmill, whenever they talk about a grudge-bearing, vindictive man, they say: "That man! Watch out! . . . He's like the Pope's she-mule, and holds back his kick for seven years."

I searched for a long time to see where that proverb might come from, and the story of that papal mule and that kick held in reserve for seven years. No one here has been able to give me information on that subject, not even Francet Mamaï, my fife player, even though he has his Provençal legends at his fingertips. Francet agrees with me that, at the bottom of it, there's some old chronicle of the Avignon region; but he's never heard talk of it except by way of the proverb.

"You'll only find that in the cicadas' library," the old fifer said to me, laughing.

That sounded like a good idea, and, seeing that the cicadas' library is right outside my door, I went and shut myself up in it for a week.

It's a wonderful library, admirably fitted out, open to poets day and night, and staffed by little librarians with cymbals who make music for you the whole time. I spent a few delightful days there, and after a week of research—on my back—I finally found what I wanted; that is, the history of my mule and that notorious kick held in reserve for seven years. The tale is a pretty one, though somewhat naïve, and I'll try to tell it to you just as I read it yesterday morning in a sky-blue manuscript that had a good smell of dry lavender, with big threads of gossamer for bookmarks.

*

If you didn't see Avignon when the Popes were there, you've never seen a thing. For merriment, liveliness, animation, the busy series of festivals, there's never been a city like it. From morning to evening there were processions, pilgrimages, the streets strewn with flowers and overhung by high-warp tapestries, arrivals of cardinals on the

Rhône, banners in the wind, galleys decked with flags, the Pope's soldiers chanting in Latin on the squares, the rattles of the monks collecting alms. And then, from top to bottom of the houses that huddled around the great Palace of the Popes, buzzing like bees around the hive, there was, besides, the click-clack of the lace frames, the to-and-fro of shuttles weaving the gold for chasubles, the little hammers of the engravers of altar cruets, the soundboards being finished in the lute makers' shops, the hymns sung by the women setting up the warp on looms; and, above all the rest, the sound of the bells, and always a few Provençal drums that could be heard rumbling there, toward the bridge. Because, where we live, when the populace is happy, it must dance, it must dance; and, since in those days the city streets were too narrow for the farandole, fife and drum players took up their station on the bridge of Avignon, in the cool breeze from the Rhône, and day and night "people danced there, people danced there" . . . Oh, the happy time! The happy city! Halberds that did not strike; prisons of the state in which wine was placed to cool. Never a food shortage; never a war . . . That's how the Popes of the County of Avignon knew how to govern their people; that's why their people missed them so when they left! . . .

There's one especially, a good old man, who was called Boniface . . . Oh, how many tears were shed in Avignon for *him* when he died! He was such an amiable and pleasing ruler! How kindly he smiled at you while seated on his mule! And whenever you passed by him—whether you were a poor little extractor of madder dye or the chief justice of the city—he gave you a blessing so politely! A true Pope of Yvetot,[1] but of an Yvetot in Provence, with something delicate in his laughter, a sprig of marjoram in his biretta, and not the slightest Jeanneton . . . The only "sweetheart Jeanneton" that that kindly father ever had was his vineyard—a little vineyard he had planted himself, three leagues from Avignon, among the myrtles of Châteauneuf.

Every Sunday, on leaving vespers, the worthy man went to pay his court to it, and when he was up there, sitting in the beneficent sunshine, his mule nearby, his cardinals all around stretched out at the feet of the vinestocks, then he had a flagon of the local wine uncorked—that beautiful, ruby-colored wine which, ever since, has been called Châteauneuf-du-Pape—and he would taste it in little sips, looking at his vineyard tenderly. Then, the flagon emptied, the sun setting, he

---

[1] A word play with reference to a humorous song text by Pierre-Jean de Béranger (1780–1857), "Le roi d'Yvetot," about a very plain-living, jolly king with a sweetheart named Jeanneton. (Yvetot is a small town in Normandy.)—Trans.

would return joyously to his city, followed by his entire chapter of canons; and, when he crossed the bridge of Avignon,[2] in the midst of the drums and the farandoles, his mule, enlivened by the music, would go into a little hopping amble, while the Pope himself beat time to the dance music with his biretta, which greatly shocked his cardinals but caused all the plain people to say: "Oh, what a good ruler! Oh, what a fine Pope!"

*

After his vineyard at Châteauneuf, what the Pope loved most in the world was his she-mule. The dear old man was crazy about that animal. Every night before going to bed, he went to see whether her stable was properly closed, whether there was nothing lacking in her feeding trough; and he would never have risen from his table without seeing prepared before his eyes a large bowl of French-style wine,[3] with plenty of sugar and spices, which he himself brought to the mule, despite his cardinals' remarks. . . . It must also be said that the animal was worth all of this. She was a beautiful black mule with red spots, surefooted, with a gleaming coat and wide, full hindquarters; she carried with pride her small, lean head that was lavishly accoutred with pompoms, bows, silver jingle bells, and tassels. In addition, she was as gentle as an angel, with candid eyes and two long ears that were always in motion, giving her a good-natured appearance. All Avignon esteemed her and, when she wandered through the streets, everyone treated her as courteously as possible; because everyone knew that that was the best way to be in good standing at the papal court, and that, with her innocent appearance, the Pope's mule had led more than one person to good fortune — as a proof, Tistet Védène and his prodigious adventure.

This Tistet Védène was basically a brazen-faced young rascal whom his father, Guy Védène, a goldsmith, had been forced to throw out of his house because he refused to do any work and was keeping the apprentices from doing theirs. For six months he was to be seen dragging his coat through every gutter in Avignon, but especially in the vicinity of the papal palace; because for some time the rogue had had a plan concerning the Pope's mule, and you're about to see that it was pretty shrewd. . . . One day, when His Holiness was on an outing, all alone with his mount, alongside the city walls, there was our Tistet, greeting him and saying, with his hands joined together in admiration:

---

[2] Every French commentator gleefully points out that Châteauneuf and Avignon are on the same side of the Rhône, so that this crossing of the bridge is an error (or a fantasy?). — Trans.

[3] Warmed-up red wine with sugar, cinnamon, and other flavorings. — Trans.

"Oh, my heavens! Great Holy Father, what a fine mule you have there! . . . Let me look at her for a while. . . . Oh, Pope, such a beautiful mule! . . . The Emperor of Germany doesn't have one like her."

And he patted her, and spoke gently to her as if addressing a well-born young lady.

"Come here, my jewel, my treasure, my precious pearl . . ."

And the good Pope, sincerely touched, said to himself:

"What a good little boy! . . . How nice he is to my mule!"

And then, the next day, do you know what happened? Tistet Védène swapped his old yellow coat for a beautiful lace alb, a violet silk short cape such as priests wear, and buckled shoes, and he joined the Pope's choir school, where never before that time had anyone been received but noblemen's sons and cardinals' nephews. Just see what intrigue will do! . . . But Tistet didn't stop there.

Once in the Pope's service, the rogue continued the game that had stood him in such good stead. Insolent with everybody, he lavished his cares and kindness only on the mule, and was always to be found in the palace courtyards with a handful of oats or a little bunch of sainfoin, amiably shaking its clusters of pink flowers while looking at the Holy Father's balcony, as if to say: "Well? . . . Who is this for? . . ." So much so, that the good Pope, who felt he was growing old, finally assigned him the task of taking care of the stable and bringing the mule her bowl of French-style wine; this did not make the cardinals happy.

*

Nor was the mule happy about it, either. . . . Now, when the time for her wine arrived, she always saw arriving in her stable five or six young clerics from the choir school, who quickly nestled in the straw with their short capes and their laces; a moment later, a pleasant, warm aroma of burnt sugar and spices filled the stable, and Tistet Védène appeared, carefully carrying the bowl of French-style wine. Then the martyrdom of the poor animal would begin.

That flavored wine she loved so much, which kept her warm, which lent her wings—they were so cruel as to bring it over to her, there in her feeding trough, to let her inhale it; then, when her nostrils were filled with it—presto, vanished! The beautiful, fiery-pink beverage would completely disappear into the gullets of those little brats. . . . And, as if stealing her wine wasn't enough, all those little clerics were like devils when they were drunk! . . . One of them pulled her ears, another, her tail; Quiquet climbed on her back, Béluguet tried out his biretta on her, and not one of those rascals imagined that, with a flick of her crupper or a kick, the good animal could have sent them all to the pole star, or even farther . . . But no! It's not for nothing that you're the Pope's mule, the mule of benedictions and indulgences. . . . No matter how the youngsters irritated her, she didn't get angry; and her rancor was directed only at Tistet Védène. . . . Now, when she sensed that *he* was behind her, her hooves itched her, and truly she had good reasons. That good-for-nothing Tistet played such nasty tricks on her! He thought up such cruel things to do when he got drunk! . . .

Didn't he get the idea one day to make her climb up with him to the bell tower of the choir school, up there, way up there, at the pinnacle of the palace? . . . And what I'm now telling you isn't a fairy tale; two hundred thousand inhabitants of Provence saw it happen. Picture the terror of that unhappy mule when, after twisting her way up a spiral staircase blindly for an hour, and after climbing heaven knows how many steps, she suddenly found herself on a platform inundated with dazzling light, and caught sight, at a thousand feet below her, of an entire fantastic Avignon, the market stalls no bigger than hazelnuts, the Pope's soldiers in front of their barracks like red ants, and, over yonder, on a silver thread, a little, microscopic bridge on which "people were dancing, people were dancing." . . . Oh, the poor animal! What panic she felt! The cry she uttered made all the windows in the palace shake.

"What's wrong? What are they doing to her?" exclaimed the good Pope, dashing out onto his balcony.

Tistet Védène was already in the courtyard, pretending to weep and pull out his hair:

"Oh, great Holy Father, you ask what's wrong? Your mule has climbed the bell tower."

"All by herself?"

"Yes, great Holy Father, all by herself. . . . See! Look at her up there. . . . Do you see the tips of her ears sticking out? . . . They look like a pair of swallows . . ."

"Mercy!" cried the poor Pope, raising his eyes. "But she must have gone crazy! But she's going to get killed. . . . Will you come down from there, you wretched thing?! . . ."

Alas![4] As for her, she would have liked nothing better than to go down . . . but which way? The staircase wasn't even to be thought of; those contraptions can be climbed up, at best; but going down them, you could break your legs a hundred times. . . . And the poor mule was in misery; while walking around the platform, her large eyes glazed over with dizziness, she kept thinking about Tistet Védène.

---

[4] The French word here, *"pécaïre!,"* is a typically Provençal exclamation.—Trans.

"Oh, you villain, if I get out of this . . . what a kick you'll get tomorrow morning!"

That thought of the kick put a little heart back into her; otherwise, she wouldn't have been able to stick it out. . . . Finally they managed to get her down from there, but it was quite a job. She had to be let down with a winch, ropes, and a litter. Just imagine how humiliating it was for a Pope's mule to see herself hanging up so high, swimming with her feet in the air like a June bug at the end of a string! And with everyone in Avignon watching her!

The unhappy animal didn't sleep all night. She kept thinking she was still turning to and fro on that accursed platform, with the laughter of the city below her; then she thought about that vile Tistet Védène and the neat kick she was going to treat him to on the following morning. Oh, my friends, what a kick! They'd see the smoke from it all the way to Pampérigouste.[5] . . . Now, while this lovely reception was being planned for him in the stable, do you know what Tistet Védène was doing? He was going down the Rhône, singing, on a papal galley, on his way to the court of Naples as one of the company of young noblemen that the city used to send annually to Queen Jeanne[6] to perfect themselves in diplomacy and fine manners. Tistet wasn't a nobleman, but the Pope desired to reward him for the attentions he had shown his animal, particularly for his active participation on the day when she was rescued.

Wasn't the mule disappointed the next day!

"Oh, the villain! He suspected something!" she thought, shaking her jingle bells in a rage. "But it's all the same; go on, you rat! You'll find your kick when you get back. . . . I'll save it for you!"

And she saved it for him.

After Tistet's departure, the Pope's mule regained her calm life style and her former ways. No more Quiquet, no more Béluguet in the stable. The good old days of the French-style wine had returned and, with them, her good humor, her long siestas, and her little gavotte step whenever she crossed the bridge of Avignon. And yet, ever since her adventure, people in town always showed a little coolness toward her. There were whispers when she passed by; old folks shook their heads, children laughed and pointed to the bell tower. The good Pope himself no longer had as much confidence in his friend as formerly, and when

---

[5] A fictitious village mentioned in several of the *Letters from My Windmill* stories. — Trans.
[6] Jeanne I of Anjou, ruler of the Kingdom of Naples from 1343 to 1382. — Trans.

he allowed himself to take a little nap on her back on Sundays on his way back from the vineyard, he always had this thought in the back of his mind: "What if I were to wake up up there, on the platform?" The mule noticed all this, and suffered from it, but said nothing; it was only when Tistet Védène's name was pronounced in her presence that her long ears quivered, and she sharpened the iron of her shoes on the pavement with a little laugh.

Seven years went by in that way; then, at the end of those seven years, Tistet Védène returned from the court of Naples. His appointed time there was not yet over, but he had learned that the chief purveyor of mustard to the Pope had just died suddenly in Avignon, and, since the office seemed like a good one to him, he had arrived in great haste to apply for it.

When that intriguer Védène entered the great hall of the palace, the Holy Father had trouble recognizing him, he was so much taller and had filled out so much. It must also be said that, on his part, the good Pope had grown old and didn't see well without his spectacles.

Tistet wasn't intimidated.

"What! Great Holy Father, you no longer recognize me? It's I, Tistet Védène! . . ."

"Védène? . . ."

"Yes, yes, you know . . . the one who used to bring the French-style wine to your mule."

"Oh, yes . . . yes . . . I remember. . . . A good little boy, that Tistet Védène! . . . And now, what does he ask of us?"

"Oh, not much, great Holy Father. . . . I've come to request of you . . . By the way, do you still have her, your mule? And is she in good health? . . . Oh, good! . . . I've come to request of you the office of the chief purveyor of mustard, who has just died."

"Chief purveyor of mustard—you! But you're too young. How old are you, anyway?"

"Twenty years and two months old, illustrious Pontiff, exactly five years older than your mule. . . . Ah, by heaven, that fine animal! . . . If you only knew how I loved that mule! . . . How I missed her when I was in Italy! . . . Won't you let me see her?"

"Yes, my child, you'll see her," said the good Pope, deeply touched. "And since you love that fine animal so much, I don't want you to be separated from her any longer. From this day forward, I attach you to my person as chief purveyor of mustard. . . . My cardinals will raise the roof, but I don't care! I'm used to it. . . . Come see us tomorrow when vespers are over, and we'll hand over to you the insignia of your office in the presence of our chapter of canons; and then . . . I'll take you to

see the mule, and you'll come to the vineyard with both of us. . . . Ho,
ho! Go now . . ."

I have no need to tell you how happy Tistet Védène was on leaving
the great hall, or how impatiently he awaited the ceremony on the
following day. And yet there was someone in the palace who was even
happier and more impatient than he: it was the mule. From the
moment of Védène's return until vespers on the following day, the
awesome beast didn't stop stuffing herself with oats and kicking out
at the wall with her hind hooves. She, too, was getting ready for the
ceremony.

And thus, the next day, after vespers had been recited, Tistet Védène
made his entry into the courtyard of the papal palace. All of the high
clergymen were there, the cardinals in red robes, the devil's advocate[7]
in black velvet, the abbots of the monastery with their little miters, the
church wardens of Saint-Agrico, the violet short capes of the choir
school, as well as the minor clergymen, the Pope's soldiers in dress
uniform, the three brotherhoods of penitents, the hermits from Mont
Ventoux[8] with their fierce expressions, the young cleric walking behind
them carrying the handbell, the flagellant monks stripped to the waist,
the florid sacristans in judges' robes, everyone, everyone, down to
the people who hand out holy water, who light candles and put them
out . . . there wasn't a single one missing. . . . Oh, what a beautiful ordi-
nation it was! Bells, firecrackers, sunshine, music, and constantly
those rabid drummers leading the dance over yonder on the bridge
of Avignon.

When Védène made his appearance in the midst of the assembly, his
noble bearing and good looks touched off a murmur of admiration. He
was a magnificent Provençal, but one of the blond type, with plentiful
hair curling at the tips and a little wisp of beard, which seemed to be
made of the filings of fine metal that had fallen from the graving tool
of his father, the goldsmith. A rumor was afloat that the fingers of
Queen Jeanne had sometimes toyed with that blond beard; and,
indeed "Lord" Védène had the boastful air and absentminded gaze of
men whom queens have loved. . . . On that day, to honor his native
land, he had exchanged his Neapolitan garments for a Provençal-style
coat edged with pink, and on his headgear there waved a large ibis
plume from the Camargue.[9]

---

[7] The theologian appointed to plead against a candidate for canonization; the entire ceremony here is wildly exaggerated in a spirit of burlesque. — Trans.

[8] A mountain in the same modern *département* as Avignon (Vaucluse). — Trans.

[9] Wetlands in the delta of the Rhône. — Trans.

As soon as he came in, the chief purveyor of mustard greeted the assembly gallantly and made his way to the high flight of steps where the Pope was waiting to hand over the insignia of his office: the yellow boxwood spoon and the saffron outfit. The mule was at the foot of the steps, completely harnessed and ready to leave for the vineyard. . . . When he came near her, Tistet Védène had a kind smile for her, and stopped to give her two or three little friendly taps on the back, looking out of the corner of his eye to see whether the Pope was watching. The position was a good one. . . . The mule started into motion:

"Here you are! Take this, villain! I've been saving it for you for seven years now!"

And she launched an awesome kick at him, so awesome that, even as far off as Pampérigouste, they could see the smoke from it, a whirl-wind of blond smoke in which an ibis feather was whirling: all that was left of the unfortunate Tistet Védène! . . .

Kicks from mules aren't usually that overwhelming; but this mule belonged to a Pope, and besides, just imagine: she had been saving it for him for seven years. . . . There's no finer example of an ecclesiastical grudge.

Jules Laforgue

SALOMÉ

To be born is to depart; to die is to return.
PROVERBS FROM THE KINGDOM OF ANNAM,
COLLECTED BY FATHER JOURDAIN OF FOREIGN
MISSIONS.

I

The dog days had come and gone two thousand times since an elementary rhythmic revolution of the Palace Mandarins had elevated the first Tetrarch, a minor Roman proconsul, to this throne (hereditary, henceforth, but through careful selection) of the Esoteric White Islands (henceforth, lost to history), but that unusual title of Tetrarch was retained because it had as sacred a ring to it as Monarch, and implied in addition the seven symbols of statehood clinging to the prefix "tetra" but not to "monos."

With pylons, three blocks of them, squat and stark, inner courtyards, galleries, vaults, and the famous Hanging Park, its jungles undulating in the Atlantic breezes, and the Observatory's one eye on the lookout six hundred feet up, near the sky, and a hundred flights of sphinxes and cynocephali: the tetrarchic palace was no more than a monolith, carved, excavated, hollowed, compartmented, and finally burnished into a mountain of black basalt streaked with white, extended by a pier of sonorous pavement, with a double row of poplars, funereal violet, in tubs, projecting far out into the shifting solitude of the sea, until it reached an eternal rock, very much like an ossified sponge, holding out a pretty comic-opera beacon toward the night-prowling junks.

Titanic hulk of gloom, streaked with pallor! Those ivory-black façades give so mysterious a reflection of today's July sun, that sun above the sea, darkly reflected, which the owls of the Hanging Park can contemplate without eyestrain from the tops of their dusty fir trees.

At the pier's edge the galley that had come, the day before, carrying those two unwelcome princes who claimed to be the son and nephew

165

of a certain northern satrap, swayed in its moorings, discussed by a few languid silhouettes.

Now, while high noon stagnated on (the festival would not begin officially until three o'clock), the palace slept away the afternoon, postponed the stretch that would end its siesta.

The followers of those northern princes and the Tetrarch's men could be heard laughing loudly, in the court where the conduits met, laughing without understanding one another, playing quoits, exchanging tobacco. A lesson was offered to these foreign colleagues on the proper grooming of white elephants. . . .

"But there are no white elephants in our country," they tried to say.

And they saw how the grooms blessed themselves, as if warding off blasphemous ideas. And then they gaped at the peacocks strutting above the fountain, moving in circles, their tails iridescent in the sunlight; and then they entertained themselves—they really went too far!—with the guttural echoes of their barbaric shouts.

The Tetrarch, Emerald-Archetypas, appeared on the central terrace, taking off his gloves in honor of the sun, universal Artist of the Zenith, Firefly of the Higher Sky, etc.; and that rabble rushed back inside to attend to their business.

Oh, see the Tetrarch on the terrace, see the dynastic caryatid!

Behind him the city, already humming festively (drying out its copious irrigation); and farther on, beyond those ridiculous ramparts and their enamelwork of tiny yellow flowers, how contentedly the fields were sprawling—the fine roads covered with small fragments of crushed flint, the checkered complexity of crops! Before him the sea, the sea, eternally novel and respectable, called the sea because there is no other name to give it.

And to punctuate this silence, nothing now but the joyous, clear barking of dogs down below, as the street Arabs, their bodies gleaming naked amid the mica of the scorching sand, whistled exotically and launched the animals against the foaming scrollwork at the rim of the sea, the sea on the surface of which these children had been converting their worn arrowheads into stones for skipping. And so, through the clematis of the terrace, through the cool hush of invisible streams, disjointed spirals of smoke arose, sadly and artlessly, as the Tetrarch, propped on his elbows, puffed sulkily on his midday hookah. There had been a moment, yesterday, after a messenger had put in a shady appearance and announced those northern princes, when his pregnant destiny on these pregnant islands had wavered between his immediate domestic terrors and an absolute dilettantism that could go for the highest stakes even at the moment of ruin.

For *he* was one of those sons of the North, those eaters of meat—he, that wretched Iokanaan, who had turned up here one fine morning, with his spectacles and his uncut red beard, hawking (in that country's own language) some pamphlets that he was distributing gratis, but delivering his sales talk in such an inflammatory style that the people had nearly stoned him—so that now he was thinking things over in the depths of the tetrarchic palace's only dungeon.

Would the twentieth centenary of the Emerald-Archetypas dynasty be celebrated by a war with the outside world, after so many centuries of esotericism, lost to history? Iokanaan had described his fatherland as a country stunted by want, famished for the property of others, fostering warfare as a national industry. And those two princes might very possibly have come to claim this fellow, who was a talented sort after all, and a subject of theirs—and they might build on this pretext, extend their rights of jurisdiction over the occidentals. . . .

But fortunately!—and thanks to the inexplicable intercession of his daughter Salomé—he had not yet interfered with the executioner's traditional, honorary sinecure, nor sent him after Iokanaan armed with the sacred Kris!

However, false alarm! The two princes were merely on a voyage of circumnavigation, looking in on dubiously occupied colonies, and they had only approached the White Islands because they were passing nearby, out of curiosity. But what a surprise! Could it be in this corner of the world that their notorious Iokanaan was going to end up on the gallows? The idea had made them eager for details of the tribulations of this poor soul, who was already so little of a prophet in his own country.

And so the Tetrarch sucked on his midday hookah, with a vacant look, his mood impaired, as it always was at this climactic hour of the day—even more impaired than usual today, with those mounting noises of the national festival, firecrackers and choristers, bunting and lemonade. . . .

The next morning, over the horizon, which was so infinite in spite of everything, but beyond which—so they said—many other races existed under the same sun, those two gentlemen and their galley would vanish.

Now, leaning across the syrupy clematis on his earthenware balustrade, throwing cake crumbs down to the fish in the ponds below, Emerald-Archetypas reminded himself that now he could no longer count on even the small income that his hidden talents might bring in, since his venerable carcass definitely resisted all impulses toward art, toward meditation, toward congenial spirits, or toward industry.

To think that, on the day of his birth, a remarkable tempest had burst over the black dynastic palace, and many trustworthy persons had seen a lightning-flash calligraph "alpha" and "omega"! How many noonday hours had he killed in sighing over that mystical folderol? And nothing out of the ordinary had come to pass. Besides, a message like "alpha," "omega"—that leaves a lot of leeway.

And so, for nearly two months now, relinquishing the interests of youth and pummeling his thighs to regain some of that old enthusiasm about resigning himself to the nothingness that had asceticzed his twentieth year, he had seriously gone about taking up a course of daily visits to the necropolis (so cool in the summer, besides) of his ancestors. Winter was on its way; the ceremonies of the Snow Cult, his grandson's investiture. And besides, Salomé would stay at his side—she wouldn't hear a word about the joys of hymeneal bliss, the dear child!

Emerald-Archetypas was about to reach for a hand bell and request some more consecrated cake for those resplendent July fish, when he heard on the flagstones, behind him, the sound of the cane belonging to the Commander-of-a-Thousand-Trifles. The northern princes had returned from a visit to the city; they awaited the Tetrarch in the hall of the Palace Mandarins.

II

The aforementioned northern princes, belted, pomaded, braided, gloved, beards combed out, hair parted along the occiput (with bangs smoothed down on the temples to suggest the medallion-profile look), were waiting, one hand of each pressing his helmet against his right thigh, the other hand caressing the hilt of his saber, with the waddling gait of a stallion that smells powder everywhere, in spite of himself. They were making conversation with the aristocrats: the high Mandarin, the Lord High Supervisor of Libraries, the Arbiter of Elegance, the Preserver of Symbols, the Tutor and Selector of the Gynecium, the Pope of Snow, and the Administrator of Death, surrounded by two rows of scrawny, nervous scribes, armed with quills at their sides and inkstands tucked in their sleeves.

Their Highnesses congratulated the Tetrarch and themselves on the "fortunate wind which . . ." "on such a glorious day . . ." "upon these islands . . ." and concluded with a eulogy of the capital, especially of the White Basilica, where they had heard a "Tedium Laudamus" played on the Hand Organ of the Seven Sorrows, and of the Cemetery of Beasts and Objects—nor were these the only curiosities of such magnitude.

A snack was served. And because the princes swore that they felt compelled not to touch meat in the company of their hosts, so orthodox in their devotion to vegetarianism and ichthyophagy, the table was a picture, with its delicate arrangement, among fine crystals, of a smattering of artichokes in the shell, swimming in iron husks that stood erect and worked on hinges, asparagus served on mats of pink rushes, pearly-gray eels, date cakes, assorted fruit compotes, and several sweet wines.

Afterward, preceded by the Commander-of-a-Thousand-Trifles, the Tetrarch and his entourage did what they could to show their guests the honors of the palace, of the titanic, gloomy palace streaked with pallor.

Their first stop would be at the panorama of the Islands, as seen from the Observatory; afterward they would descend from one story to the next, through the Park, the Menagerie, and the Aquarium, all the way down to the vaults.

Hoisted to the heights (and pneumatically at that), the procession hastily crossed, on tiptoe, the apartments that Salomé occupied, to an accompaniment of countless slamming doors into which disappeared two or three Negresses' backs, with vertebrae of oiled bronze. What was more, in the exact center of a room tapestried with majolicas (so very yellow!) they found an abandoned and enormous ivory basin, a good-sized white sponge, some moist satins, a pair of pink sandals (so very pink!). Then, a room filled with books; next, another crammed with metallotherapeutic equipment; a spiral staircase; and finally they breathed the upper air of the platform—ah! just in time to see the disappearance of a young girl, harmoniously bemuslined in spidery jonquil with dots, who was manipulating the pulleys so as to let herself glide into space, down toward the lower stories . . . !

The princes were already falling all over themselves with gallant salaams about their intruding, but they quieted down altogether when they saw a ring of astonished eyes, full of the apparent confession: "Well, well, after all, nothing up here is any of our business."

And then a promenade in the open air, with terse expressions of stifled appreciation, around the Observatory Dome, which contained a huge equatorial telescope fifty-four feet long, a movable dome, decorated with waterproof frescoes, whose bulk of one hundred tons was balanced on fourteen steel bars in a vat of magnesium chloride and could rotate in two minutes, the story ran, under a single pressure from Salomé's hand.

Come to think of it, suppose these exotic freaks should dream up the idea of pitching us over the edge, these two princes thought, with a simultaneous shudder. . . . But they were ten times more vigorous, the two of them in their skin-tight uniforms, than this whole dozen of nobles, all pale, hairless, their fingers laden with rings, wrapped up like priests in their shining gilt brocades. And they diverted themselves by singling out their galley, down below in the harbor, like a coleopteron with a thorax of rubbed sheet-iron.

And they listened to an enumeration of the islands, an archipelago of natural cloisters, each one with its own caste, etc.

They descended through a chamber of Perfumes where the Arbiter of Elegance made a note of the gifts which Their Highnesses would like to take along, all of them secretly sabotaged by Salomé: make-up without carbonate of lead, powder without white lead or bismuth, rejuvenators without cantharis, lustral waters without mercurial protochloride, depilatories without arsenic sulphide, milk without corrosive sublimate or hydrated lead oxide, genuinely vegetable dyes without silver nitrate, hyposulphide of soda, copper sulphate, sodium sulphide, potassium cyanide, acetate of lead (can such things be!) and two demijohns containing perfume bouquets for spring and for autumn.

At the end of a dank, interminable corridor with a smell of ambush about it, the Commander opened a door that was green with moss, covered with fungi as sumptuous as jewels, and they were surprised to find themselves in the midst of the vast silence of that famous Hanging Park — ah, just in time to see, around the bend of a path, the disappearance of a svelte young form, hermetically bemuslined in spidery jonquil with black dots, escorted by molossine bats and greyhounds, whose playful barking, almost sobbing for sheer loyalty, gradually faded away into distant echoes.

Oh, everywhere, echoes from unknown passages, filling that austere green solitude, kilometrically deep, sprinkled with patches of light, furnished exclusively with an army of rigid pines, whose bare trunks of a salmon-flesh tint spread, far above, far above, their dusty horizontal parasols. The bars of sunlight lay down between these tree trunks with the same gentle calm they might have between the pillars of some claustral chapel with grillwork vents. A sea breeze tried to penetrate this lofty timber, with a strange distant murmur, like an express train in the night. Then the high-altitude silence took shape again and made itself at home. Nearby, oh, somewhere, a bulbul discharged some rewarding remarks; from a great distance another answered; just as if this were their home, their century-old dynastic aviary. And the group moved on, hazarding guesses as to the thickness of this artificial soil, with its thick felt of dead leaves and pine-needle cushions left by a thousand yesteryears, forming a comfortable lodging for the roots of those pines, so patriarchal! Next were vast gulfs of lawn, grassy slopes like dreams about a faun's kermis; and stagnant sheets of water where swans that wore earrings far too heavy for their spindle necks were immersed in ennui and old age; and endless decamerons of polychromatic statues with fractured pedestals, but posing with surprising — nobility.

Finally, the gazelle enclosure acted as a transition — it didn't pretend to be anything else — between the orchards on one extreme, the Menagerie and the Aquarium on the other.

The deer hardly condescended to raise their eyelids; the elephants shifted their weight to the tune of a harsh crack-crack of plaster, but their thoughts were elsewhere; the giraffes were dressed modestly in soft coffee-and-cream, but they had exaggerated mannerisms and stubbornly stared over the heads of this brilliant court; the monkeys never for a moment interrupted the domestic scenes of their phalanstery; the aviaries' glitter was deafening; the reptiles, for nearly a week, had been endlessly shedding skin; and the stables just happened to be deprived of their finest animals, stallions, mares, and zebras, which had been lent to the municipality for a special cavalcade in honor of the day.

The Aquarium! Ah! That is it, the Aquarium! We'll stop here. How silently it gyrates . . . !

Labyrinth of grottoes, corridors to the right, to the left, each compartment revealing through glass luminous vistas of undersea nations.

Their moors, everywhere dolmens studded with viscous gems, arenas with graded basalt seats, where crabs wallow together in couples, stubborn and fumbling in their after-dinner good spirits, their small eyes roguish and hard-bitten.

Their plains, plains of fine sand, so fine that it sometimes lifts in the breeze after the waving tail of some flat fish just arrived from far away, fluttering like a liberty banner, scrutinized, as he passes and leaves us behind and goes his way, by large eyes that dot the sand in spots and have no other interest in life.

And the desolation of their steppes, housing only one blasted and petrified tree, colonized by trembling clusters of sea horses . . .

And, crossed by natural bridges, their mossy hollows, where the slated carapaces of king crabs with rattails ruminate, wallowing, some capsized and flailing, but no doubt intentionally, so as to exercise . . .

And, below the chaotic ruins of their arches of triumph, the sea needles moving along like frivolous ribbons; and the haphazard navigations of hairy nuclei, a tuft of bristles around the matrix, which can fan itself thus when traveling becomes tedious . . .

And their fields of sponges, sponges like lung remains; thickets of truffles, all in orange velvet; and a great cemetery for pearly molluscs; and those plantations of asparagus, tumefied and pickled in the alcohol of Silence . . .

And, as far as the eye can see, their prairies, prairies dotted with white anemones, fat and healthy onions, bulbs of violet mucus, bits of intestine that got lost and, indeed, began existing again, stumps with antennae that blink at a coral reef nearby, a thousand aimless warts; an entire flora, fetal, claustral, vibratile, fermenting that eternal dream, of someday achieving a mutual whisper of congratulations among themselves about their condition . . .

Oh, just look, that high plateau: hanging on like a leech, a polyp keeps its vigil, the area's gross and glabrous minotaur . . . !

Before departing the Pope of Snow turns to the halted procession and speaks, as if reciting an ancient lesson:

"No day, no night, my friends, no winter, nor spring, nor summer, nor autumn, nor any other weathercocks. Loving, dreaming, without a change of position, in the cool repose of the imperturbably blind. O world of contentment, yours is a sightless, supreme beatitude, while we, we are being dehydrated by other-worldly hunger pangs. And why are our antennae, our own senses, not bounded by the Blind, the Opaque, the Silent, why do they follow a scent that leads outside of our realm? And why are we so incapable of curling up in our own little corner and sleeping off the drunken stupor of our sad little Self?

"But, O submarine villegiatures, we do have two feasts to glut our other-worldly hunger pangs that are worthy of you: the face of the too-beloved, shut up tight on the pillow, a flattened headband glued down by the final sweat, an agonized mouth opening on pallid teeth in an aquarium ray of the Moon (oh, pluck not, pluck not!)—and the Moon herself, a sunflower, yellow, crushed, desiccated by agnosticism. (Oh! Try, try to pluck her!)"

And this was the Aquarium: but could those foreign princes have understood?

And, in single file, speedily and cautiously, they moved down the main corridor of the Gynecium, with its paintings of callipedic scenes and the rotten melancholy of its feminine odors: all they heard was the trickle of a waterspout—to the left? to the right?—whose freshness moistened the thin thread of a cantilena, unforgettably oppressed, miserable and sterile.

And lest their ignorance of the fertility rites might lead them to commit some fatal error, the princes continued at the same discreet pace across the tetrarchic necropolis: two rows of cupboards, masked by life-size portraits, containing urns and thousands of realistic relics, but only affecting to the family, you know what I mean.

But, look here, what they absolutely insisted upon, was seeing their old friend Iokanaan again!

So they followed an official with a key embroidered at right angles to his spine, who stopped at the end of an old sewer that smelled of niter, and, pointing out a grating, lowered it to waist height with a mechanism; and they could approach and perceive, inside a small cell, that unfortunate European, who was getting to his feet, having been interrupted as he lay flat on his stomach, his nose in a mess of ragged papers.

Hearing two voices wish him a polite good-morning in his native tongue, Iokanaan stood erect and straightened his thick spectacles, which had been patched up with wire.

Oh, good Lord, his princes had come! How many dirty winter nights, with his clogs soaking up the muddy snow, he had been at the head of all the paupers going home after a day of wage-earning, and, pausing for a moment there, while tyrannical policemen on horseback restrained the crowd, he had watched these two dismount, covered with plumes, from their heavy, pompous coaches, and climb between two banks of drawn sabers up the great staircase of their palace, that palace with *a giorno* windows at which, as he moved on, he shook his fist, muttering every time that an "era" had to come! And now, it had come, that era! In his own country, the long-promised revolution was a fact! And its poor old prophet, Iokanaan, was a belated god! And this personalized royal measure, this far-flung heroic expedition his princes had undertaken to deliver him, was certainly the moving ceremony the people had demanded in confirmation of the advent of this Universal Easter Day!

At first he automatically doubled up in a bow, in the manner of his own country, having to think of a speech that would be memorable, historic, fraternal of course, but dignified as well. . . .

Illico, his words were cut off short by the northern satrap's nephew, an apoplectically bald army veteran, who insisted on mumbling irrelevantly to everyone that, following the example of Napoleon I, he detested "ideologists": "Ah, ha! Look at you, an ideologist, a scribbler, a dishonorable discharge, a bastard of Jean Jacques Rousseau. So this is where you finally decided to be hanged, you classless pamphleteer! Good riddance! I hope your grimy pate is quick about finding your colleagues from the Bas-Bois at the bottom of a guillotine basket! Yes, I mean the Bas-Bois conspiracy, yesterday's fresh heads."

Oh, the brutes, the indestructible brutes! And the Bas-Bois plotting had failed! His brothers, assassinated! And there was no one to give him the affecting details of the affair. Finished, finished; nothing left but to be ground, like his brothers, under the Constitutional Heel. The wretched publicist resolved to stick to a rigid silence, waiting for the upper classes to leave so that he could accept death in his corner; two long white tears flowed out under his spectacles along his emaciated cheeks toward the meager beard. And suddenly they saw him raise himself to his bare feet, stretching his hands after an apparition, to which he gurgled some of the softest diminutives of his mother tongue. They turned around—ah!—just in time to see the disappearance, in a tinkling of keys, through the lambency of that *in pace*, a young form unmistakably bemuslined in spidery jonquil with black dots. . . .

And Iokanaan once again fell flat on his stomach among his litter, and, noticing that he had upset the inkwell into his stack of papers, he began blotting the ink, tenderly, like a child.

The procession climbed away, without comment; the northern satrap's nephew fingered the stickpin of his military collar and chewed over his principles.

III

In a mode uniting joy and fatalism an orchestra of ivory instruments was improvising a unanimous miniature overture.

The court came in and was hailed by a lush hullabaloo from two hundred luxurious guests who raised themselves on their fine couches. A brief halt was made before a pyramid of shelves containing presents offered to the Tetrarch on this occasion. The two northern princes nudged each other with their elbows and excitedly took from around their necks the Necklace of the Iron Fleece, which they bestowed on their host. But neither one dared to put it around his neck. The aesthetic mediocrity of that necklace was glaring enough, especially here. And as for its honorific value, they felt, not having observed anything similar around them, that the explanations required to make it clear definitely risked falling flat, or at best merely achieving a polite success.

Everyone took his place; Emerald-Archetypas introduced his son and his grandson, two magnificent specimens (magnificent, that is, of course, from the esoteric, white point of view), emblematically attired.

And then, in that windy hall strewn with rushes as yellow as jonquils, those deafening aviaries intoning on all sides, while in the center a fountain sprang up and at its height pierced a gaudy velarium of India rubber, on which the water could be heard falling back in a fine rain, icy and pelting; there were all told, paralleling the semicircular tables, ten rows of couches, each decorated with an eye to the guests' specialities—and, facing them, an Alcazar stage, amazingly deep, where the cream of the mountebanks, jugglers, beauties, and virtuosi of the Islands would come to be tasted.

A wily breeze scuttled along the velarium, but weighted down in spite of itself by that incessant downpour from the fountain.

And the aviaries, overjoyed by the clashing colors, regretfully stopped their noise when the music began to accompany everyone's supper.

The poor Tetrarch! This assortment of music, this audience of sumptuous effusion on this pompous occasion grieved him in his heart. He barely nibbled at that ingenious sequence of sweetmeats, pecking at them with spatulas of hardened snow, his attention wandering like a child's, gaping at the bizarre circus frieze that was evolving on the Alcazar stage.

On the Alcazar stage there appeared:

The serpent girl, thin, viscous scales of blue, green, and yellow, her bosom and belly soft pink: she undulated and twisted, never tiring of her own touch, and lisped that hymn that begins, "Biblis, Sister Biblis, you, yes, you have changed into a wellspring!"

Next a parade of costumes, all sacramentally curtailed, each one symbolizing a separate human desire. The refinement of all this!

Next the entr'actes, presenting horizontal cyclones of electrified flowers, and a horizontal waterspout of berserk bouquets . . . !

Next came musical clowns, wearing over their hearts their insignia, the crank of a genuine hand organ, which they turned with the look of Messiahs who refuse to be influenced and will go to any lengths to follow their apostleship.

And other clowns took the roles of the Idea, the Will, and the Unconscious. The Idea rattled on about everything, the Will beat his head against the scenery, and the Unconscious made big, mysterious gestures, like a person who is sure of being far better informed than he can express in words as yet. Moreover, this trinity had one single, unchanging refrain:

> Our Canaan, I guess,
> Is nothing less
> Than good old Nothingness.
> Non-being, I mean,
> The Meca far-seen
> Toward which libraries lean.

It obtained a howling success.

Next virtuosi of the flying trapeze, describing nearly sidereal ellipses . . . !

Next, a rink of natural ice was brought in, and there emerged an adolescent skater, his arms crossed over those Brandenburg trimmings in white Astrakhan fur on his chest, only stopping after he had described every combination of all the known curves; then he waltzed on his points, like a ballerina; then he etched on the ice a flamboyant Gothic cathedral, not omitting one rose window or grill! Then he designed a three-part fugue, and ended with a labyrinthine twirl, like that of a fakir possessed *del diavolo*, finally leaving the stage, his feet in the air, skating on his steel fingernails . . . !

And it was all concluded by a batch of living pictures, nudities as chaste as vegetables, symbols becoming ever more eurhythmic, by means of a Crucifixion of the Aesthetic.

The calumets had been carted in; the conversation moved into the general; Iokanaan, who could hardly have been amused at hearing this

festival going on over his head, was the chief staple of news. The northern princes spoke in favor of armed authority, the supreme religion,
that guardian of repose, of bread, and of international competition, but
they lost the thread and tried to make an end by quoting this distich, as
a kind of epiphonema:

> *Besides, every decent person preaches*
> *The perfectibility of the Species.*

The Mandarins were of the opinion that the sources of social competition should be atrophied, neutralized, that society should be orga-
nized into cliques of exclusive initiates, scraping along in peace, with
great walls of China between them, etc., etc.

And the music, playing on alone, seemed to complete the sense of
what the speakers were too ephemeral to formulate.

In the end, you could hear the silence growing larger, like the pale
mesh of a fish net cast out on an evening of fishing; the company arose;
apparently it was Salomé.

She entered, descended the spiral staircase, tense in her muslin
sheath; with one hand she signed to them to recline again; a small,
black lyre dangled from her wrist; with the tips of her fingers she flicked
a kiss toward her father.

And she came and took her place, facing them, on the platform,
behind her the drawn curtain of the Alcazar stage; she waited for them
to exhaust the possibilities of observing her, but saved appearances by
pretending to sway on her pallid feet, spreading their toes wide apart.

She took no notice of anyone. Powdered with exotic pollens, her hair
fell loosely onto her shoulders in flat locks, while on her forehead it was
entangled with yellow flowers and bits of straw; supported over her bare
shoulders by two armlets of pearl was a dwarf peacock's spread tail, with
an ever-changing background, silken, azure, golden, emerald, a halo
against which her pure face was etched, that superior face, but politely
indifferent to the knowledge that it was unique, that pinched neck,
those eyes exhausted by their iridescent expiations, those lips, a cir-
cumflex accent of pale pink setting off those teeth, and those gums, of
an even paler pink, in that too crucified smile.

Oh! The celestial, sweet creature, so understandably aesthetic, the
delicate recluse of the White Esoteric Islands . . . !

Hermetically bemuslined in a spidery jonquil with black dots, which
several fibulae pinned together here and there, exposing the arms in
their angelic nudity and forming, between those soupçons of breasts,
whose nipples were dotted with tiny pinks, a sash embroidered on her
eighteenth birthday; then, a little above that adorable umbilical dim-

ple, joining a jeweled girdle of an intense, jealous yellow, casting an inviolable shadow into the hollow between those meager thighs, and halting at her ankles only to reascend her back as two sashes, fluttering apart, finally joining again at the pearl armlets below the dwarf peacock's tail and its changing background, azure, silken, emerald, gold, a halo for that pure superior face; she swayed on her feet, her pallid feet, spreading their toes wide apart, bare except for anklets from which rained a dazzling fringe of yellow silk.

Oh! The little Messiah, complete with womb! How burdensome her head was for her! She didn't know what to do with her hands, even her shoulders seemed ill at ease. Who was it that crucified her smile, that poor little Immaculate Conception? And who exhausted those blue eyes?—Oh! Their hearts exulted, how simple her skirt must feel! Art is so long and life so short! Oh, just to chat with her in a corner, near a fountain, to find out not her Why, but her How, and then to die . . . ! To die, unless . . .

Do you think she may make a speech, after all . . . ?

Craning forward out of his heap of silken cushions, his wrinkles dilating, his pupils jutting out from the battlements of his tarnished lids, pretending to be interested in fingering the Seal, which hung around his neck, the Tetrarch had just handed a page the pineapple he had been nibbling and his towered tiara.

"Look inward! Look inward, before you do anything, O Idea and Contour, Caryatid of these islands without history!" he pleaded.

Then he smiled at everyone, like a contented father, as if to say: "You will see what you will see," giving the necessary information to his guests, the princes, in highly disorganized form, so that the two of them gathered that the Moon had been bled white in order to cast the horoscope of the little creature before them, and that she was generally admitted (a council had been devoted to the question) to be the foster sister of the Milky Way (she has everything!).

Now, delicately planted on her right foot, her thigh raised, her other leg bent behind her in the manner of Niobe, Salomé, permitting herself a small coughing laugh, perhaps with an idea of suggesting that the last thing to do was to imagine that she took herself seriously, plucked on her lyre until she drew blood, and, in a voice without timbre or sex, like that of an invalid calling for his dose, which neither he (nor you, nor I) ever actually needed, she improvised as follows:

"O Non-being, by which I mean the latent Life to come day-after-tomorrow, but no sooner, how worthy you are, how forgiving, coexisting with the Infinite, the ultimate in clarity!"

Was she mocking? She went on:

"Love! That compulsive mania that refuses to accept an absolute death (feeble subterfuge!). O traitorous Brother, I cannot honestly say that we have reached a time for mutual explanations. For all eternity, things are as they are. But how real it would be to make each other some concessions in the realm of the five existent senses, in the name of the Unconscious!

"O latitudes, altitudes of those Nebulae of good intentions, filled with little fresh-water jellyfish, please do me one good turn—come and graze in empirical meadows. O transients on this earth, so eminently *idem* as incalculable others, all equally alone in a life indefinably infinite in its strivings! The active Essence loves itself (listen carefully, now), loves itself dynamically, more or less freely: it is like a profound soul forever playing solitaire with itself, exactly as it pleases. I command you, be the passives of nature; enter the Discipline of the Benevolent Harmony, but automatically as Everything! And let me know how it feels.

"Yes, you hydrocephalic theosophists, you are like the tame fowls of the people, nothing but arbitrary groups of phenomena without any guarantee of being governed from beyond: go back to existences tainted by negligence, and in my name browse, for your daily meal, for your seasonal sustenance, on those deltas without sphinxes, whose angles equal two rights in spite of all. O you generations of incurable pubescence, behold the true decorum; and whatever else you do, pretend to be utterly enmeshed in the irresponsible limbo of the potentialities of which I speak. The Unconscious *farà da se.*

"And you, O fatal Jordans, O baptismal Ganges, insubmergible sidereal currents, cosmogonies like Mamas! When entering, wash yourselves clean of the more or less original stain of the Systematic; first of all, let us be minced into lint to help out the Great Curative Power (or should we call it Palliative?), which sews up all holes, in the prairie, in the epidermis, etc.—*Quia est in ea virtus dormitiva.* Go . . ."

Salomé stopped short, brushing back her hair (powdered with exotic pollens), and her soupçons of breasts churned so that the pinks fell away from them (widowing their nipples). Trying to recover herself, she took her black lyre and plucked out an irrelevant fugue. . . .

"Oh! Go on, go on, tell all you know!" Emerald-Archetypas moaned, clapping his hands like a child. "I give you my tetrarchic word! You will be given anything you desire: the University? my Seal? the Snow Cult? Inoculate us with your Immaculate Conception charm . . . I am so bored, we are so bored! Am I wrong, gentlemen?"

Actually the company was breathing a murmur of unspoken discomfort; some of the tiaras tottered. Each one felt ashamed of the others, but the weakness of the human heart, even among so correct a race . . . (neighbor, you get my drift).

Having summarily slaughtered a number of theogonies, theodicies, and formulas of national wisdom (all in the offhand tone of a chorus master who says: "All right, now, one measure to get our breath?), Salomé, a little delirious, returned to her mystical gabble, her head quickly thrown back, her Adam's apple leaping frightfully—her whole being soon becoming little more than a spidery fabric, her soul like a transitory meteor drop.

O tides, lunar oboes, promenades, twilight gardens, obsolete breezes of November, hay-gathering, missed callings, animal gazes, vicissitudes!—Jonquil muslins with funereal dots, exhausted eyes, crucified smiles, adorable navels, peacock halos, dropped pinks, irrelevant fugues! There was a rebirth of non-culture granted to all, and their youth was restored besides, the systematic spirit died in spirals amid showers with a turmoil that was doubtlessly definitive, for the earth's own good, thoroughly understood everywhere, touched by Varuna, the Omniversal Atmosphere, who gave each one the test of readiness.

And Salomé insanely insisted:

"It is pure being, I tell you! O sectarians of the consciousness, why label yourself as individuals and therefore indivisible? Why not breathe on the embers of some other sciences, in the Sunrise of my Septentrions?

"Do you call it life to inquire stubbornly after the details of self and whatever else there is, with the inevitable question after each step: Ah! well, whom am I deceiving now?

"Get rid of contexts, species, realms! Nothing is lost, nothing is gained, everything belongs to everyone; and everything is already full of submission, no need for confessionals, ready for the Prodigal Son (he won't be allowed to explain, only to relax).

"And these are not just devices for expiations followed by relapses; they are the trampled vintage of the Infinite; not experimental, but inevitable; because . . .

"You are the other sex, and we are the little darlings of childhood (always as unattainable Psyches, at that). So, before the evening is over, let us immerse ourselves in the harmonious mildness of pre-established moralities; let us drift along, exposing our flourishing abdomen to the air; surrounded by prodigality's perfumes and some appropriate hecatombs; toward the beyond where no one will hear his heart's beating or the pulse of his consciousness.

"It all advances as in stanzas, my pulse rate swells like cannon shells, in our lust's furor no caesura, our priestly dress a flattened mess, leave it behind and let us wind along the shore of Nevermore; I must vault up out of me!—(You can see it's not my fault.)"

The little yellow oratress in black dots broke her lyre over her knee and reclaimed her dignity.

The company, intoxicated, kept up appearances by mopping their brows. There passed a silence of ineffable confusion.

The northern princes were afraid to look at their watches, and even more so to ask, "And when is her bedtime?" It couldn't possibly be later than six o'clock.

The Tetrarch examined the embroidery of his cushions; it was all over; Salomé's hard voice suddenly made him look up.

"And now, Father, I want you to tell them to bring up to my room, in a plate or something, the head of Iokanaan. That's right. I'll go upstairs and wait for it."

"But my child, you can't mean it! That foreigner . . ."

But all those present in the hall fervently urged the tiara to fulfill Salomé's will on that occasion; and the aviaries ended the discussion by resuming their deafening glitter.

Emerald-Archetypas sneaked a side glance at the northern princes; not the slightest sign of approval or of disapproval. Doubtless it was none of their concern.

Decreed!

The Tetrarch threw his Seal to the Administrator of Death.

The guests were already dispersing, changing the subject, in the direction of the evening bath.

IV

Leaning her elbows on the Observatory parapet, Salomé, fugitive from festivals of state, listened to the familiar sea sound of beautiful nights.

A full outfit of stars on one of those nights! Eternities of braziers in the zenith! Oh, for the means of making an escape, so to speak, on an Exile Express, etc.!

Salomé, the foster sister of the Milky Way, never really gave of herself except to the stars.

According to a color photograph (ectoplasmic) of the stars called yellow, red, white, of sixteenth magnitude, she had had diamonds cut in precise imitation and sprinkled them into her hair and her other charms, even her evening dress (funereal violet muslin with gold dots), in order to commune *tête-à-tête* on terraces with her twenty-four million stars, just as a sovereign about to receive his peers or satellites will wear the insignia of their territories.

Salomé had nothing but contempt for vulgar trinkets of first, second magnitude, etc. Up to the fifteenth magnitude, no star was her social equal. Besides, her special passion was nebulae matrices, not fully formed nebulae with already planetiform disks, but the amorphous, the perforated, the tentacled. And the Orion nebula, that gaseous pasty of sickly rays, had always remained the favorite son of all the jewels in her flickering crown.

Ah, dear companions of the astral prairies, Salomé had ceased to be our little Salomé! And that night was to inaugurate a new era of relating and etiquette!

In the beginning, after being exorcised from her dress's virginity, she felt a new connection with those nebulae matrices: that she, like them, had been impregnated with an orbital path.

Later, this drastic sacrifice to the cult (although she was really lucky to have extricated herself so discreetly) and made it necessary, if she wanted to dispose of the originator, that she perform the act (a serious one, in spite of what they say) called homicide.

Finally, in order to bring about the silence of the tomb for the Originator, she had had to present a diluted specimen to all those present of the elixir she had been distilling in the anguish of a hundred nights formed like this one.

Well, after all, that was her life; she was a speciality, a minor speciality.

Now in her presence, on a cushion, among the fragments of her ebony lyre, the head of John (in the tradition of the head of Orpheus) glowed, dipped in phosphorous, rouged, curled, grimacing at those twenty-four million stars.

When the object was handed over, Salomé had cleared her scientific conscience by trying out those notorious experiments after decapitation that have caused so much talk, but as she had anticipated, all the electric shocks produced only a facial rictus of minor consequence.

Now she would try her own theory.

But, think of it, she had stopped lowering her eyes before Orion! She steeled herself and stared at that mystical nebula that had presided over her puberty, for ten full minutes. How many nights, how many future nights, to the winner of the last word . . . !

And those choristers, those firecrackers, below her, in the city!

Finally Salomé consulted her reason, shook herself, and pulled up her shawl, then she unclasped the opal of Orion from her person, a mottled jewel, sprinkled with gray-gold, put it in John's mouth like a Host, kissed the mouth mercifully and hermetically, and sealed the mouth with her own corrosive seal (an instantaneous process).

She waited, a minute passed . . . ! Nothing signaled to her out of the night . . . ! With a "Well?" that sounded rebellious and irritable she picked up that jovial object in her little feminine hands . . .

She wanted the head to fall intact into the sea, without first smashing against the cliff rocks, and so she exerted all her strength. The missile described a convincing phosphorescent parabola. Oh, such a noble parabola! But that unfortunate little astronomer had failed abominably in calculating her distance, and, flying over the parapet, she gave her first human cry, and she fell, winding down from rock to rock, to rattle her last in a picturesque channel bathed by the tides, far from the sound of that festival of state, lacerated to the bone, her sidereal diamonds tearing into her flesh, her skull shattered, paralyzed by vertigo, in short sick unto death, in agony for more than an hour.

Nor did she finally attain the viaticum of seeing the head of John, a phosphorescent star, upon the sea . . .

As for the endless distances of heaven, they remained distant . . .

Thus ended the existence of Salomé, I mean the one from the Esoteric White Islands; she was less a victim of illiterate destiny than she was one who wanted to live in the world of artifice, instead of simply from day to day, as all of us do.

DOVER · THRIFT · EDITIONS

FICTION

All books complete and unabridged. All 5³⁄₁₆" x 8¹⁄₄," paperbound. Available at your book dealer, online at **www.doverpublications.com**, or by writing to Dept. GI, Dover Publications, Inc., 31 East 2nd Street, Mineola, NY 11501. For current price information or for free catalogs (please indicate field of interest), write to Dover Publications or log on to **www.doverpublications.com** and see every Dover book in print. Dover publishes more than 500 books each year on science, elementary and advanced mathematics, biology, music, art, literary history, social sciences, and other areas.